Love the Way You Dance

Allison M. Boot

Dedication

♥ *This story is dedicated to Dylan Boot, who has shown me that familial connection goes beyond biology. Thank you for loving and accepting me and for being part of my forever family, sweetie!* ♥

Acknowledgements

Firstly, I would like to acknowledge my mother, Kimberly Hughes. She encouraged me to try wheelchair ballet as a teenager, which subsequently led to my lifelong love of dance. Perhaps more importantly, she persuaded me to dance as a soldier in a performance of *The Nutcracker*. This was an unbelievable, exhilarating experience that I will remember for the rest of my days; it also provided one of the themes for this story. Most notably, though, my mother has always told me that I can do anything I set my mind to.

Secondly, I'd like to acknowledge my loving husband, Dylan Boot. Thank you again for supporting me throughout the writing and publishing process. And as always, thank you so much for going through this crazy journey called life with me... ILYSMSM!

Thirdly, I'd like to acknowledge Merry Lynn Morris, who invented the Rolling Dance Wheelchair that inspired the Dancer Dazzler, which you will see featured in the story that is to come. Thank you so much for inventing something to help audiences focus on the talents and ABILITIES of dancers with disABILITIES instead of their differences.

Additionally, I would like to acknowledge my friend, Erin Kelly. Thank you for supporting me through writing and publishing this book. If it weren't for you, I may not have finished this long-awaited sequel. Thank you for encouraging me to trust my characters and myself. You will always be my fellow Raider and sister!

Last, but certainly not least, I would like to acknowledge my editors without whom *Love the Way You Dance* would not be what it is today. The secret to great writing is good editing. I can't thank my editors enough for lending their skills and expertise to this book and for helping me to be a great writer.

Chapter 1

Once upon a time, in a faraway land called Starrycrest, there lived a princess named Kara. Like other princesses before her, she was beloved and regarded as special in her realm. As far as the princess was concerned, she was special not because of her royal status per se, but because of how it was bestowed upon her.

Unlike other princesses, her royal status was not a birthright, but rather a perk of the king and queen adopting her two years earlier. Despite having to keep up with homework, chores, and various royal duties, life had been pretty perfect since that day.

By far, dance was the aspect the princess loved most about her new life. She and her adoptive mother, Misty, were both in wheelchairs because of disabilities that left them unable to walk. But Derrick Dennison, the kingdom's dignified and fair ruler as well as its most loving husband and devoted father, quickly taught the two most important women in the world to him that their disabilities didn't have to prevent them from loving dance.

The tiny family had bonded over dance so much that the king had implemented an adaptive ballet class, the Starrycrest Dancing Starlets, shortly after Kara's adoption. Sitting in the class one afternoon with 13 other kids she fidgeted apprehensively in her chair, as he assigned parts for an upcoming performance of *The Nutcracker. Uh oh, I look even more nervous than I feel*, she realized as she noted her wide-eyed frazzled reflection in the focal point mirror covered wall. *This is so weird. I'm used to feeling so comfortable and confident here in the studio.*

Looking at the jewel covered phonograph at the front of the room, she closed her eyes and tried to imagine the soft, melodic stylings of the Fairy Lullaby from *A Midsummer Night's Dream* filling the room. After a long moment, she took a deep breath, opened her eyes, and flashed a smile at Derrick.

Her smile fell instantly as, "Sally Levinson will dance as Clara," left his mouth. *I can't believe he chose Sally. What was he thinking?* she thought to herself. She understood that he didn't want to give her preferential treatment for being his daughter and the royal princess, but she hoped that her talent and the fact that her name rhymed with that of the star of the show would earn her the part. Biting the inside of her cheek with gumption, she managed to not make a peep despite her overwhelming desire to protest.

"And last, but certainly not least, the lovely Kara Dennison will be our Sugar Plum Fairy," Derrick announced, pride coloring his voice.

A squeal left the young girl's lips as her confidence in her adoptive father was instantly restored.

Derrick let out a roar of laughter. "I hope you are all as happy with your part as Kara is with hers. That's all for today kiddos. Go home and study up because, come December 3rd, we are going to celebrate Starrycrest's birthday by putting on the best performance of *The Nutcracker* this kingdom has ever seen."

Derrick and Kara were left alone in the dance studio after a chorus of cheers followed his announcement.

"I am so glad you're happy with your part sweetheart. You seemed nervous for a minute there."

The young girl giggled, her adorable dimples popping out against her skin. "I tried to hide it, but I was hoping to be the star of the show," she admitted, her voice suddenly soft and quiet.

Derrick smiled, the love he felt for Kara shining in his eyes. "Sweetheart, I'm going to tell you a little secret but first you must promise to keep it just between us, okay?"

Kara nodded eagerly, her dimples still exposed. "I will. I promise."

"Clara may spend the most time on stage in *The Nutcracker* and be the character who most people consider the star of the show, but truth be told the Sugar Plum Fairy character dances one of the most beautiful, intricate, and challenging ballet routines of all time. I gave you the role of the Sugar Plum Fairy because, in my humble opinion, the most difficult dance in the piece deserves to be performed by my best, and most dedicated, dancer. There is no doubt in my mind that's you." Pausing briefly, he flashed a smile. "Besides, as the most beautiful person in this kingdom, you are the only one who can do the part justice."

The little girl smiled mischievously; her eyebrows furrowed. "What about Misty? Don't you think she's the most beautiful person in the kingdom?"

Kneeling to look her straight in the eye, his expression thoughtful, Derrick contemplated for a moment then answered, "I could no sooner choose between the two of you than I could destroy this kingdom…you two are definitely tied, but I'll tell you another little secret." Smiling wider, Derrick dropped his voice to a whisper,

"You aren't the best dancer in the Starrycrest Dancing Starlets just because your appearance is gorgeous. You're the best because, when you dance, you let people see your beautiful heart."

Throwing her arms around Derrick's neck, Kara squeezed tightly. "You are the best."

Derrick shook his head, still smiling. "No sweetheart, you are. I only hope that someday you can learn to love the way you dance."

"Hmm?"

Ignoring the tiny dancer's question, Derrick returned her hug and flashed a smile. "What do you say we go and start on dinner before Dex and Cliff riot and break into the fridge?"

With that, Kara let out a chorus of giggles and the two of them walked happily back to the castle proper.

***

"Guess what? Guess what? Guess what?" Kara charged enthusiastically at her adoptive mother as she burst through the door of the castle dining room that evening.

Misty beamed at her daughter's excitement, her emerald eyes sparkling with love for the little girl. "What, sweetie?"

With a smile that lit up her whole face, Kara sat up straighter in her wheelchair and announced, "I'm going to dance as the Sugar Plum Fairy in the Starrycrest Dancing Starlets' production of *The Nutcracker*!"

Misty instantly hugged the little girl, squeezing gently as an enthusiastic squeal escaped her lips. "I'm so happy for you, sweetheart!" She locked eyes with her husband, and they shared a grin as she sent Kara off to set the table for dinner.

"You're going to be great, you really are," Misty told her as she put plates and forks at three places. "You're such a radiant dancer, and you can bet I'm getting a seat in the front row."

Once everything was ready, the tiny family sat down to a delicious dinner of fried chicken, mashed potatoes, and buttermilk biscuits.

"I'm so glad Derrick asked me to be the Sugar Plum Fairy," Kara mused conversationally between bites of food.

Hearing these words, Misty couldn't help the sigh she exhaled looking at the young girl before her. "Kara, honey, it's been two years since your adoption. You're not going anywhere, and neither are we, so I think it's okay if you call us Mom and Dad."

Kara focused her gaze on her shoes. "I love you guys so much," she whispered instead of responding to her adoptive mother's thought. *I really do want to call them Mom and Dad, but I can't bring myself to do it,* she sighed. An awkward silence settled like a cloud over the trio.

Clearing his throat after a few minutes, Derrick turned to Misty, valiantly trying to diffuse the tension with his, "So, how was your day?"

"Well, Kara's not the only one who received big news today," Misty admitted hesitantly.

"Enlighten us!" the king urged, taking a bite of chicken.

"After I finished with today's audiences, I went to the doctor," she elaborated, apprehension darkening her features.

"Misty, why didn't you tell me you were feeling poorly?" Derrick could not mask his alarm. He took her hand and squeezed it.

"Yeah, why didn't you tell anyone? Are you okay?" Kara asked, echoing Derrick's concerns.

Returning Derrick's solid grip, Misty looked at Kara and took a deep breath. "Well I've been feeling poorly in the early hours of the morning for a while now, but I didn't want anyone to know until I was sure."

"Sweetie, what did the doctor tell you?" Distress poured from Derrick's question. "Please tell us," he pleaded before taking another bite of his fried chicken.

"I'm pregnant," the queen blurted, smiling nervously as the words tumbled into the space between them.

Eyes watering, Derrick's face turned purple in seconds as he tried to cough up a piece of chicken that had lodged into the back of his throat upon hearing about his wife's delicate condition.

"Oh God. He's choking… he's choking… help… help!" Misty shouted, anxiety overtaking her muscles and creating a spasm that ran up and down her legs. The jerky movement of her limbs made her seatbelt pop off, at which point she was practically standing upright in her wheelchair.

"I'm on it," Kara declared, signaling for Dex, the family service dog, to follow her before she raced out of the room in search of help.

Upon returning the young girl watched, her eyes glued in amazement to Derrick, as he leaned himself against the dining room table and, after three abdominal thrusts, effectively displaced the fried fowl.

Marie, a personal assistant and beloved member of the castle staff, looked at the little girl. "Oh, my heavens, why didn't you tell me what was going on?" the caregiver asked as she rushed over to the leader of the realm. "Are you all right, your Majesty? What on earth happened?"

"Water," the king croaked out, his voice quiet and weak. "I need water."

"Take this," Kara said, quickly satisfying his request by offering him her glass.

After taking a large gulp of water, the king took a deep breath and smiled. "I'm okay. Just startled by Misty's announcement."

Flashing him a nervous half smile, Marie nodded. "Oh, I see. I'm glad you're okay. Let me know if you need anything else your Majesty. And please take smaller bites." The family's laughter in answer to this message followed her out of the room.

As everyone's laughter quieted, Derrick reached over, buckled his wife's seatbelt, and reclaimed his seat at the dinner table. Having the clang of forks against plates be the lone sound in the room for the next few minutes, brought back the memory of another quiet dinner for Kara held some time ago. Misty and Derrick had tried to stage a meeting between their feuding parents over food shortly after she'd come to live in the castle. The past fading, and her plate empty, Kara fixed her gaze on Misty. "So. You have a bun in the oven?"

The queen smiled uncertainly. "Yes," she answered, her voice small and quiet. "Where did you hear that expression?"

Kara giggled, exposing her dimples. "A few years ago, I got mad when I heard that Alicia, the oldest girl in the group home, was suddenly allowed to get an apartment and live on her own. When I asked Betsy why, she said it was because Alicia had a bun in the oven. Then, a few days later, a lady named Doula came by to tell everyone where babies come from. I put things together."

Giggling, Misty looked at her daughter. "Kara, sweetheart, I think you mean a doula. That's what people who deliver babies are sometimes called. I was actually thinking of using a doula instead of a doctor," she said casually.

Suddenly wide-eyed, a shocked Derrick joined the conversation again, "What? Okay, we'll talk about that decision later," he directed at his wife. Then, he addressed his daughter; he was anxious and completely incapable of hiding his inexperience talking about the subject he was broaching, "What did the doula tell you about the baby thing, sweetheart?"

Kara's cheeks, usually a rosy pink, instantly became a deep red. "Uh, shouldn't you know that already?" she questioned, her laughter more nervous than happy.

Misty chuckled at the joke, her pleasure reaching all the way to her eyes. "It's okay, Kara, we just want to be prepared to fill in whatever gaps may come up in the future."

Kara beckoned the winged and fur-covered members of the family, who had already been sitting nearby, closer; she needed a morale boost before she imparted her information. "Oh – well – she told us that, sometimes, if two people love each other enough, God allows their souls to join and create another one. According to the doula, this new soul is protected for nine months in the mother's stomach before it comes into the world."

As the queen listened to, and fully absorbed, Kara's words, her eyes brimmed with moisture. "That's the sweetest thing I've ever heard!" Misty sobbed, tears coursing down her cheeks. Overcome with emotion, she pulled Kara toward her, across the table, and hugged her.

The young girl's body went into the embrace, but her limbs stayed stiff. Her blonde hair swinging as she shook her head, confused, and looked to Derrick, "What's happening?" The words collapsed into a faint croak as Misty tightened her hold.

"Sweetie, I believe we're witnessing the first of many hormone-induced mood swings," Derrick chuckled.

Misty nodded in agreement. "I know it's crazy to cry, but I can't help it." She gently freed Kara from her grasp, wiping her eyes and smiling. "I couldn't be happier, but I'm so scared," she added wonderingly, fresh tears welling in her eyes.

Kara locked eyes with Derrick, breathing sagely, "Mood swing."

With a small, thoughtful grin the king told his wife, "We'll get through this, really, we will. I promise. I know it's unknown territory but try not to worry too much. It won't be good for you or the baby."

Continuing to cry, Misty shook her head. "It's not about the pregnancy," she admitted slowly. "I mean, I am scared about that, but…" Her voice lost the little strength it had; her family had to strain to hear: "I'm more frightened about Trovella's family."

"What're you talking about?" Derrick asked, calm but confused.

Drawing a deep, steadying breath, the beautiful monarch explained, "The royal guard has records that identify every member of Trovella's family, going back five generations. Yesterday, the captain reported that some of his soldiers spotted her cousin Victrollia's footprints on the outskirts of the kingdom. I have a sinking suspicion that she's here to avenge Trovella's death."

Hearing that evil name made Kara's heart race. Trovella, a malevolent troll, had tried to destroy the two beloved kingdoms that had joined to form Starrycrest in the not-too-distant past. Misty had ultimately defeated her, but the fight had not been an easy one. *Of course, she's worried about Trovella's family coming after us. She wants to see that we, and the kingdom, are protected. It makes so much sense.* The princess realized that Derrick was having similar thoughts when she saw him pull Misty into his arms comfortingly.

"You could have told me what was troubling you, the king informed his wife, his voice full of the love he had for her. "You don't have to concern yourself with anyone from Trovella's family." Standing before she could respond, he continued, "That's my job. Your only job is to make sure you and the baby stay healthy."

The queen denied his request swiftly, "No." Her head moved from side to side in a gesture of denial. "I came after her. Now, if she comes after me, or this family, it's only right that I be the one who protects us. *That's* my job," she insisted forcefully. "That's why I visited Cinder's Edge after I defeated Trovella to ask the trolls there the best way to track the most dangerous of their kind."

"Misty, traveling that far is dangerous, especially with trolls involved. Why didn't you tell me you felt the kingdom needed to be protected from Trovella's family and let me handle it?" Derrick queried, his eyes wide with disbelief.

"Please don't be angry, Derrick. Like I said, I felt a responsibility to protect the kingdom myself since I was the one who got us into the mess with Trovella. Besides, my friend, Isabel, promised the trolls there were nice and would help me," she explained.

"I see," Derrick nodded. "And the trolls helped you?"

Nodding her head vehemently, Misty assured him. "Yes, one in particular: the Cinder's Edge Ambassador of Happiness, a treasure troll name Murlyn. He couldn't put a protection spell on the entire kingdom for fear of messing with someone's destiny, but he told me that troll footprints are just as unique as their gemstones. I wished for a way to identify Trovella's relatives and he gave me an extensive collection of her family's tracks which I passed onto the royal guard and asked them to memorize." Pausing, Misty let her explanation sink in then continued. "Knowing there is a chance that Victrollia has a vendetta against me only heightens my desire to protect this family and this kingdom," she declared.

As soon as her suspicions were confirmed aloud a second time, Kara jumped in. "No, Derrick's the one who's right. Your only job is to stay safe and in good health during your pregnancy. We'll take care of everything else," she assured confidently, smiling wide.

Misty's eyes grew moist again as she considered the depth of emotion in her loved ones' sentiments. "You two are the sweetest."

The young girl rolled her eyes in exasperation before she allowed them to find Derrick. "We're in for a long nine months, aren't we?"

The queen beamed brightly. "Seven months," she hurried to correct. "I'm already eight weeks along. The baby's due on Valentine's Day."

"How exciting!" Kara proclaimed. "I hope the baby's a girl."

"I don't care what the baby is as long as he or she is healthy," Derrick put in. He permitted himself a short moment to fully appreciate the situation at hand before his demeanor turned serious. Glancing between his wife and his daughter, he earnestly divulged, "This is not going to change the relationships any of us have with each other. Our family may be about to change, but nothing will ever change the love we feel for one another." Pausing for a moment, he let his words sink in, after which he enjoined Kara, "Like Misty said earlier, we're your parents and you're not going anywhere."

Misty, continuing in the tradition of what appeared to be her strongest emotion for the foreseeable future, began to cry. "I couldn't have said it better myself," she sniffled. "I think we need a group hug."

After the heartfelt family embrace, Kara finished her homework and went to bed, thrilled by the idea that, soon, she'd have a tiny sibling in her life.

Chapter 2

"Hey, Dex. Hey, Cliff, how was your day?" Kara asked, the furry and feathered members of family when she returned home from school the following day.

As the princess entered her beautiful, daisy adorned bedroom with the animals in tow and plopped her backpack onto her desk, she noticed a note. *Meet us in the library as soon as you get home please. Big news. Love, Derrick.* Studying the message for a moment, Kara chuckled. *Big news, huh? What news could be bigger than Misty having a baby?* she mused. Glancing from Dex to Cliff and back, she furrowed her eyebrows and smiled. "Any idea what this is about boys?"

When her canine and winged friends responded by enthusiastically retrieving and bringing her a tennis ball, Kara laughed again, accepting it from Dex's mouth. "Wish I could, but I gotta go check in with Misty and Derrick. We'll play fetch later, okay?" she questioned sweetly.

Dex and Cliff both hung their heads clearly disappointed.

Kara sighed. "I know you guys have been waiting all day for me to play, but Derrick's note said he's got big news so I'm pretty sure it's important. I'll make it up to you guys later, okay? I promise," she insisted.

After the dog and bird offered a squawk and lick of approval respectively, she flashed them a smile and headed to the castle library.

What the heck? The princess coughed as she entered the castle library only to be practically engulfed by a cloud of dust. *I didn't think there was a speck of dirt in this castle. Guess I was wrong*, she realized. The library, housed in one of the largest rooms of the castle, had floor-to-ceiling shelves full of the most beloved novels, biographies, and reference books in the kingdom. It wasn't until that moment that Kara realized just how old some of the books must be.

"I found it!" Derrick shouted excitedly as he stood up from a table covered in books that he and Misty had spent the afternoon pouring over. "I found the enchantment."

Leaning forward, Misty peeked into the thick brown book in front of Derrick and went wide-eyed. "You did! You found it! We're safe," she exclaimed, her voice coated in a mixture of excitement and relief.

Kara rolled her eyes as Derrick pulled Misty into a hug before kissing her on the lips. *There they go again. Always so lovey-dovey.*

Clearing her throat, she gained their attention. "Sorry to interrupt. I got your note."

Misty pulled away from Derrick, her cheeks turning slightly pink. "You're not interrupting anything, sweetheart," she assured. "We're just excited."

Nodding, Kara giggled. "I can see that. You guys want to tell me what this is all about?"

"After you went to bed last night, Misty and I spoke more about how we can protect our family from trolls as well as other possible threats. I remembered that my great grandfather used to mention an old magical enhancement that the family has used from time to time to call upon our ancestors," Derrick explained.

Kara's eyebrows furrowed in confusion. "Aren't you a little old to believe in magic, Derrick?"

"Ah, that's where you're wrong, sweetheart. I may be too old to believe in ordinary magic, but as a proud Denison I'll always believe in the power of the Denison Dynasty."

"The Denison what?" Kara queried, her eyebrows even more furrowed than just moments before.

"Dynasty is another way of saying family line, sweetie," Misty clarified.

"I don't get it. How is calling upon family members who aren't with us anymore going to protect us?" the tiny royal asked, her voice coated in skepticism.

"Sweetheart, firstly, we Denisons have always protected our own as well as our kingdom. Secondly, just because our ancestors aren't physically with us doesn't mean they've stopped protecting us. In fact, me finding this magical enchantment proves the exact opposite. It shows that this family and our crown jewels will always be safe."

Misty nodded. "I know I wasn't a Denison then, but I could've used the enchantment a couple of years ago when facing Trovella."

Smiling, Derrick took Misty's hand and gave it a gentle squeeze. "I'm sure my ancestors could sense how much I loved you even then and would've helped you, but you didn't need it. You literally kicked that overgrown gemstone thief 's butt and it was awesome."

Misty blushed. "Thank you, my love, but trust me when I say I would have used an enchantment as it is so much easier." Biting her lip, she paused, nervously glanced at the book Derrick had been studying and then continued, "I'm sorry, sweetie. I shouldn't have said that. I didn't mean that using a magical enchantment was taking the easy way out. I know that protecting our family from potential threats isn't going to be easy at all."

Derrick shook his head. "No need to apologize, sweetheart," he assured. "I know that you know I'd never take the easy way out when it comes to this family. All this is just precaution," he reminded her. "Everything will be all right. We just need to memorize the enhancement in case we ever have to use it," he explained calmly.

How can Derrick be so calm? Kara wondered. *He may be right about how all of this is a just precaution, but we still shouldn't take any chances. We can't,* she decided.

"Uh guys, I'm sorry to keep interrupting with questions, but don't you think we should make sure the enchantment will work before we memorize it?" she questioned warily.

Derrick shook his head. "No need. Like I said, we Denisons protect our own. We're all Denisons so the enchantment will work for all of us. We just have to trust and believe it."

The king's words of encouragement and warm smile usually calmed Kara and made her feel safe, but at that moment neither did anything to quiet her concerns or inner thoughts.

For such a smart guy, Derrick is being somewhat dumb. How can he trust in the enchantment so blindly?

"How can we trust it without testing it?" the pint-sized royal insisted. Taking a deep breath, she looked from Derrick to Misty and back. "If the enhancement is really meant to protect our family shouldn't we be 100-percent sure it will do just that?"

Leaning down to the young girl's level, the loving, adoptive father looked her straight in the eye. "Kara, sweetheart, are you certain you're going to nail your routine every time you go out and dance?" he queried.

Sighing, the princess shook her head. "Of course not, but I practice to make sure that I am as good as I can be," she pointed out.

Misty giggled, eyeing Derrick. "She's got you there."

Derrick nodded, his soulful blue eyes sparkling with love for the little girl. "You mean to tell me that you've never danced a routine without practicing?"

Groaning, Kara eyed him. "C'mon, you know I have. I'm a good dancer and I believe in myself."

"Exactly," Derrick exclaimed. "Sweetheart, I'm only asking you to believe in the enchantment and this family as much as you believe in yourself as a dancer. Can you do that?" he questioned anxiously. "Can you live the way you dance?"

Derrick looks as pathetic as Dex at feeding time, she mused. *How can I resist?* "Okay, okay," she relented after a moment. "I'll memorize the enchantment with you, but can we start tomorrow please? I had a long day at school."

Nodding, Derrick flashed her a proud grin. "I suppose finding the enchantment and convincing you to learn it is enough victory for one day."

"I agree," Misty added, looking at the little girl. "Take some time to relax before supper. Just don't forget to also finish your homework."

"Of course," Kara agreed. "I'll see you at supper."

With that, the tiny princess sped out of the library, happy to be able to go play a round of fetch with Cliff and Dex as promised.

Chapter 3

"Well, if it isn't our favorite royal!" Tyler, a boy with spiky red hair and a lopsided smile greeted Kara in much the same way every time she visited Starrycrest Group Home.

The princess sighed heavily, annoyed. "Nice try, Ty. I may be royalty now, but I'm still me. I'll always be Kara. I just happen to be in line for the throne now."

"That's a scary thought," Tyler joked. Taking Kara's purse off of the back of her chair, he threw it into the waiting hands of his buddy Ben, who was chubby and sported short black hair in addition to glasses that didn't quite fit his face.

Shrugging, Kara chuckled. "Go ahead, keep it. Not even you two goofballs can bug me today. A couple nights ago, I found out I'm going to be an older sister. I'm only stopping by today so I can tell Betsy the good news," the princess explained happily as the boys tossed her bag around the room.

This information was enough to distract Tyler from his game. His expression became grave in seconds. "Man, I'm really sorry, Kara. That's a tough break."

Tyler was a year older than Kara and had been messing with her for as long as she could remember. In the nine years that she'd known him, she'd never seen him be anything close to genuine and he'd never shown anyone compassion. At this moment, though, his features were not only kind, but resolutely solemn. *What is he thinking? Why's he acting so weird all of a sudden?*

"What do you mean? I love babies – they're adorable," Kara said honestly, her smile never faltering.

The boy nodded, his face still earnest. "Yeah, babies are adorable and all that, but you better hope that Misty's bundle of joy ain't too cute. If it is, you're gonna be sent packing and end up back here." Tyler held her gaze, making sure she understood the truth of his message.

Kara's curls bounced against her shoulders as she laughed. "No, don't be silly. Having another child won't change the way Misty and Derrick feel about me. They already told me it wouldn't."

"'Course they did. Wait 'til that baby makes its first adorable face. Your pretty blonde ringlets won't look so shiny after that," Tyler cautioned. "Don't you remember Felicia?" he asked rhetorically. "She was part of her family for two years before they kicked her to the curb. All I'm sayin' is: it happens."

A wave of nausea swept over Kara then, but she couldn't be sure if the feeling stemmed from the smell of Betsy's chili wafting through an open window in preparation for dinner that evening or the terrible realization that Tyler might be right.

Holding a hand to her stomach, she let out a shaky breath. "I'll talk to Betsy some other time. I should go. I'm not feeling very well."

Giving Kara her purse back, Tyler shook her shoulder lightly, advising, "Keep your head up, go home, and take care of what's yours."

Kara laughed through her queasiness. "I will."

With that, Kara headed out, her brain overwhelming her as she made her way back to the castle. *What if Tyler is right?* she mused. *What if the baby changes things so much that I'm forced to go back to the group home?* Despite the cool weather, the little girl's cheeks heated in time with her mounting thoughts. *Oh no,* her mind went on. *The baby is eventually going to call Misty and Derrick 'Mom' and 'Dad'– what if that makes them feel more attached to the new addition than they feel about me? I really wish I could use those names with them. I need to know things are permanent, though. A piece of paper means nothing.*

These revolving thoughts were interrupted when she opened her front door and was greeted by a very enthusiastic Dex and his equally exuberant partner, Cliff.

Petting Dex's head and allowing him to snuggle into her lap, Kara eyed her surroundings. Though she had called the castle home for two years now, she remained in awe of the structure most of the time. The marble pillars and richly colored granite floors throughout were indeed breathtaking but, for a kid who had been used to living in a four-bedroom, two-bathroom facility with twenty-nine other children, they proved to be quite intimidating. For her, the most soothing accouterment of the castle was the floral scent left behind by the blooms that populated most of the flat surfaces in the space. The atmosphere in the group home had been characterized by sadness and tension, but life at the castle was usually happy and calm. Kara couldn't help but believe that it was due, at least in part, to the décor choices. Letting the repetitive motion of patting Dex distract from her concerns somewhat, she smiled at him. The smile disappeared moments later as she realized, *I'll miss him and everything else about this place so much if they make me leave.*

Kara's ponderings were cut short when Misty came into the room, appearing very chipper.

"Hey, sweetie, Derrick made your favorite dinner – chicken tenders, French fries, and brownies. Go wash your hands and come to the table, please."

After delivering this direction, the regal parental figure turned toward the dining room, spinning back a breath later. She lowered her voice conspiratorially, revealing, "I'm going to take you out of school early tomorrow and we're having a mother/daughter afternoon. I could use some bonding time with my oldest child."

Basking in the delight that this plan brought into her heart, Kara followed Misty into the dining room, her worries put aside for the time being.

***

Kara sat in Starrycrest Schoolhouse, trying to concentrate as her teacher, Ms. Ryder, a rail-thin 50-year-old with a high-pitched voice, long gray hair, and a dark brown mole on her left cheek illuminated the best way to multiply double digits. However, she couldn't stop herself from glancing expectantly at the clock every few minutes. There was only an hour and a half left in the school day and Misty hadn't picked her up yet. Rationally, the young girl knew that the pregnant monarch had probably been tied up with matters of state or medical appointments, but she still worried. *Something must be wrong, I just know it. This isn't like Misty,* she fretted internally. When the final bell of the school day sounded, Kara's heart began racing fast enough that she feared it would burst from her chest. She rushed home, ignoring even Dex and Cliff as she tore into the castle.

"Misty!" she shouted, alarmed, as she rolled down the main corridor and into the master bedroom.

"What is it, sweetheart?" Misty's eyes widened with worry as she registered Kara's fretful demeanor.

Releasing her held breath into the room, Kara tucked a stray strand of hair that threatened to go into her face safely behind her ear. "You were supposed to pick me up from school this afternoon? Early?" Her tone queried whether Misty recalled yesterday's conversation.

The princess saw the queen's mouth drop open in surprise. "Oh, my goodness! I'm so sorry, Kara! I had such a hectic day that I completely forgot," Misty said regretfully. "Please don't be mad." Pulling Kara into her, she encircled her daughter tightly. At times, hugging ended up being awkward for the two of them, given that the bulky nature of their wheelchairs made it difficult for them to get close to one another. Misty's ever-expanding stomach hindered the process even more, but that didn't stop Kara from rolling her chair toward her mother's and returning the embrace.

"I'm not mad," Kara assured against her adoptive mother's shoulder. "I'm just glad you're okay. When you didn't show up, that's what really upset me." She pulled away to conclude, "Don't be so hard on yourself. Stress isn't good for you or the baby, remember?"

The queen reluctantly ended the familiar contact, drying her eyes with a sleeve. "I know you're right, sweetie. I'll try to stop, but I'm definitely making this up to you, I promise. Starting Wednesday."

At this last piece of information, Kara's eyebrows knitted together in puzzlement and excitement laced through her voice. "What's Wednesday?"

Misty's delighted face far outshined Kara's own thrilled countenance as she began to expound, "I have an ultrasound that afternoon, and Derrick and I would like for you to come with us. Will you do that for me? I thought maybe we could go for pizza afterward, just the two of us. How does that sound?"

The princess took some time to compose herself and mentally sort through her feelings. She hoped Misty didn't notice any of the disappointment in her eyes. *This baby is already invading my life,* she lamented. At that moment, she wanted nothing more than to vehemently say no and suggest bringing home a pizza. *Look how happy she is, though. I can't ruin that,* she decided, nodding at Misty.

After a timid 'sure' escaped her lips, most of the anxiety Kara had felt when she entered the castle dissipated; only then did she catch sight of the chaos around her. The young girl had often heard castle staff say that the master bedroom was the most serene room on the premises , but the princess felt anything but tranquil as she noticed the astounding amount of baby supplies that had been collected within its walls. Surveying the space from one side to the other, she catalogued at least half a dozen bassinets, five swings, three changing tables, countless baby bottles, pacifiers, burp cloths, and packs of diapers scattered in various spots. "Ummmm…" she hesitated. "What's going on?" she finally managed, biting her lip to keep from cackling. "It looks like Starrycrest Baby Boutique blew up in here."

The queen sighed forlornly and placed a palm to her forehand as if that might help her straighten her notions. Her eyes seemed to be permanently moist now. "I went to get a few things for the baby and started thinking about everything he or she is going to miss out on because he or she has me for a mother. Then I felt guilty because of what I'd been contemplating and, to make up for it, I bought anything and everything I thought might be good for the baby." Tears rolled down her cheeks as she made this confession. "Now, I know how stupid my shopping spree was because, I mean, look at it," she flung an arm out to point at her purchases. "I couldn't help myself, though. It was like some weird out of body experience. I wasn't sure whether I should give in to the adrenaline rush or vomit." Grabbing a tissue off the nightstand by her and Derrick's bed, Misty blew her nose. Kara's urge to laugh was replaced by heartache as she watched her adoptive mother sob.

"What do you mean?" she asked after a long pause, gentle, quiet, and concerned.

"I just don't know if I can do this." The queen stared down at her stomach, sniffling all the while.

Kara shook her head, hard and fast. "What are you talking about? You're a great mother," Kara promised, catching her guardian's eye and refusing to look away. "Trust me. I, of all people, can tell you that with certainty." A small chuckle fell into the air between them, breaking some of the strain of the moment.

Kara was pleased when Misty smiled at this declaration, even if it only lasted for a heartbeat.

"It's true that I do the best I can for you and I always will, but it was different when you came along. You were older, so I didn't have to know about feeding you, changing your diapers, bathing you, or any other strenuous things like that. I can't imagine how I'm going to make everything work," Misty cried despairingly.

In the next second, laughter escaped from the princess's core even though she could sense her adoptive mother's pain.

Misty gaped at her daughter. "This isn't funny," she reasoned, clearly stung by Kara's insensitivity.

The young girl rushed to placate Misty. "I agree! I'm only laughing because you should be taking your own advice, and I don't know why you're not. You've always told me that people with disabilities can do everything able-bodied people can, we just have to do it a little bit differently. That's still true, isn't it?" she queried sharply.

"Yes, sweetheart, but there's more–"

Kara's head shook even more vehemently than it had only moments ago. "Nope, no buts. I'm gonna be here to help, always. Between the two of us, we have three limbs that work. Add in Derrick's, and that's seven. If we count Dex and Cliff, we have more body parts than a person would ever need to take care of a baby. Now that I think about it, that number doesn't even include any of the other people here. You know the staff will be more than happy to help." Cautiously, she reached out and placed her hand on Misty's stomach. "My baby brother or sister is going to have all the help anyone could ever need. I was without a parent until I met you," the small royal cleared her throat, tears pricking at her eyes. Looking around the room and trying to pull herself together, she took her hand out of its position, reassessing the large piles of baby accessories around her. "All of these things won't replace a mother's love. They can't. All you can do is love your baby and let the rest fall into place, okay?" the princess advised sweetly.

"How did you get so smart?" Derrick's voice carried into the room, full of sincerity.

Although he made every effort to avoid frightening the girls, they both startled at the sound. Relaxing, as she realized it was the king, Kara grinned. "I'm a chip off the ol' block," she teased good-naturedly.

His eyes alight with love, Derrick replied, "Yes, you sure are," and clasped her hand in his.

Laughing playfully, he looked to Misty. "Worry about this later. Come join us for a dance, my love," he implored his wife. His ecstatic smile contagious enough for her to mirror it with one of her own.

Nodding eagerly, she moved to fill the hole in their family circle. Derrick's idea succeeded in erasing both Misty and Kara's fears and insecurities, at least for the rest of that evening.

***

Holding a tennis ball, Kara rolled down the front ramp of the castle and glanced up at the sky, her feathered and furry friends in tow. She looked warily at the black cloud coated sky to the animal members of her family and back. "Probably not a good idea to play fetch today boys. It's looking a little stormy out," she explained, turning to go back up the ramp.

Sneaking and flying past her respectively, Dex hit her with his best sad puppy dog eyes while Cliff stilled and hung his head.

"C'mon guys, don't do this to me," she groaned. "You know I can't stand to see you all pouty and sad."

Dex whimpered in response while Cliff stayed eerily still and quiet.

Sighing again, the princess relented, "All right, all right I give. Five minutes and then we head back inside, got it?"

Cliff perked up and started flying around just barely dodging the wagging tail of his canine partner in crime.

Kara's lips broke into an ear-to-ear smile, exposing her dimples. "Go on you two," she urged, enthusiastically throwing the tennis ball onto the lawn out in front of the castle.

"Guys, where are you going?" Kara called out as Cliff and Dex rushed past the tennis ball, through the front gate, and toward some tall, richly green cypress trees beyond the castle.

What's gotten into Cliff and Dex? We never go out this far for a round of fetch, let alone leave home. The pint-sized majestic pushed the wheels of her chair as hard as she could, but still struggled to keep up with her beloved comrades who soon disappeared into the forest of trees.

Whoa, either this forest is really creepy or it's getting ready to storm fast, Kara thought as she hesitantly made her way deeper into the forest only to realize she was headed toward pure darkness.

"Dex... Cliff..." she called out, her voice shaky and fretful despite her trying to shout, as she searched for them. "C'mon guys, she persisted after receiving no response. This isn't funny! Come back... I want to go home!"

Relief washed over Kara when, after a long moment, Dex appeared with Cliff perched on his back, as per usual, and dropped something onto her lap.

"Oh my Gosh!" she exclaimed as the trio walked out of the forest and into the light toward the castle. "That's not a tennis ball! That's a –AAAAAAAAHHHHH," Kara woke with a start and sat up in her full-sized canopy bed only to find Derrick looking at her, his usually bright, blue eyes, dark and full of concern.

Carefully sitting on the edge of her bed, Derrick attempted to calm the little girl. "Sweetie, relax. I'm here. You're safe," he soothed, his voice quiet and reassuring despite the anxious look in his eye.

Kara let out a breath. "Oh, thank goodness. It must've just been a nightmare."

Derrick's eyes widened, but his apprehension never left them. "A nightmare about what, sweetheart?"

"I was playing fetch with Dex and Cliff and instead of bringing back the tennis ball, they brought me a snake," she explained, her nose wrinkled in disgust.

"A snake, huh?"

Kara shivered. "Those creepy, crawly things have always given me the willies," she admitted, her voice a hesitant whisper.

Derrick chuckled. "Snakes gave me the creeps when I was a kid too, sweetie, but then my great grandfather let me in on a little secret about our creepy crawly foes."

This time it was Kara whose eyes widened. "Really? What's the secret?"

Taking Kara's hand, Derrick squeezed it gently. "Sweetie, I'll share the secret with you, but you have to promise to keep it within our family. If it gets out to the kingdom then it's likely that too many people will try to test the theory and that could have some serious repercussions."

What kind of family secret could help me handle my fear of snakes? she wondered. *Whatever the secret is, I have to get Derrick to tell me before he and Misty have the baby and decide I'm not part of the family anymore,* she reasoned. Shaking her head, she dismissed the idea and flashed her adoptive father a smile. "I have no idea what you're babbling about, but if the secret will help to not be scared of snakes then I swear I'll never tell anyone," she said earnestly.

Chuckling again, Derrick nodded. "That's my girl. The secret to conquering snakes is realizing that they are dark magic."

"Dark magic? You mean you actually believe in that stuff?" she queried, her voice laced with disbelief.

Nodding vehemently, Derrick agreed. "I believe it as much as I believe in our family enchantment."

Kara groaned, "Oh well, that's just great. If snakes really are dark magic, then that means I really do have reason to be afraid of them."

Derrick shook his head. "You, my sweet girl, do not need to be afraid of snakes or any other form of dark magic for that matter. To conquer dark magic, you only need to remember two things. First, remember that dark magic feeds on dark magic. Secondly, always know that you, sweetheart, are a Denison and my little girl. I'll always protect you, no matter what," he reassured her, placing a kiss on her forehead. "Sweet dreams, my sweet girl. I'll see you in the morning," he whispered before leaving her in the quiet of her daisy-adorned bedroom.

If only I knew that Derrick truly would protect me forever, Kara thought wistfully before drifting off to sleep for the second time that evening.

Chapter 4

Kara's Sugar Plum-induced performance anxiety set in as soon as she rolled into the studio, her dance class about to begin. She and the other students aimed questioning looks at Derrick and the mystery woman standing next to him, whom none of them recognized.

"Hello, everyone! I see you all have some questions, so I won't leave you lingering in suspense." The king laughed, finding his daughter in the crowd, and glancing between her and his guest. "This is Stella Dixon. She's from the kingdom of Eclipston, about four hours away by carriage, but has recently moved here to Starrycrest. Please trust me when I say that she is a fantastic dancer. My wife, our lovely queen, is feeling a bit under the weather, and I need to be with her. As such, Ms. Dixon has graciously agreed to run class today as well as whenever help is needed in the coming weeks." He smiled encouragingly at his charges. "You'll all do your very best, as always," he said, by way of bidding them goodbye as he theatrically danced out of the room.

What in the world? Derrick has never abandoned class before. This stupid baby is ruining everything and it isn't even born yet. It took every ounce of strength Kara possessed to not make a scene and ask Derrick what was so wrong with Misty that it warranted him leaving class. *It's never good to bring problems into the studio unless you plan to dance them away,* Kara reminded herself, biting her bottom lip to keep from calling out.

Eyeing the woman before her suspiciously as she performed first through fifth position with her arms largely from muscle memory, the princess drifted into her head for the rest of the hour. *I cannot believe he stuck us with this crazy woman,* she ruminated as the small, lithe dance instructor with piercing hazel eyes, and close-cropped pink hair finally dismissed the class.

It wasn't until 'Kara, could you please stay behind a minute?' reached her ears that the young girl realized she had been on autopilot.

"Can't this wait?" she retorted haughtily. "I really should check on my–"

"Nope, sorry to disappoint you. Your mother and the baby are just fine. Turns out it was only a bad bout of morning sickness." Stella's rigid comportment left little to no room for argument.

"How did you–" Kara spat her question through her confusion, cheeks turning crimson with the force of her anger. *Great. I bet a really nice, mandatory discussion about my feelings is right around the corner.*

"Your father told me the family's good news. I have the strange feeling that you, Ms. Kara, are just as happy with the little bundle of joy comin' your way as you are about me bein' here," Stella hazarded gently.

"Whatever, lady, you don't know any–" Kara began to fire back. The color had not drained from her face, and her rage seemed to mount as time passed.

"Oh, I know more than you think. I have pink hair and you're royalty. I'm still the adult here, though, and that means that you're going to respect me. Are we clear?"

At that moment, Misty and Derrick's voices and teachings flooded her mind: *Always respect your elders. Never use your royal status for selfish gain.* Thanks to this intervention, despite her fury and every bone in her body screaming at her to give in to her desires and tell this woman off, she resisted.

"Yes, ma'am," she acquiesced instead, knowing she'd eventually have regretted not heeding her upbringing.

Stella nodded her approval. "That's more like it. Now let's dance it out," she suggested mischievously.

Confusion completely overshadowed any contempt that may have remained in the princess's features.

Her teacher smiled broadly, more radiance playing in her eyes than in an early morning sunrise over the ocean. "I'm going to help you with your Nutcracker solo."

This reveal elicited a giggle from the attentive student. *She really is crazy.* "No offense, Stella, but I doubt you can help me with adaptive dance."

"Oh, really?" the dance teacher retorted playfully, not upset in the least about being doubted. "Ever heard the phrase 'don't judge a book by its cover'?"

Kara nodded, telling herself: *This woman is definitely nuts.*

"Wait right here, then." Without another word, Stella left the dance studio the usual way, using her legs and feet, but she did not return like this. Her entrance was unexpected and very different.

As the princess watched with wide eyes and an open mouth, Stella performed a series of turns from a clear circular seat set on wheels similar to those of a motorized wheelchair. "Wow," she breathed.

"Nice, huh?" Stella gestured to the bottom and sides of the chair like Vanna White would have, laughing the entire time. "It's called the Dance Dazzler. Watch this." She twirled with purpose now, performing first through fifth positions with perfectly raised arms.

When it dawned on Kara that the chair did not have any kind of joystick, she was even more impressed. *She's doing all of this without her hands.*

"Oh my gosh! How did you do that?" Kara rushed to ask Stella as soon as she finished performing.

"I can show you how to do even more than that for your solo," she promised, exuding a palpable confidence that soon transferred to the princess.

"Awesome! I'll surprise Derrick and Misty with how great I get. I'm going to own my solo."

After setting up a rehearsal schedule with Stella, the youngest member of the royal family returned to the castle. *I can't believe that I'm going to be able to treat Misty and Derrick to an amazing dance in a fabulous wheelchair*, she chattered to herself, so excited that she had to keep reminding herself not to tell them when she sat down to dinner that evening.

***

Did Derrick leave us in the hands of a dancer or a drill sergeant? Kara wondered as Stella performed five consecutive pirouettes as though she'd just had an espresso with five extra shots of caffeine before encouraging her young proteges to do the same.

No wonder Stella is treating us like robots. Everyone's acting like a bunch of obedient drones, she mused. Glancing in the mirror wall, the princess noticed that she and her classmates had unconsciously formed a line from one end of the room to the other and were each trying their best to mimic Stella's fluid movements. As she took in the eager, determined expressions of her classmates, the princess's anger was replaced by sadness. *Derrick would be so proud if only he wasn't so consumed by the baby,* she sighed and attempted to focus on the petite pink-haired ballerina twirling in the center of the room as though she were preparing to take flight at any moment. The tiny royal tried her best to focus on the light as air dance instructor, but her concentration broke as Tiphany Hendrix, her friend and fellow dancer, took a loud swig from her water bottle.

"Whew," The young girl sporting a bright green leotard that complimented her olive-green eyes let out a breath. "I used to think that savior of yours put us through our paces, but he's got nothin' on Stella," she whispered.

Rolling her eyes, Kara chuckled quietly. "I'll be sure to tell the ruler of our kingdom that he doesn't compare to a pink-haired, caffeine-crazed dance coach."

Clearing her throat, Stella eyed the tiny dancers, bringing their quiet conversation to a halt. "Some of ya seem more focused on gabbin' than dancin'," she declared pointedly. She paused for a moment, sighed, and then turned her attention to the entire class. "Let's take five and get back to it."

Kara frowned, her eyes downward, "Sorry, Stella."

Tiphany's shoulders slumped as she nodded. "Yeah, sorry."

The dance instructor's hazel eyes instantly softened as she returned her focus to the formerly chatting ballerinas. "It's okay girls. Just finish gabbin' quickly so y'all can focus," she flashed a reassuring smile before adding, "And don't forget to hydrate."

Nodding simultaneously this time, the girls agreed before settling on the floor catty corner from the studio ballet barres.

"So, are you going to stay to watch me and the other girls rehearse the March of the Nutcracker tonight?" The young royal's dark braid-sporting comrade questioned before taking another drink from her water bottle.

"Sure," Kara agreed. It's been a long day, but I think I can make that hap–"

"Whoa," Tiphany shouted, cutting her off. "Maybe I was wrong. It looks like Derrick is the crazy one."

Kara opened her mouth to question her friend but closed it as Derrick rushed over to her, his eyes wide and full of concern.

Uh oh, Derrick would never interrupt dance class unless something was seriously wrong, Kara realized.

Clearing his throat, Derrick looked to Stella. "So sorry to interrupt, but I'm afraid that the princess is needed elsewhere," he explained, his voice coated in urgency.

What could have made Derrick so nervous? Kara wondered as she struggled to listen despite suddenly feeling the rapid pound of her heartbeat in her ears.

Shaking her head, Stella's eyes clouded with worry. "Don't worry about the interruption. Is everything okay, Derrick?"

Nodding, Derrick looked from Stella to his adoptive daughter and back. "Royal duty calls. We really must be going. Come along Kara," he urged, his voice and eyes coated in more apprehension than moments before.

"Derrick, what's going on? The princess called out as she followed him out of the dance studio and into the castle proper. What's wrong? Are Misty and the baby okay?"

Derrick nodded, walking through the dining room and down the castle's center corridor. "Misty and the baby are fine, but the family crest is not," he explained.

"What're you talking about? What happened?" she barely managed to get the words out, her mouth going dry, as she followed him down the hallway.

Stopping abruptly, Derrick turned to face Kara. He grasped both of her shoulders and squeezed gently. "Sweetie, don't worry. Everything is going to be fine," the loving father assured.

"Derrick, what's going on? Just spit it out," the pint-sized majestic insisted.

Looking her straight in the eye, Derrick answered, his voice just above a whisper, "Sweetheart, the family crest has been stolen and the royal guard suspects Victrollia is the culprit."

Kara shook her head. "W-what? H-how?"

Pulling the curly-haired royal in for a hug, Derrick reassured her. "I don't know, sweetheart. However, it's going to be okay. We're going to use the family enchantment to get it back."

This can't be happening. This is all just a horrible nightmare, Kara told herself, reluctantly pulling away from his embrace.

"Sweetie, come quick," Misty insisted as she raced to Derrick's side, her eyes wide and clouded with fear. "Dad says the longer the crest is gone. The more the kingdom is at risk. We have to do this now."

Nodding, Derrick comforted her, "Don't worry, my love. All will be right soon enough. We just have to believe in ourselves and this family and the rest will be easy."

Oh, yeah, easy peasy, except for when you're not sure if you're really part of the family, Kara groaned inwardly as they all walked to the vault where the family crest was housed.

Chapter 5

"Oh, my Gosh, what the heck happened to this place?" Kara questioned as she looked around and saw that the usually meticulously organized vault looked as though a tornado had ripped through it.

Several drawers and cabinets were open yet bare, while generations' worth of heirloom accessories, in the form of tiaras, handmade high heels, and everything in between, featuring infinitely shiny sapphires, rich rubies, and elegant emeralds were strewn across the floor.

Breathtaking examples of every precious gem ever discovered, were scattered haphazardly about the enclosed space. It gave the impression that the perpetrator was indeed after a specific treasure.

The disheveled state of the riches of the kingdom, made the princess feel most uneasy. But it was not until she spotted that the curio cabinet– which normally housed the gold-plated shield featuring the etchings of a crown, a shoe, and a ballerina performing demi pointe that represented the Denison family crest– was empty, that her heart began to race and panic set in.

Oh my gosh… Derrick's right. We're in big trouble, she realized, looking at the shards of glass scattered on the floor beneath the cabinet, wide-eyed and horrified.

"Victrollia happened, sweetheart," Archibald explained. "Don't you worry your pretty little head. We've got a plan to get it back."

"We sure do," Marguerite agreed. "This is all going to be fixed quicker than you can say Denison Dynasty," she assured, flashing a sweet smile at the tiny royal.

Derrick's parents seem so sure. I wish I felt half as certain as they seem to be about all of this. Sighing, she looked to Archibald. "Derrick told me that we are going to use the Denison family enchantment, but how does that work exactly?"

Archibald looked to Derrick, eyebrows furrowed. "Son, have you not told her how our family crest works?" he questioned pointedly, his boleros voice brimming with disappointment.

Shifting his weight from one side to the other, Derrick ran his fingers through his chocolate brown hair. "I've always planned to father, but–" he began his voice hesitant and quiet.

"No!" Archibald declared, cutting him off. "Son, I know how much of a challenge it is to rule over this great kingdom, but that's no excuse for not carrying on family traditions."

Uh oh, did Derrick not tell me about the family crest because he doesn't feel like I'm really part of the family? she wondered. *Was Tyler right? Are Derrick and Misty going to send me back to the home after the baby comes?*

"You're absolutely right father," Derrick agreed, interrupting her thoughts.

Bending down to Kara's level, Derrick took her hands in his and explained, "Sweetheart, it's time that you learn the Denison family crest isn't just a family crest. It's also a key."

The princess's eyebrows wrinkled in confusion. "A key? A key to what?"

"Our family crest is the key to our ancestral magic. It holds all the love and goodwill of the Denisons who came before us which ties it to light magic," Derrick elaborated as though the concept were as easy as 1-2-3.

"Wow," Kara exclaimed. "It's cool to know that we always have people watching over us."

Nodding, Derrick agreed. "Yes, it is. Our ancestors protect us, but that could change if Victrollia tampers with the crest using dark magic." Sighing, Derrick squeezed her hands gently. "Sweetheart, I won't lie to you, Victrollia having the crest puts not only our family, but the kingdom as a whole in grave danger."

"Whoa, don't you think you should've told me about this a long time ago?" Kara queried her eyes wider than they were even a moment before.

Derrick nodded hesitantly. "Misty and I always meant to tell you, but we wanted to make sure you're ready for such a huge responsibility."

"Well, ready or not, she's going to have to take on the responsibility now," Archibald explained, his voice coated in the authority only a wise, elderly father can possess. "Each of you must recite the enchantment since you're all represented in our family crest. Son, we'll start with you. Do you know the enchantment?"

Taking a deep breath, Derrick focused on the cabinet in which the crest was normally proudly displayed and said, "A royal treasure has fallen into evil hands. Here and now I call upon the Dynastic Denison Divination to return it to its rightful place and protect our lands."

How can something be so creepy and so cool at the same time? Kara mused as a puff of golden smoke appeared and dissipated from the cabinet in seconds leaving in its wake the initial portion of the shield featuring a crown etching. Following suit, Misty grasped Derrick's hand and recited the chant just as he had, making the second portion of the shield featuring an etching of a dancer's silhouette appear out of thin air and float through the air to its proper place in the cabinet just as quickly.

Moments later all eyes were on Kara. "It's your turn, sweetheart," Derrick coaxed sweetly.

Glancing at her feet to avoid the hopeful yet apprehensive eyes of her loved ones, Kara bit her bottom lip. "Uh, um, are you sure that—" she began after a long moment, her voice meek and quiet.

Shaking his head, the king kneeled in front of the princess once again putting himself at her eye level. "Sweetie, you can do this," he assured her. "You mustn't doubt yourself or our ancestors. You don't have to repeat what Misty and I said exactly. You can put your own spin on it. You just have to believe in the magic of the Denison family," he insisted pleadingly.

"Yes," Misty agreed. "Believe in our family magic and everything will be fine."

"There is no pressure, sweetheart. Just believe in the Denison family magic," Archibald echoed.

Oh sure, no pressure. No pressure at all, Kara mused. *I just have to try and save a family I'm not even sure I'm really a part of, not to mention an entire kingdom to boot,* she chuckled nervously at the mere thought. *This is absurd.*

Closing her eyes, the tiny royal took a deep breath in an attempt to calm herself.

"Sweetheart, I don't mean to pressure you, but the longer the crest is in Victrollia's possession the greater the risk of—" Archibald began.

"I know," she insisted, cutting the elderly, former king off. "Just give me a minute." *Calm down,* the little girl told herself. *You can do this. You just have to believe in the Denison family magic.* As much as Kara wanted to do just that in the moment, doubt soon crept into her mind. *What if this doesn't work? What if I can't save the kingdom? What will happen to the kingdom? What will happen to me? Will they send me back to the group home before the baby even comes?* Shaking her head, she dismissed the thoughts and focused on the spot in the curio cabinet where the final piece of the crest should be and declared, "Royal treasures have fallen into evil hands. Here and now I call upon the Dynastic Denison Divination to return them to their proper place and ensure peace in our lands."

Kara's face fell as seconds ticked by and nothing happened.

***

I knew it wasn't going to work, Kara groaned inwardly as an awkward silence settled over the room. *After all, I'm not actually a part of the Denison Dynasty,* she sighed. *Why did I let them talk me into this?* she wondered. *This is so awkward. No one is even saying anything.* As that thought crossed her mind, she panicked for the second time that afternoon. *Oh my gosh! No one is saying anything. Are they mad? Are they disappointed? Are they–*

"It's okay, sweetie," Archibald assured her, abruptly interrupting her rumination.

Eyebrows wrinkled in confusion, Kara looked at him. "Okay? How is it okay? The enchantment didn't work for me. We didn't get the whole family crest back. Doesn't that mean the whole kingdom is in grave danger?" she queried pointedly, her voice coated in horror.

The usually confident Archibald looked down at his feet, avoiding her gaze. Eyeing him, Marguerite flashed the slightest of smiles and said, "Sweetheart, it's confession time."

"Confession?" Derrick echoed. "What do you mean?" he questioned, his voice laced with pure curiosity.

Closing the space between herself and her son, Marguerite placed a hand on his shoulder and squeezed it gently. "Derrick, sweetheart, Victrollia doesn't have the family crest. Your father set this whole thing up."

The wrinkles in Derrick's forehead deepened as he looked at his mother. "What are you talking about?" he asked.

"Sweetheart, we've talked about the family enchantment since you were a little boy. You know how powerful it is. We want to make sure you each know how to utilize it properly," the loving mother, and former queen explained.

Derrick studied his mother, bewildered.

Kara's eyes widened as she watched the exchange between Derrick and his mother. *Oh great, first I failed at using the family magic and then I caused a family feud. Even if the Denisons did believe I was part of the family before, they definitely won't after all this. Could things get any worse?* she wondered.

"I don't understand," Derrick said after a moment, looking from her to his father and back. "Don't you guys trust me and my family to use the enchantment properly?"

Sighing, Archibald jumped into the conversation. "Of course, we trust you son. It's just that you've never had to call upon our ancestors before. Your mother and I just wanted to make sure you all were able to utilize such powerful magic," the apprehensive king reiterated.

"Exactly," Marguerite agreed. "Now we have our answer; we know that we have to work with Kara a little bit more before she's ready."

Flashing a smile, Archibald looked to Kara. "What do ya say sweetheart, you up to learning a thing or two from us old folks?"

I guess that answers my question, Kara groaned inwardly.

"I, for one, think that's a wonderful idea. What d'ya say, sweetie?" Derrick questioned, his voice edged with excitement.

Biting her lip, Kara contemplated her response. *Honesty is the best policy*, she reminded herself. "I'd like to, but I'm scared I'll disappoint you," she admitted after a moment, her voice meek and quiet.

Derrick opened his mouth to respond but closed it when Misty spoke up first. "Aww sweetie, as long as you try your best, you'll do no such thing."

"How can you be so sure?" Kara questioned, her voice innocent yet skeptical.

Rolling her wheelchair forward, Misty pulled Kara into a hug, closing the space between them. "I love you, sweetie. We all love you," she assured. "As long as you try your hardest to believe in the family magic, there's no way you'll disappoint us."

Misty freed Kara from her embrace after a long moment and looked to the others, smiling. "Isn't that right, everyone?"

Kara fidgeted in her chair a bit as the others nodded in agreement and looked to her, eyes pleadingly.

"Say you'll do it," Misty urged. "For you, for your future sibling, and for our family."

Ugh. Why did she have to go and put it like that? Kara groaned. *I guess it's better to risk disappointing them by trying rather than giving up*, she decided. As pleading eyes continued staring back at her, she flashed a nervous smile. "Well, when you put it like that, how can I say no?" she asked.

With that, the adults in the princess's life all breathed a sigh of relief and exchanged hugs before parting for the evening with the promise of lessons in ancestral magic to come.

***

Why is this stupid enchantment so difficult for me? Kara groaned after failing at her third attempt to call upon the Denison Divination and return the family crest to its rightful place during her fourth lesson in ancestral magic with Derrick's parents.

Sighing, she looked around the still ransacked cellar, feeling more scattered than the priceless gems and treasures thrown about. *I don't know what's more of a mess*, she groaned. *This place or me.* "This is not working," she admitted after a moment. "I appreciate you guys trying to help by recreating the family crest, but it's not worth it. I can't do this," she said, her voice solemn and quiet. "It's no use."

"Sweetheart, you're overthinking this whole thing. Just believe in the Denison family magic. It's as simple as that," Archibald assured her. "Take a deep breath and try again," he suggested. The former king took a deep breath and let it out, as though demonstrating the action would somehow help the princess.

Seriously? How dense does Archibald think I am? This is ridiculous, she decided. *But, I can't disappoint him or anyone else,* she sighed. Rolling her eyes, Kara relented and followed suit, but it did nothing to calm her.

"I'm tired," she whined. "I don't want to try again!"

Archibald nodded. "Sweetheart, I know you're tired. Grandma Marguerite and I are, too, but we know you can do this. "You must keep trying," he insisted, his blue eyes pleading with her to understand. "You're a Denison and this is important to our family."

"If I am a Denison then why didn't Derrick and Misty tell me about the family connection to light magic when they first adopted me?" the princess blurted out as a single tear rolled down her cheek.

"Kara, sweetheart, don't cry," Archibald soothed. "I know my boy and I know he and Misty always intended to tell you about our familial connection to light magic eventually. Like he said, it's a big responsibility. I'm sure he and Misty just wanted to wait until—"

Shaking her head, Kara disagreed. "Being princess of this kingdom is a big responsibility, too, and I've handled that just fine, haven't I?" she shouted.

Nodding his head vehemently, Archibald agreed. "Of course, sweetheart. You're an amazing princess, but–"

"No buts," Marguerite asserted, eyeing him as she cut him off, joining the conversation. "Kara does a great job handling her duties as princess and I will not let you or anyone else tell her otherwise," the older woman declared resolutely.

The former king flashed his wife a smile. "You're absolutely right dear. I wouldn't dream of saying otherwise."

"Good." Returning Archibald's smile, Marguerite looked from him to Kara and back. "I think we could all use a break. How about some tea?"

"Good idea, honey. Some tea will help us clear our heads. It might be just what we need," Archibald said, his tone hopeful as he looked to the princess. "What do you think, sweetheart? Would you like to take a break and have some tea?"

Focusing on Archibald's kind eyes, Kara fought the urge to roll her own again. *Why do old people always think tea will fix everything?* she wondered as she considered her response. After a moment, she replied, "A break would be nice."

"That settles it then. Come along. Both of you," Marguerite urged before leading them into the castle's informal dining room.

How do they know their way around here so well? Kara asked herself as Marguerite pulled a few bags of tea from the mahogany cabinet while Archibald retrieved a kettle from a shelf above the stove. "Shouldn't we ask a member of the staff for help before we start moving stuff around?" she suggested as the elderly Denisons continued to rummage through the kitchenette in the far-right corner of the room.

"Nonsense," Archibald shook his head. "This was my kitchen before most of the current staff had their third birthdays."

Chuckling, Marguerite nodded. "And besides, I've been making tea since I was your age. You like chamomile, right?"

Nodding, Kara waited for the tea to brew while Derrick's parents busied themselves with getting cups from the cabinets. She sighed quietly as the older royals turned their backs to her. *Would they notice if I slipped out and went to the dance studio?* she wondered as she began to slowly roll backwards into the dining room doorway.

"Where are you headed, sweetheart?" the former queen questioned, making her stop cold.

"What do ya mean?" she feigned innocence.

Shooting her a knowing look, Marguerite chuckled. "I know we old people can be boring, sweetie, but don't go running off. We want to talk to you."

So much for dancing out my feelings. Biting her lip to keep from groaning, Kara forced herself to smile. "Yes, ma'am."

Smiling sadly, Marguerite crouched down to Kara's level so the two were eye to eye. "Sweetie, I've told you a dozen times, call me grandma. Archibald and I are your grandparents, whether you like it or not, and we wouldn't have it any other way, isn't that right?" she questioned her husband but continued to focus on the princess.

Archibald nodded, blowing gently into his mug of hot tea as he sat down at the table. "Of course, dear."

The curly-haired majestic found herself groaning inwardly yet again, as she anticipated the conversation that she and the elder Denisons were about to have. "I love you both very much, you know that, don't you?" Kara opened as she and Marguerite sat across from each other, joining the Denison family patriarch at the table.

"Of course, we do," Archibald assured her as Marguerite reached across the table for her hands and squeezed them gently, tears welling up in her eyes.

"We know you love us, sweetheart," the elderly woman reassured her. "We just wish that you could love the way you dance."

If Derrick's parents love me as much as they say they do then I have to ask them the hard questions, Kara decided as she looked into Marguerite's kind, green, moisture-filled eyes. After a moment, she took a deep breath and asked, "If you guys love me so much then that means I'm definitely part of the Denison family, right?"

Nodding his head vehemently, Archibald spoke first, "Indeed, you are, sweetie and you always will be."

"That's right," Marguerite agreed. "You've been a true member of our family since the day our Derrick and Misty adopted you and truth be told we considered you to be part of the family well before that. Kara, honestly, we've loved you since the day we met you," the former queen explained, her voice meek and quiet as a tear rolled down her cheek.

Leaning across the table, the tiny princess squeezed Marguerite's hand, took a deep breath, and pressed on. "If that's the case then why didn't you guys tell me about the family connection to light magic or at least make sure that Derrick and Misty told me?"

"Aww sweetie, is that why you're having such a difficult time with the enchantment? Are you questioning whether you are part of our family?" Marguerite queried, a lump forming in her throat as more tears escaped from her eyes.

Oh no! I didn't mean to make anyone cry. I hate upsetting them. I have to say something to fix this. But, what? the pint-sized royal wondered as she bit down on her bottom lip to keep from crying herself.

"Kara, sweetie, please. Honesty is the best policy," Archibald coaxed. "We want to help you and to do that we have to know how you're feeling."

Kara sighed. *Archibald sounds just like Derrick. Honesty may be the best policy, but it's not the easy one.* Squeezing Marguerite's hand again, she managed to croak out a quiet, "You're right," before she, too, burst into tears.

Letting out a breath, Archibald retrieved a handkerchief from his coat pocket and handed it to the tiny young girl. "I've suspected as much since the first time I saw you attempt the enchantment, sweetheart," he admitted. "But don't worry. I have something I think will help you."

"You do?" Marguerite and Kara questioned simultaneously.

Nodding, Archibald left the dining room and returned a few moments later, book in hand.

"Sweetheart, I retrieved this from the royal library. It's a biography about my grandfather, Maxwell Denison. He was very influential to this family and Starrycrest as a whole. I strongly encourage you to read about him. I think you'll find it…" Pausing, the former king tilted his head to the right, searching for the right word. After a moment, he finished, "…enlightening."

Sniffling, the princess wiped her eyes with his handkerchief then held it out to him. "What do you mean?" she asked, her voice a mixture of shyness and curiosity. "Oh, and before I forget to ask, what do you mean by you hope I learn to love the way I dance? Derrick said the same thing the other day and I'm not sure what he meant by it."

"Sweetie, Maxwell was an–" Archibald began.

"There you guys are," Derrick said as he rushed into the room unknowingly interrupting his father. "I've been looking everywhere for you, sweetie. I'm afraid royal duty calls," Derrick urged, looking to his beloved little girl.

"Uh oh, did I forget a commitment this afternoon or something?" Kara queried worriedly.

Derrick shook his head. "No, sweetie, but we really should be going."

"Yes, sweetheart," Marguerite flashed a smile at Kara, but it didn't reach her still moist eyes. "When royal duty calls, you must answer quickly."

Nodding, Archibald chuckled. "Besides, we old folks can tell when we're not needed." He smiled and looked to Kara. "Sweetie, remember what we discussed, read the book I found for you, and we'll see you on Thursday for more enchantment practice, okay?"

The young majestic forced herself, agreeing even though she dreaded the mere thought of any further enchantment practice. "Sounds like a plan," she answered after a moment.

With that, the princess bid the elder Denisons goodbye and followed Derrick.

***

"Wait, we're leaving the castle?" Kara questioned as her adoptive father led her outside. "Where are we going?"

Derrick flashed a mischievous grin. "You'll see. Just follow me and try to keep up. If we don't get there soon, we'll miss it."

"Miss what?" Kara persisted.

"Come along," Derrick urged. "We're almost there."

Relenting, Kara chuckled and forged ahead. Minutes later, she found herself groaning as they came upon Starrycrest Sweets and Petals, the shop owned by the kingdom's florist and chocolatier. "Don't tell me Thomas and Maurice are fighting again. I thought Misty talked some sense into them."

"Oh, she did," Derrick confirmed, his voice brimming with pride. Maurice and Thomas are getting along great now and, thanks to Misty, we get to reap the benefits."

Rolling her eyes, Kara looked at him. "Derrick please, stop talking in riddles and tell me what's going on."

Throwing his head back, Derrick laughed and opened the door for her.

The smells of peppermint, peanut butter, and chocolate wafted into the princess's nostrils as they entered the specialty shop. Taking a deep breath in, the little girl smiled, exposing her beloved dimples. "Something smells good in here."

Misty, who was sitting at the counter in the back of the shop, smiled from ear to ear. "I'm so glad you guys made it. The new chocolates are all so good. I can't be objective."

Looking past Misty, Kara eyed the sweets on the counter, an assortment of milk chocolate covered strawberries, white chocolate drizzled pretzels, and dark chocolate truffles, her eyes widened instantly. "Oh, new chocolates. I wanna try."

Maurice and Thomas smiled. "Feel free to try as many as you like, your highness," Thomas urged, his gentle hazel eyes glittering with excitement.

"We need all the help we can get," Maurice added.

"I'll help with anything that requires eating chocolate," Kara assured them as she pulled up next to Misty, settling on the queen's right while Derrick settled to her left.

"Mmm... I love the fresh flavor of this one!" she exclaimed after biting into a dark chocolate, peppermint truffle.

"Try a chocolate peanut butter covered strawberry," Misty urged, handing one to the little girl. "They practically melt in your mouth."

Accepting the fruit, Kara chomped into it enthusiastically. "Delicious," she agreed after a moment. "Have you tried the pretzels yet?"

Derrick looked from Misty to Kara and back, his eyes sparkling with love. "Pace yourselves ladies. We're here to help Thomas and Maurice not get tummy aches."

The little girl eyed the florist and chocolatier, her eyebrows scrunched in confusion. "What's troubling you today, friends?" she asked sweetly.

Maurice sighed, his shoulders slumping slightly. "The problem, sweetie, is we only have enough room here at the shop to sell one of these new chocolates and we can't decide which one is best."

Chuckling, Thomas added, "We thought you and your lovely parents having a taste test would help but..." glancing to Misty, he paused and flashed a sly grin.

The queen bit into a chocolate truffle, her cheeks turning slightly pink. "I don't mean to make this more difficult for you guys," she said sheepishly after a moment. "It's just the chocolates are all so good. It's impossible to pick just one."

Nodding, Derrick frowned at their friends. "Sorry boys. I agree with my lovely wife."

"Why don't you just let customers decide?" Kara suggested.

Maurice looked at her, eyebrows furrowed. "Hmm?"

The princess chewed into another chocolate covered strawberry, actively resisting the urge to roll her eyes. *How could two smart guys like Maurice and Thomas miss something so obvious? This must be why Misty seems so annoyed during some personal audiences,* she realized. After a moment, the princess finished her strawberry and addressed them, using the quiet, nonchalant, positive voice she normally reserved for royal engagements. "You could sell one of the chocolates each month until you earn enough to buy a bigger shop then put whichever one sells best in your new shop permanently."

Maurice's dark brown eyes widened in disbelief as he studied the tiny royal. That's brilliant!" The kingdom chocolatier exclaimed, excitedly slapping his hand on the counter.

"It sure is," Thomas agreed. "Why didn't we think of it?"

"Well, ya know what they say, like mother, like daughter," Derrick winked at Kara. "Misty's advice solved your last conflict and hopefully Kara's advice will solve this one."

Wow, I didn't think they would like my idea that much. Maybe Archibald and Marguerite were right. Maybe I'm better at this princess thing than I thought, Kara smiled.

"You're right your majesty. That's a great idea," Thomas praised. "I don't know what we'd do without you."

"You'll never have to worry about that," Misty assured them.

Maurice nodded. "Good. This kingdom needs you." Placing a hand on Misty's belly, he smiled affectionately. "All of you."

The happiness Kara had felt moments before evaporated like dew in the morning sun as she realized Misty had told their florist and chocolatier friends about the baby. *Is Maurice right?* She wondered. *Does the kingdom really need all of us? Is there room for another young royal?* The princess's stomach began to churn as her mind flooded with questions. Within moments, she had four sets of worry- filled eyes focused on her.

"Forgive me for saying this, your highness," Thomas said sheepishly after a moment, his bushy eyebrows knitted in concern. "You don't look so good. Are you feeling okay?"

Uh oh. They know something is up. I can't talk to them about what's worrying me. It's not the time or place, she decided. *But I should still be honest.* "Derrick was right. I think I gave myself a tummy ache," she admitted meekly.

"Awww, okay sweetheart, let's get you home," Misty said as she backed away from the counter.

"Yes, we should be getting home," Derrick agreed. "Thank you for the chocolate, gentlemen, and best of luck," he added, smiling as he led the girls out the specialty shop.

"Kara, sweetheart, you were thinking so hard back there I could practically see the wheels turning in your head. Are you sure a tummy ache is the only thing that's bothering you?" Derrick queried as the three of them walked back to the castle.

Kara groaned inwardly. *I should've known Derrick would ask questions. Nothing ever gets past him.* "I guess I'm just a little nervous about how much things are going to change soon," she admitted, her cheeks growing hot at the mere thought of the future.

"Aww, sweetie, it's okay to be nervous. Misty and I are nervous too," he reassured her.

"That's for sure," Misty agreed. "I've tried to hide it, but truth be told I transformed into a basket of nerves the moment I found out about the baby."

"That's perfectly understandable, sweetheart," Derrick assured Misty as he gave her hand a gentle squeeze. "I'd be worried if you weren't nervous. Everything is going to be fine as long as we have each other."

Am I included in that 'we'? Kara wondered. *I really want to be, but I'm just not sure if there's room for another princess in this kingdom.* Sighing, the tiny royal shook her head, attempting to dismiss her thoughts.

Derrick flashed a reassuring smile. "I know what you girls need."

"A good night's sleep?" Kara queried.

Derrick chuckled. "Yes, that would do us all some good, but not before we dance out our feelings. How about it loves?" he suggested, his voice brimming with affection. Are my beautiful girls up for a dance party?"

With that, the royal family raced each other to the castle dance studio where they laughed and twirled to their hearts content before turning in for the evening.

Chapter 6

Dragging herself out of bed Wednesday morning, the princess lifted her arms over her head for a moment in a luxurious stretch, transferred into her wheelchair, and chose her outfit for the day.

"Okay, I'm ready," Kara called out after selecting a pair of tights to wear.

There's that stupid clubfoot again, she murmured inwardly, glaring down at her lower half. While her mother's disability was neurological, her disability stemmed from her spinal cord not developing properly and her lower limbs being paralyzed as a result. The paralysis didn't bother her much because it was all she had ever known. However, another aspect of her disability, her clubfoot, was a constant imposition. *I'll never look as delicate as other dancers*, she reflected mournfully as her personal assistant Ashleigh, a copper-skinned woman in her twenties, with long black hair and an incandescent smile, walked into the room.

"Good morning, miss," Ashleigh greeted, perusing the princess's selection of clothes. She held an item up. "This is such a wonderful dress! I love the sequins and its emerald color."

"Thank you," Kara responded. "I like it too. It was a gift from Misty."

"That's sweet. It also reminds me, you must be so excited about today," Ashleigh offered cheerfully, kneeling in front of her mistress to pull on her tights, tugging them when the material got caught on the troublesome clubfoot.

"Ouch!" Kara cried.

Massaging the princess's foot gingerly, Ashleigh frowned. "I'm so sorry, miss! I didn't mean to hurt you," she apologized.

Wiping her eyes, the princess assured her helper. "It isn't your fault, Ash. My foot just got in the way again, that's all. I'll handle this myself," *I wish I could just get rid of my ridiculous foot. I can't feel it anyway... except for the pain... and it just makes it harder to dance*, she groused to herself as she deliberated on her clubfoot preventing her from wearing pointe shoes and looking as graceful as other dancers. Taking a deep breath, the tiny majestic pushed thoughts of her clubfoot aside, locked her wheelchair into place, pushed herself up on her feet so that she was halfway standing up in her chair, and pulled up her tights.

"You're pretty good at that, your highness," Ashleigh complimented. "What do you need me for?"

The princess shrugged. "I do okay. Having help just speeds things up," she explained. "Well, most of the time anyway," she added under her breath as the young woman turned her back in search of a brush.

"Pardon me, miss." The personal assistant said as she turned around, brush in hand. "I didn't catch the last thing you said."

"Oh, it was nothing," Kara assured the assistant, her cheeks turning red slightly. You were saying you thought I'd be excited about today. Why is that?" she queried, quickly changing the subject.

"I was told you're to attend an ultrasound with your parents." Ashleigh spoke as though this were the most obvious statement in the world. The words pulled the young dancer out of her thoughts and she became aware that Ashleigh had moved on to brushing her unruly curls.

"I completely forgot about that!" Kara exclaimed. This remembrance rejuvenated her, lifting her spirits exponentially. She was going to get the chance to spend some long overdue one-on-one time with Misty today, no matter what else took place.

The anticipation that Kara had felt earlier tripled when Misty and Derrick pulled up to Starrycrest Schoolhouse in a horse-drawn carriage to pick her up that afternoon. The tiny family arrived home in plenty of time to meet the midwife, Tabitha Middleston, though they had had to stop at several points along the way in order to address the concerns of citizens who were apprehensive about their beloved queen's condition.

I hope he doesn't drop her, Kara thought anxiously as Derrick lifted Misty up onto an examination table. The conscientious midwife had already set up everything she'd need in one of the castle's bigger rooms. In this room, the future nursery, the walls were adorned with myriad representations of Lisianthus flowers, in a range of yellow hues. *Wow! Misty's stomach has really grown*, she marveled as the queen revealed her baby bump in preparation for the sonogram machine. *Just keep smiling*, she coached herself. *I love her so much, I can't bear to hurt her feelings*. She brought her focus toward Misty's face, steadfastly avoiding her midsection.

Tabitha, a towering woman in her mid-fifties, had gray hair, dark brown eyes, and permanent frown lines around her mouth, got straight to work, offering the royal family not even the smallest of pleasantries. "Oh my," she breathed wonderingly as her examination began. "Someone's gotten quite big."

Who does this lady think she is? How can she be so insensitive? More than a little taken aback that the medical professional didn't reach her own level of decorum, Kara vowed to stay silent about it. Glancing over at Derrick, she saw, from his clenched teeth and unamused glower, that he had interpreted the woman's comment similarly.

"Not too big though, right?" Misty worried. "I'm trying to keep my diet balanced, but I'm so hungry all the time that I sometimes slip up. Especially when it comes to sweets. I figured the hunger came from a combination of morning sickness and my body not absorbing enough nutrients." The queen went on for far longer than she'd intended to, her anxiety ramping up the more she talked. Kara brought their hands together, providing comfort as best she could.

Misty's eyes darted between her daughter and her spouse. "What if something *is* wrong? Kara, sweetheart, maybe you should wait outside."

Placing a hand on the expectant royal's shoulder, Tabitha tried her best to soothe her. "Take deep breaths and try to relax, your majesty. It's perfectly normal for a woman to experience substantial weight gain throughout her first pregnancy. Before you work yourself up into a frenzy, let me check on some things and make sure the baby is on track, okay?" The midwife smiled, but it didn't reach her eyes.

Kara's eyes stayed glued to Misty while the midwife searched for the baby's heartbeat. *I know that I haven't been the best baby cheerleader*, she admitted. *That doesn't mean I want something to be wrong...*

Within minutes, Tabitha's face lit up, brimming with genuine delight. "I know exactly what's happened here," she gasped, giving off positivity for the first time in Misty's appointment so far. "I hear two heartbeats, not one," she announced.

"Sure. Mine and the baby's, right?" Misty's question belied her still-present nerves.

Tabitha's amusement skyrocketed. "If I'm accounting for yours as well, I hear three heartbeats."

Kara's gaze pivoted from her parents to their midwife. "Twins?" she whispered urgently.

Nodding to acknowledge the little girl, Tabitha confirmed, "Yes, that's right. You're about to get yourself two siblings."

Two babies! I'm definitely in trouble now, the princess's mind declared for her before pushing her recent conversation with Tyler to the front of her mind.

She opened her mouth to reply but closed it as Derrick enveloped her in a hug, solid and meaningful. "Did you hear that, sweetheart? We're getting twins," he sighed, disbelief and joy running through every syllable.

Returning the king's tight hold, Kara kept track of Misty over his shoulder. Her adoptive mother was beaming from ear to ear. "Congratulations," she managed to tell her after a moment.

"Thank you! Congratulations to you as well," the queen reciprocated through a mist of tears.

Once the family had exchanged best wishes, Tabitha gave the queen a couple tidbits about what being an expectant mother really entailed – that the job was more than dietary restrictions – before departing for her next appointment.

Grinning at his wife and daughter, Derrick was the epitome of pure happiness, recommending, "How about we celebrate by taking a scenic carriage ride? Then I'll fix us a celebratory dinner." He put all his energy into transferring Misty safely from the examination table into her wheelchair.

"That sounds nice," the queen told him jovially while he clicked her seatbelt into place.

"Wait!" Kara protested plaintively, staring at Misty. "Shouldn't Derrick be staying at home? Aren't we having girls' night?" Her breezy tone took so much effort that it faltered almost as soon as her questions started.

The downward spiral didn't end there because the pregnant mother's spasm was an unmistakable sign that the disappointment of days previous was about to be repeated. Misty had forgotten their plan for the evening.

"Sweetie, I'm so sorry! I completely spaced, *again*. Pregnancy brain, I guess." Misty put a hand to her stomach. "I'm really overwhelmed by the news of the twins and, honestly, I don't think my stomach can handle pizza right now. Do you mind if we do it another night?" Before Kara had even had a chance to think of an answer, the queen went on, "We'll bring Ashleigh and Marie along too! We'll all make a day of it – go shopping, eat a fancy lunch, get manis and pedis, anything else you want. Would that be okay?"

No, it wouldn't. I miss you. I'm having a hard time dealing with this, too, and I need you right now, Kara's inner voice wanted to protest.

"Of course, it would! Kara knows we all have a ton of responsibilities before the babies come." Derrick winked at his daughter, but nothing could make up for the fact that he put words in her mouth.

This is pointless. They both have pregnancy brain, the princess groaned to herself. She'd been defeated, so she told herself, and her parents, as much when she agreed to dinner at home. She stayed quiet throughout their meal of cheese-and-spinach stuffed chicken, asparagus, and chocolate covered strawberries, escaping to the studio as soon as she could. She danced out all her feelings until she went to sleep that night.

***

"Hey there, little lady. How're you doin' today?" Stella's upbeat voice rang out from the chair Kara had been introduced to a few days before. The talented instructor wore a black leotard and was ready to dance.

The princess sighed, her shoulders slumping. "Can we just dance? Please?"

"Oh my, you're having quite a day, aren't you?" Stella looked the young girl up and down, further assessing her state of mind. "In that case, I'll get down to business. Tell me everything you know about the Sugar Plum Fairy dance."

"I only know that the role is performed by a principal dancer," Kara recited easily. "Why does that matter?"

Stella stared at her student in barely contained disbelief. "For more reasons than you know, my little friend. A dancer can't truly sign on for and/or do a part justice until he or she knows, and understands, its intricacies backward and forward."

"Oh, I'm going to learn the part, trust me." Kara's oath was a vehement one. "I'm going to be the best Sugar Plum Fairy this kingdom has ever seen."

Stella gave a single quick nod in praise of the young girl's dedication. "Good. I'm glad to hear such resolve from you. I wasn't tryin' to criticize you, little lady. What I'm trying to tell you is that dancin' is about more than just learning the part," Stella elaborated, pausing as she decided on her next words. "A dancer must embrace, and embody, his or her role in order to dance it as it was meant to be danced and share a memorable performance with audiences," the eccentric dancer advised, the passion and earnestness she felt for her calling filling the studio.

What on earth is she babbling about, and when am I going to get to dance? Kara's brain whined at her. "I thought we were dancing?" was all the princess permitted herself to say aloud.

Shooting Kara a withering look, Stella pleaded, "Hold your horses." After convincing herself that the young girl was ready to listen to what she had to say, she resumed her train of thought. "You must embody every inch of the Sugar Plum Fairy. Your character is the leader of the Kingdom of Sweets, yes, but, perhaps more importantly, know that she is strong, beautiful, and whimsical. I have no doubt that you can bring this role to life in the most spectacular way. That's why your father cast you. He wouldn't steer an entire production wrong."

"Yeah, yeah, yeah," the princess huffed, rolling her eyes. "I appreciate the vote of confidence. Now tell me what you've got planned for my solo before I turn all gray and wrinkled."

"Such enthusiasm!" the teacher deadpanned sarcastically.

Kara flicked her eyes at her seatbelt, sighed heavily, then looked up at Stella. "I don't mean to be rude, I really don't. I just had a tough day yesterday, and dancing will help me get over it."

"Twins weighing heavily on your mind, are they?"

"Is there anything Derrick doesn't tell you?" Kara chuckled wetly, frustrated.

Spinning quickly around in her chair, Stella once again amazed Kara with her ability to ease the tension in a room. "I can tell you don't want to talk about it, so I won't push. I'm always here if you change your mind." She smiled openly, highlighting the truth of her proposition. "Now onto lighter subjects. Remember how I told you that this beauty," she patted the clear seat affectionately, "is called the Dance Dazzler?"

The princess verified that she did, absently, still in awe of the powerful machine. *It's so cool – I just wish I could figure out how it works.*

"Well, it does its name proud. It allows every dancer, no matter the limitations they might be facing, to dazzle audiences."

Beginning to show the first signs of an improving mood, Kara asked, "How can it work without a joystick?"

Waving a dismissive hand, Stella laughed. "That's an easy one, girlie! All you have to do is wear this," she pointed a finger at a small remote pinned to her chest that Kara hadn't noticed against the black backdrop of her leotard. "As long as it stays in contact with your body, it can use your movement to control the chair," she explained, making it seem like the easiest thing in the world. Finished with her introductory spiel, she took a steadying breath. "Ready to take it for a spin?"

"I've never been more ready for anything!" the princess proclaimed confidently.

"Good! But, it's kind of high off the ground so you can't transfer into it yourself. Once I lift you into it, I'll give you the controls, and then it's all up to you, little lady." Stella maneuvered the chair backward, hit a button on the remote to lock it into place, stood up from the seat, and helped her pupil replace her, just as she'd said she would.

From the comfort of the Dance Dazzler, the young royal's thoughts swirled contently. *This is exactly what I imagine sitting on a throne feels like… I've never been this tall before. It's awesome!*

Unable to keep her excitement at bay, the princess quickly hit the button on the remote, now attached to her dress, to unlock the Dance Dazzler's brakes and turned her body to the right. She giggled nervously as the unique wheelchair jerked in that direction.

"We've got a lot of work to do," Stella laughed. "First things first, take a breath and relax."

The young royal followed her teacher's instructions, bargaining with her body and hoping it would help her rather than hold her back. The result seemed to please the woman in front of her, who proceeded, "Good. Now, do you know why the Dance Dazzler comes with a clear seat?"

Kara had no clue, and she wasn't about to lie. "No, I don't. It makes it look really awesome, though."

Stella agreed with an amused laugh. "It ain't just the seat color that makes it awesome – it's the purpose of the seat."

"What do you mean?" she countered, distracted by how tall she still felt in this chair.

Pulling a stool over from a corner, the older woman arranged her placement so that she and Kara were across from each other, in a perfect line. "What do you want the audience to be looking at when you dance?" she asked, spinning around on her stool.

"Me, of course." Kara giggled at the sight of her mentor making circles around her.

Stopping her progress suddenly, Stella smiled proudly. "Exactly! The seat of the Dance Dazzler is clear so that people will focus on the dancer, not the apparatus he or she is in."

"That's really neat! Can I try spinning around you?" the pint-sized royal changed topics excitedly.

"Yes but, before you do, there is something you must understand," the dance instructor warned, her tone hardening a bit ominously. "The Dance Dazzler is meant to be an extension of your body so, to use it properly, a dancer must be comfortable moving his or her body in time with the music. That being said, I'm going to turn on the Sugar Plum Fairy Suite and I want you to try and spin, okay?"

Nodding in confirmation, Kara waited for Stella to start the music, took a deep breath, and slowly turned her body until she'd succeeded in guiding the Dance Dazzler through a complete circle.

***

"Hey, sweetheart, Stella and I have a surprise for you," Derrick said by way of greeting as Kara entered the dance studio the next day.

"The two of you have a surprise for me? Should I be scared?" the princess joked.

The leader of the realm shook his head. "No sweetie, it's a good surprise," he smiled genuinely. "Stella and I have been trying to decide who should play the prince in *The Nutcracker* for weeks now because we weren't sure any of the boys in the adaptive ballet class could pull it off." He explained, his tone thoughtful and quiet. "Then when Misty and I visited the group home the other day we got an idea and well–"

Eyebrows furrowed, the princess quickly interrupted; "What are you getting at? And why would you guys go to the group home without me?" she questioned urgently.

"Tyler, come on out here please," Derrick called out, grinning mischievously.

Oh my gosh. The princess's mind spun as the spiky-haired boy who had messed with her for years at the group home entered her beloved dance studio. *This can't be happening. They just can't be serious.*

Putting a hand on both of Tyler's shoulders, Stella jumped in, grinning from ear to ear. "Girlie, this here is Tyler and he will be playing the prince in the *Starrycrest Starlets* rendition of *The Nutcracker* this year," she declared excitedly.

Kara's cheeks instantly turned from rosy pink to bright crimson. "Oh, c'mon, you guys cannot be serious! Derrick, do you even know who this is? He has tortured me for years."

Chuckling curtly, Tyler smirked. "That's just because you're such an easy target, *princess*. How do ya think I feel? No one told me that *you* were going to be dancing in the stupid thing."

Rolling her eyes, Kara looked to Derrick. "See what I mean?"

Stella laughed. "Don't be so dramatic, girl. Tyler is gonna be a great dance partner, aren't ya bud?"

The boy shrugged. "Yeah, whatever," he muttered. "I'm just here to avoid another chili night at the group home. I don't care about this stupid thing."

Letting out a huff, the princess shot Tyler a look. "The thing is called a ballet. And it's not stupid. You're the one who is stupid."

"That's enough!" the king shouted, his voice filling the entire dance studio.

Stunned, Kara sat up straighter in her wheelchair. *Whoa, since when does Derrick raise his voice?* she wondered. *I didn't know he was capable.* A quick glance at Tyler's wide eyes and Stella's deeply wrinkled forehead told her that they were just as shocked and confused.

After a moment, Derrick took a deep breath and addressed the children. "It is clear that you two know each other and perhaps have a bit of a past, but from this point on, you must act in a manner befitting of a princess and befitting of a gentleman because that is what you are. Even more importantly, you must respect each other because respect is something that all dance partners must have when performing together. From now on, you are to treat each other with nothing but kindness and respect. That is in order, do we all understand each other?" Derrick queried, his usual calmness and quiet sincerity once again intact.

While the boy nodded, the young majestic opened her mouth to object. "But–" she began.

Derrick shook his head earnestly. "Kara, this is what Misty wants and we need to do everything we can to keep her happy right now for the sake of her health and the health of the babies. With that said, I'll remind you that I need you to act in a manner becoming of the princess of this kingdom and respect Tyler as your dance partner. Is that understood?"

Are you kidding me? Kara mused. *Could he be treating me any more like a subject right now? This is ridiculous. These babies are changing everything.* At that moment, she wanted to do nothing more than demand his understanding even if it meant throwing a tantrum, but she couldn't bring herself to do so. *I have to do what's right for Misty and the babies,* she lamented.

Glancing down at her feet, she answered, her voice meek and quiet. "Yes, Derrick."

The king nodded. "Good. I must go. I expect nothing but a good report from Stella when I return," he advised. Poking his head in the door just moments after leaving the studio, he looked to the dance teacher. "Good luck with these two."

Smiling briefly, the ballet instructor wasted no time getting right down to business. "Okay, before I determine how the two of you will dance together, I have to assess your individual abilities. I already have an idea of what Kara can do because I've seen her in class and we have been working on her solo which means, Tyler, you are in the hot seat," she announced, smiling with anticipation. "Show me all of that talent that the queen was bragging about."

Talent… Misty spotted talent? What is she talking about? What did I miss? the princess wondered as Tyler flawlessly moved into fourth position, his feet pointing in different directions one in front of the other; his right arm rounded in front of him and his left arm open to the side. Eyes wide, she watched in amazement as he extended both arms and bent his knees slightly before rising gracefully, executing a seamless plié, then brought his arms together while rising up on the ball of his left foot into a perfect demi pointe. He then flawlessly bent his right knee so that his big toe touched his left knee, performing a textbook passé, then zipped through 10 consecutive turns effortlessly before landing, his feet parallel to one another and back in fourth position.

"Wow!" Stella shouted, her voice brimming with amazement and disbelief. "The queen wasn't lying. That was amazing. You are quite the talent," she praised enthusiastically.

Tyler shrugged, his cheeks turning slightly pink. "Eh, I'm actually a little rusty," he admitted sheepishly.

The princess's eyes widened in utter astonishment. "That's what you call rusty?" she butted in, her voice colored with surprise. "Why didn't you ever tell me you can do that? That was the best passé I've ever seen. Why have you been holding out on me?"

Letting out an exaggerated sigh, the boy shot Kara a look, his brown eyes dark with frustration.

"Really *princess*?" he asked sarcastically. "Do you really think I would last a minute in the group home if any of the kids knew that I dance?"

Kara waved a dismissive hand. "After the other kids see you in *The Nutcracker* there's no way they're going to make fun of you," she smiled encouragingly. "You are a good dancer, Ty. Derrick and Misty always say that a good dancer shouldn't waste their talents."

"Whatever," Tyler muttered. "I'm only here because the stupid queen opened her big mouth to Betsy."

"How dare you come into the castle and call Misty stupid. She is the leader of this kingdom and my mother. You have no–"

Tyler's face grew more and more crimson by the minute. "I've got news for you, Misty is not your mother. She is about to have two babies and when she has those babies you are going to be just as much an orphan as I am!"

Sitting up a bit taller in her wheelchair, the princess fired back, "Oh yeah well, at least–"

"Enough!" Stella yelled, her voice filling the entire studio. "This is a mess. Were either of you even listening when Derrick spoke about respect?"

"I was," the young royal insisted. "But he–"

"No," the dance instructor shook her head vehemently. "I won't hear it. I don't even know where to begin so I'm goin' to insist that the two of you leave here and take some time by yourselves to consider whether you even want this performance of *The Nutcracker* to happen and then come back to rehearsal ready to learn a lesson and work your butts off. Is that understood?"

Jeez, Stella looks serious, Kara mused, nodding absentmindedly. *We're lucky that the yelling in here today didn't knock all the mirrors off the walls. This is all Tyler's fault, but I guess I'm going to have to make the best of it,* the princess lamented before leaving the studio.

***

Kara walked into the dance studio a couple days later and saw Tyler performing a grand jeté, a ballet move that had been famous in the kingdom ever since Misty used it to ultimately defeat Trovella. "Showing off before I even get here, are we?"

"You can't always be in the spotlight *princess*," Tyler quipped, a proud smirk across his face.

Shaking her head vehemently as she walked into the dance studio, Stella looked from Tyler to Kara and back. "No, no, no. I will not listen to any more ridiculous arguments between the two of you. Forget what I said the other day about ya havin' a decision in this. The queen insisted on the two of you dancing together in *The Nutcracker* so now you two must work together whether you like it or not, got it?"

The children nodded simultaneously.

"Good. The three of us are going to have to work together a lot, so I thought we'd start today off a little differently by learnin' a little somethin' about each other," the eccentric dance instructor smiled encouragingly. "So, before we start rehearsal today, we're gonna go around and tell each other why it is we love to dance," she looked at Kara, still smiling. "Why don't you go first little lady?"

What is she thinking? That we're all going to bond over why we love dance and then suddenly be able to work perfectly well together? Ha. This should be interesting, the princess thought, pretending to take the time to consider her answer. "Well, for me, the answer to that question is easy. Dancing is something that helped to bring Derrick, Misty, and me together. It is something that we have always enjoyed. I have loved to dance ever since the first day they brought me into this studio and I always will," she explained, her voice cluttered with happiness.

Nodding, Stella smiled genuinely. "That's very sweet Kara," she said kindly before turning toward Tyler. "What about you, Tyler? How did you gain your love of dance?"

"Sorry ladies, I don't know either one of you well enough to start spillin' my guts," the young boy replied half-jokingly.

Throwing her head back, the princess chuckled. "C'mon, Ty, they stuck you in the group home two months after I ended up there. We've known each other practically our whole lives. Are you afraid I'm going to blab or something?"

Glaring at the small majestic, Tyler let out a huff. "Not everybody has such a sweet connection to dance Kara," he shot back, his voice laced in irritation.

"Whoa," Stella placed her hand on Tyler's shoulder and squeezed gently. "Take it easy there, tiger." She looked at him and then glanced at the young royal. "Remember what I said. You must work together and respect each other, no ifs, ands, nor buts about it. That bein' said, I agree with Tyler," she smiled at the young, gifted, male dancer. "If ya don't think that ya know us well enough to tell us about your connection with dance then ya shouldn't have to."

"But–" the pint-sized monarch began.

Standing quietly in front of the children, the eccentric dance instructor stared at them intently as if considering what to say next. After a long moment, she spoke. "I'm going to tell you about my connection to dance even though I don't know you that well because I feel that it would help both of you." Pausing, she found a stool, took a seat, and continued, "Ya see, we have a lot more in common than you might think. I, too, was an orphan at one time. And I personally gained a love and appreciation for dance while living with Madam Sterling," she said proudly.

The kids offered her nothing more than blank stares in response.

Stella laughed wholeheartedly, her tone colored by sheer surprise. "You guys know Madam Sterling, right? As in *the* Madam Sterling?" the dance teacher queried, her tone more than a little expectant.

The princess shook her head. "No, who is Madam Sterling?" she asked innocently.

"And what do you mean you lived with her?" Tyler added, eyebrows knitted together in confusion.

Eyes widened in astonishment, mouth slightly opened, the spiky pink-haired woman stared at the kids for a moment. "You call yourselves dancers and you don't know who Madam Sterling is?"

Kara and Tyler laughed. "Is she *that* important?" the young majestic queried.

The dance instructor looked from Tyler to Kara and back, her expression suddenly very stern. "This is not a laughing matter, kiddos. Madam Sterling is the reason why we are allowed to dance today."

The princess's forehead wrinkled in confusion. "Huh? Allowed to dance… why wouldn't we be?"

"Yeah, what are you babbling about?" Tyler asked, echoing her perplexed feelings.

"Long ago, before your grandparents were even born, dancing was banned in Starryton, Mooncrest, Eclipston, and all surrounding kingdoms, because it always awokeTromelia, Trovella's great grandmother, from her slumber in her cave. This made her very angry and put all the realms at risk, but Madam Sterling changed all of that," the dance instructor explained, her voice suddenly quiet and serious, a lump forming in her throat as she struggled to continue. The atmosphere of the dance studio turned from relaxed to tense as the reality of what Stella said sank in. *I can't imagine dancing ever being banned in this kingdom or any other*, Kara shuddered at the idea, struggling to listen as Stella went on. "She was brave like Misty. Her family was from a faraway kingdom called Rubiesville, where dancing was among the most beloved and respected forms of art. When she and her family first moved to Eclipston and heard about the ban she traveled to Tromelia's cave and wished that dance no longer be a trigger for the troll's anger so that everyone in Eclipston and the surrounding kingdoms could dance whenever they pleased."

Grinning happily, the princess exposed her beloved dimples. "Well, the ban was lifted, so everything went according to plan, right?" she asked, excitement sparkling in her eyes.

Tears instantly welled into Stella's eyes. "Her wish was granted, but she, like your mother, learned that all magic comes with a price. The one thing that Madam Sterling loved just as much as dance was family," the dance instructor explained, her tone quiet and defeated, as tears began trailing down her cheeks.

Stella doesn't seem like the type of person who cries much. This can't be good, Kara realized, her own tears beginning to blur her vision as she saw the pain behind the eccentric dancer's eyes. Wiping her tears, the little girl spoke a moment later, her voice meek and hesitant. "What price did Madam Sterling have to pay?"

"She had to give up her ability to have a family in the traditional way. That's why she became a kiddo keeper and eventually let me into her home for a little while."

"You said that before… what's a kiddo keeper?" Tyler asked, his voice colored with curiosity, as he rejoined the conversation.

"In Eclipston, there is no group home. Instead, we have the *Eclipston Kiddo Keeper Program,*" Stella explained. "The program allows families and individuals to house children in need, while deciding whether to adopt them. Sometimes it works, other times it–" Pausing briefly, the eccentric dance teacher considered how to finish her sentence, tears welling up in her eyes again. "Doesn't," she finished solemnly.

"Oh. My. Gosh! That sounds awesome," Kara shouted excitedly. "I've said for years that more kids in the group home would get adopted if families had a real chance to get to know us, haven't I, Ty? I mean, after all, that's what worked for me." The princess continued before her dance partner could respond, "A program like that would be great here in Starrycrest. It would do so much good. Why don't we have one?"

Chuckling, Tyler furrowed his eyebrows at the princess. "As a member of the royal family, shouldn't you be the one to answer that?" he queried pointedly.

Oh. My. Gosh. He's totally right. I can fix this. This is how I'm going to make the kingdom better. Misty and Derrick will be so proud that they will never forget about me, the princess was instantly energized by the idea.

"Ty, I–" the princess began.

"Okay guys, that's enough," Stella said, her voice calm yet firm. "We should really plan the performance."

Shaking her head, the pint-sized royal disagreed, "Sorry, Stella, I cannot believe I'm saying this but, Tyler is right. I gotta go talk to my parents about this right now."

"But–"

Ignoring Stella's objection, the princess hurried into the castle proper, more than ready to tell Derrick and Misty about her great idea.

***

Kara's excitement about her plan to help the children without families in Starrycrest faded slightly the moment that she found Derrick and Misty in the master suite meeting with Tabitha.

"Hey guys, I didn't know Misty was having another ultrasound today. How are the babies lookin'?" she asked as she slowly wheeled into the room.

"Oh, hi, sweetheart, you don't want to be in here," the king said, his voice full of anxiety as he motioned her out of the master suite. He quickly shut the door behind them and flashed her a nervous smile.

Looking her adoptive father up and down, the toe-headed young girl studied him, her eyebrows scrunched together in bewilderment. "Why are you acting all spazzy? Are Misty and the babies okay?"

Derrick nodded. "Of course… of course they are," he said, a hint of anxiety still present in his tone. "I'm just happy to see you, how about we have a movie night? Just you and me."

"Sounds good," Kara smiled genuinely. "But I need to talk to you abo…"

"Okay, I'm going to pick out the snacks. You pick the movies, and go easy on the rom coms," the king shouted, cutting her off as he walked toward the castle kitchen.

Derrick's acting really weird, Kara realized as she made her way to the castle theater. *Something is definitely up, but what? He just said that Misty and the babies are doing fine and he wouldn't lie about that.* As soon as that question crossed her mind, it filled with more uncertainties. *Would Derrick lie? Is there something he doesn't want me to know? Is something wrong with Misty?* She physically shook her head to stop the rumination. *No, he wouldn't lie. I should just focus on the positive*, she decided, continuing to pick titles from their film library. *Derrick and I are going to get some one-on-one time and I'll have the chance to tell him about my idea that could help families here in Starrycrest.* The sheer anticipation of telling Derrick about the idea filled Kara with so much joy that she literally had to bite her tongue to keep from bursting with excitement the moment he came in. *This idea is very important and could mean a lot for the kingdom. I have to wait for the right moment,* she realized.

"Didn't I tell ya to go easy on the romantic comedies sweetie?" Derrick joked as the first film Kara had chosen for the evening commenced on the big screen in the castle theater. "We've seen *Just the Way You Are* at least six times." The princess laughed. "It hasn't been that many and besides, it's awesome. You know it's based on—"

"How we became a family. I know. I know. It's just a bit cutesy for me," the king explained, before chomping on a handful of popcorn. "Don't get me wrong sweetheart," he said after finishing the buttery, salty snack. "I love you and our movie nights, and I always will, but I'm kind of hoping a boy will be added to our family in a few months because movie night could use a little testosterone," he chuckled.

This is it. Families are the perfect opening. Taking a breath, Kara faced Derrick. "Speaking of growing families, I've been thinking about a way that we can help the families here in Starrycrest grow a little," she said, her voice suddenly quiet and meek.

Oh my gosh. That sounded so lame, the princess cringed inwardly at her weak segue.

Looking away from the movie screen, the king focused on his daughter. "Sweetie, the royal status of our family affords us a lot of privileges but controlling the rate at which families grow in the realm is not one of them."

Kara couldn't help but giggle. "Derrick, that's not what I meant," she said, her voice a bit higher, but still timid.

"Okay then, what did you have in mind?" the gentle majestic questioned before eating another handful of popcorn.

"Today, Stella told Tyler and I about the Kiddo Keeper Program in Eclipston which–"

"I know what the Kiddo Keeper Program in Eclipston is, but we can't establish anything like that in Starrycrest," Derrick said matter-of-factly the moment he'd finished swallowing.

Scrunching her eyes, the princess studied him. "But why not? It would be great. It'd help so many kids in the kingdom."

"Oh look, your favorite part is coming up," he flashed a half-smile, pointing at the screen.

The princess watched intently as a scene replicating the moment that her parents had given her a daughter's ring and announced that they wished to adopt her flickered across the screen.

There's no way that they could ever forget about me after a moment like that, the young regal thought, suddenly feeling a lot more hopeful that Misty and Derrick would love her no matter what happened in the future.

"Establishing a kiddo keeper program here in Starrycrest could allow more kids to have moments like that," she said as the credits for the movie began to roll. "Wouldn't that be great?"

"Yes, it would," the king nodded hesitantly. "But we just can't… it's… complicated," he admitted solemnly.

"Derrick, if you really aren't going to even consider establishing a kiddo keeper program in Starrycrest then I'm going to need a better reason than 'it's complicated,'" Kara persisted, looking him straight in the eye.

"Sweetie, it's not–"

"Derrick!" Misty called out, abruptly interrupting their conversation.

"Sounds like Misty needs you," the princess said, her voice slightly deflated. "You should go, but we are going to talk about this later," she insisted.

The joy and hope Kara had felt faded as Derrick ran toward Misty's voice, ignoring her persistence.

How can Derrick be so dismissive about something so important? What does he mean by 'it's complicated'? the princess pondered, as she headed from the theater to the one place where she could always clear her head: the dance studio.

Kara groaned as she approached the studio and spotted Stella and Tyler rehearsing without her. *Ugh, my dance studio isn't even mine anymore. What has happened to my life? I'm so over changes. What's next? Is Tyler going to live here instead of me?*

"Hey girlie, is everything okay?" Stella interrupted her spiraling thoughts.

"I'm sorry. I didn't realize anyone was in here. I'll go," the tiny royal muttered.

Quickly shaking her head, the eccentric dance instructor disagreed. "Don't be silly," she chuckled. "Join us. Queen Misty said we could rehearse anytime, but this is your studio after all," Stella explained, flashing her a slight smile.

I can't believe they are already giving other people special privileges to use the dance studio after class. This has always been a special place for the three of us. How could they do this?

"I don't feel like dancing," Kara managed, her voice as solemn as her mood. Biting her lip to keep from crying, the princess inched toward the door.

Wide-eyed, Tyler questioned her, "*You* don't feel like dancing? Are you sick?"

"Something like that," Kara said solemnly, inching even closer to the door.

Stepping between her and the doorway, Tyler stopped the curly-haired royal. "C'mon, Kara, stay and dance. I don't wanna go back to the group home yet and rehearsing alone blows. Stella is turnin' into more and more of a drill sergeant every day."

Chuckling, the dance teacher quickly protested, "Hello, still here, and not a drill sergeant last I checked."

"I'm just messin' around," the boy explained, his cheeks quickly turning the color of his hair. "Help a brother out," he insisted, flashing her a grin. "Tell the princess that she should stay and rehearse with me."

Kara let out a huff, moisture behind her eyes. "Ty, please, just let–"

"I agree that we all should stay, but not to rehearse," Stella grinned. Running over to the phonograph, Stella turned on The Fairy Song from *A Midsummer Night's Dream*. "Who's up for a little freestyle?" she queried excitedly, still smiling.

"Oh my gosh! This is my favorite song," Kara exclaimed. "How did you know?"

"Let's just say a little birdie told me," the eccentric pink-haired woman reached for her. "Don't just stand there – dance – both of you," she insisted.

Why can't everything in life be this much fun? The princess wondered, twirling around the studio with Tyler as soft, melodic sounds filled the room. *I'm going to miss this studio almost as much as I'll miss Misty and Derrick if they make me leave after the babies are born. At least if we established a kiddo keeper program I could maybe-*

"For cryin' out loud, Kara," Tyler groaned. "You're thinking so hard it's makin' my head hurt. What's on your mind?" he asked, pointedly.

"You wouldn't understand."

"Try me," Tyler persisted. "I'm smarter than you think," he added, his tone laced with amusement.

"You gotta' promise not to laugh," the pint-sized royal stopped dancing and looked him straight in the eye.

"Just spill your guts already," Tyler contended as he also slowed to a still.

"I talked to Derrick about starting a kiddo keeper program here in Starrycrest, but he won't even consider it. He says it's complicated."

Frowning instantly, Tyler shook his head ardently. "How can he make huge decisions concerning the entire kingdom daily, but say that helpin' some kids find a family is too complicated?"

"I know, right? I tried to tell him how much good it would do for the kingdom, but it was like he didn't even care." Sadness clouded the princess's features in spite of the beautiful music that filled the dance studio.

"At least you tried," the young male dancer encouraged after a moment. "I'm glad to know you're using your royal status for good instead of evil," he quipped, flashing a crooked grin.

Chuckling, Kara questioned him. "Are you calling me evil?"

Tyler shrugged. "At least I got ya to laugh."

Stella, who had been quietly watching the exchange between them finally chimed in. "I'm glad to see you two finally getting along, but I'd like to see less talkin' and more dancin'," she insisted, putting Kara's hand into Tyler's. "If you really want to establish a kiddo keeper program here in Starrycrest, you'll find a way," Stella smiled at the princess. "Just relax and dance. Everything will work itself out," she encouraged.

The words, *'If you really want to establish a kiddo keeper program here in Starrycrest, you'll find a way,'* swirled through the little girl's mind until well after she and her comrades left the dance studio that evening. Tossing and turning in bed that night, she could think of nothing else. *Stella is right. If I want to establish a kiddo keeper program here then I have to find a way and I will*, Kara decided as she finally drifted off to sleep.

Chapter 7

"Isn't this awesome?" Kara asked, her voice laced with excitement, as she spun around slowly in the Dance Dazzler.

"What is it?" Tyler questioned, eyebrows furrowed, as he studied his dance partner.

Performing an even larger circle, the young royal answered, her voice chipper, "It's called a Dance Dazzler and I'm going to use it during the Sugar Plum Fairy Dance, right Stella?"

Grinning, the dance teacher shook her head. "You'll not only be using it during your solo, but also your dance with this guy right here," Stella explained, pointing her head toward the young male dancer.

"What?" the kids asked in unison.

"That's right," Stella nodded. "And we are going to get started right now." She looked at the princess, still smiling. "Bring the Dance Dazzler to the center of the room."

Leaning, Kara did as instructed and brought the unique wheelchair forward.

"Good, now face Tyler, hold your arms out in front of you, and sit very still," she said calmly before turning toward the little boy. "And as for you… you're going to run toward her and jump," she said, her voice full of anxious excitement.

"Jump? What do you mean?" the spiky-haired boy queried.

Looking at the princess, Stella nodded, smiling mischievously. "Into that little lady's arms," she answered, feigning nonchalance.

"You want me to what?" Tyler shifted his weight from one side to the other, wide eyed.

"You're going to jump into Kara's arms and then she is going to lift you up onto her shoulder. Basically, we are going to do a shoulder lift with a slight twist because the ballerina is the one performing the lift instead of the one being lifted," the dance instructor explained, her tone still casual.

Kara stared blankly at Stella. *It's official… Stella has gone from eccentric to downright crazy,* she mused.

"Are you nuts?" Tyler asked, echoing the princess's feelings, his voice colored by utter disbelief. "There's no way that *she* can lift me," he eyed the princess momentarily and then looked himself up and down.

Stella chuckled. "Ya need to get to know your dance partner a little better, bud."

"Oh, please," Tyler groaned. "I know her as well as anyone. We've known each other our entire lives."

"So, then, did you just forget that your partner has a service dog who she has to lift once a month because he doesn't like water?" the ballet instructor said pointedly.

Biting her lip, the princess chimed in, her voice hesitant. "Well, Dex weighs about 60 pounds, but that's different; he's got four legs to stand on when I put him down."

"And what do you weigh, Ty? About 80?" The dance instructor studied him, deliberately ignoring the young majestic. "It'll take lots of practice, as lifts always do, but I don't see why we shouldn't give this a shot," she smiled encouragingly. "Ty, since you don't feel comfortable practicing jumpin' into Kara's arms first, we'll just go straight to the dance steps. Go to the other end of the room, perform an assemblé, and then allow her to lift you onto her shoulder."

"But–" Tyler objected.

Shaking her head, Stella stopped him. "Do as I say, or Queen Misty and I will be having a discussion later."

Shoulders slumped, the boy walked to the other side of the room. Reluctantly, he planted his feet into a classic ballet pose; one foot in front of the other, his feet turned so that the heel and toe of each foot was adjacent to that of the other, in fifth position. He then brushed his right leg across the floor with his foot in pointe, demonstrating a beautiful battlement glisse while simultaneously performing a pliéwith his left leg. He then launched into a jump bringing his feet together, causing them to meet in pointe while still in the air, Finally, with a shy grin, Tyler landed, his feet back in fifth position, performing a perfect assemblé. "Great job with the assemblé, Ty," Stella encouraged. "Now, do it again, but after you land in fifth rise up on your toes into relevé," she instructed, smiling happily. Sighing audibly, the spiky-haired boy shook his head before begrudgingly performing as she asked.

"You have great form, Ty," the dance instructor nodded as she studied him. "Your mother must have been an impeccable dancer. Keep repeating this move set until you are in front of Kara and ready to jump," she said, her voice energized and cheerful. "But don't forget about your arm movements," she warned. "The arm movements used in lifts vary, but I prefer starting in first for lifts like the one you two are performing because it is simple yet beautiful when paired with an assemblé. Just remember to extend them as you jump. Allowing them to flutter a bit before you land. Act almost as if you're painting something in the air," the instructor explained as she demonstrated the motion.

Shaking his head, the boy could no longer hold back his frustration. "That's where I draw the line," he said, his cheeks instantly red. "I'll let Kara perform the lift if I have to, but I'm not goin' to do anything to make my steps more girlie."

Kara and Stella laughed simultaneously.

"C'mon, little man, if ya are going to do the lift just commit to it fully," Stella insisted. "Besides, Starrycrest seems like a fairly enlightened kingdom, no one will care if we switch up gender roles, right Kara?" the dance instructor queried, her voice hopeful.

Nodding, the princess agreed. "No, no, of course not." Eyebrows furrowed, the pint-sized royal looked to Tyler. "How did you get to be such a good dancer? And did Stella say something about your mother?" she asked, her voice laced in disbelief.

Tyler's face instantly fell into a frown.

"Sorry if I'm being nosy," Kara said quickly. "It's just you never talk about your mother, so–"

Clapping her hands together, Stella interrupted, "Now isn't the right time for that conversation. We have a lift to rehearse. Let's get to it."

"Right," Tyler agreed, rising slowly onto his tiptoes, into the start of a perfect relevé.

Arms shaking slightly, the princess grunted as she struggled to lift him up onto her shoulder. *Whoa. I can't believe I actually managed to lift him up*, she mused as her dance partner sat in the anointed spot, also trembling a little.

"Great job, kiddos," Stella grinned. "That was an awesome first attempt."

Wide-eyed, the princess questioned her, "You're kidding, right?"

"No, it's like I said earlier, lifts take a lot of practice. Kara, next time lift Tyler up as high as you can and then lower him onto your shoulder. That should make the lift just a bit easier. I know you struggled but, trust me, that really was a good first try," the dance teacher reassured, smiling brightly. "We just have to tweak it a little bit, so that's what we'll do starting tomorrow. That's enough lifting for today."

The princess let out a breath and smiled. "Great. I so need a break. I'll see you both tomorrow," she declared, her tone cheerful as she began to unfasten the seatbelt of the Dance Dazzler.

***

Chuckling, Stella stopped her from unfastening the seatbelt, "Not so fast, little lady. I said the two of you were done practicing, but *you* still need to work on your solo."

The young royal sighed. "I'm tired. Can we practice my solo tomorrow, please?" she pleaded innocently.

Before Stella could even respond, Tyler broke out into laughter, shoulders shaking as he looked at the princess.

"What's with the cackling?" she asked, brow furrowed.

"Nothing," the young male dancer shrugged his shoulders. "It's just funny how someone who supposedly loves dance so much could get tired of it so easily. I guess you don't have to work too hard when you live in a big, fancy castle." He eyed her, smirking mischievously.

How dare he even go there? I am the hardest working dancer in this kingdom. The small majestic suddenly felt more angry than sleepy. *I'll show him,* she decided.

Nostrils flaring with determination, Kara looked to the dance instructor. "Stella, tell me how to do figure eights like you mentioned the other day, Tyler is going to stay and witness all of my hard work."

The ballet teacher readied her hand for a high-five. "Way to go," she whispered. Smiling, the spiky red-haired boy slapped his hand against hers.

Looking from Stella to Tyler and back, the princess blinked. "Wait… you guys set me up."

The dance instructor chuckled. "You got your second wind and Tyler gets to avoid the group home a bit longer. What's the harm?"

"Yeah, *princess*, What's the harm? Shouldn't a hardworking dancer like yourself be more excited about your solo?" he teased.

"Aren't audiences just supposed to be quiet spectators?" the tiny regal shot back.

"Okay, okay, that's enough," Stella chuckled and looked to the little girl. "Let's rehearse, you've got a solo to perfect. I'll go get what we need so we can get down to business," she said before rushing out of the studio.

"Wait… where are you going?" the princess called out.

When Kara received no response, she looked to Tyler. "What's she up to?"

"Heck if I know." Shrugging his shoulders, the boy chuckled. "Whatever Stella has up her sleeve has got to be more entertaining than game night at the group home."

A moment later the princess's question was answered when Stella returned to the dance studio with a group of young, muscular men, holding fake giant red and white candy canes and Christmas presents covered in various shades of pastel wrapping paper, adorned with sparkling snowflakes and splendid mistletoe.

"Thank you so much gentlemen. Your muscles and generosity are greatly appreciated," the dance instructor said, excitement coloring her voice, as the men arranged the sculptures throughout the room.

"Uh… what the heck is all of that for?" the princess asked, her eyebrows scrunched in confusion.

Stella let out a laugh. "It's for your performance, of course." The instructor motioned to the props that had been placed around the studio. "All of these props will be on stage during your solo, so you'll be dancing a figure eight between them."

At that moment, Kara noticed the small amount of space between the props. She looked from Stella to the props and back, her eyes full of disbelief. "You've got to be kidding."

"C'mon, Kara, where is your sense of adventure?" Tyler joked.

Shooting her dance partner a look, the princess let out a huff. "Have you seen the space, or lack thereof, between those props?"

Tyler nodded. "Yeah, and fancy wheelchair or not, I'll bet you can't dance a figure eight between them. They are way too close together. I mean, c'mon, look at them," he eyed the props warily.

Following his gaze, Kara's heart began pounding inside her chest. *Tyler is right*, she realized. *This is going to be hard, but I can't let him know that. I must seem confident.* Despite her every instinct telling her to do the opposite, a moment later, she heard herself saying, "Am I hearing a challenge?"

Tyler laughed, his cheeks turning slightly crimson. "Sure," he agreed. "I challenge you to do a perfect figure eight between those props."

"Prepare to be amazed as I conquer your challenge," the princess declared, giggling nervously, still eyeing the props.

Shaking her head, Stella interjected. "Don't get ahead of yourself, little lady. Ya gotta crawl before you can walk and walk before you run."

Nose scrunched in confusion, the pint-sized royal shot her dance instructor a look. "Uh Stella, where have you been? I can't do any of those things."

Stella's eyes lit up as she broke into a fit of laughter that made her shoulders shake. "I was speakin' metaphorically, little lady. What I mean is that you must first become comfortable in the Dance Dazzler. After that, you must become comfortable actually dancin' in it, and then you can begin perfecting your solo."

The princess's shoulders slumped, a sigh quickly escaping from her lips. "That's going to take forever," she said, her voice suddenly void of enthusiasm. "What do we do first?"

Stella looked her straight in the eye. "Do ya remember what I told ya the other day about the Dance Dazzler?" she asked in a calm yet serious tone.

"You mean all of that stuff about how the Dance Dazzler is supposed to be an extension of a dancer's body?" Kara asked after a moment.

"Yes, exactly. The Dance Dazzler is an extension of you that is meant to help you reach your full potential as a dancer. So, sit up straight, smile, relax, and just let yourself dance," the instructor directed, her tone still stern yet hopeful.

The young royal wasted no time doing as she was told. *This song really is beautiful*, she thought, listening to the romantic melody that filled the room as she extended her arms out into first position, aligning them with her belly button. The moment she did Derrick's voice popped into her head. *'Remember to always extend your arms out directly in front of your belly button, sweetheart. That way they'll never be too high or too low.' So many of Derrick's dancing tips have become second nature,* she laughed, rounding her arms slightly. A moment later, she extended them into second position, and leaned a tad forward. "Whoa," she shrieked as the Dance Dazzler jerked forward.

"You're okay," Stella encouraged. "That's why we're doin' this. Just keep moving and remember that the Dance Dazzler is meant to be a continuation of you, so just take it easy, and try to have fun. Just spin like you did the other day."

Taking a deep breath, the young royal turned her body ever so slowly to navigate the dazzler. Over the next few minutes, she formed a series of circles in the Dance Dazzler, quicker and with more ease than she had just a few days prior.

"I'm finally getting the hang of this thing," she said, pride coloring her voice. "But I am starting to feel a little dizzy."

"Of course, you are," Stella laughed. "You've done nothin' but go in circles, so I'd be worried if ya weren't." The instructor once again looked Kara straight in the eye and spoke sternly. "You accomplished a lot today, so I am going to help you get back in your chair. But I want you to promise that you'll be back tomorrow prepared to do your best, so that eventually you can meet Tyler's challenge and give a great performance, okay?"

"You bet." Kara flashed a smile as Stella sat her back in her chair and fastened her seatbelt. The little girl glared at her dance partner, "I'm definitely up to the challenge."

With that, the princess bid her dance instructor as well as her partner goodbye and raced out of the dance studio.

***

Wow, we're actually getting pretty good at this lift. Hard to believe that's the fourth one of the day, Kara mused, as she and Tyler rehearsed in the studio a couple of days later.

"Excellent job today, kiddos," Stella said. "Even I worked up a sweat," she chuckled. "I'm going to call it for today, but be ready to get right back at it tomorrow, okay? You both need to be on top of your game for the big performance."

"Can't we stay just a little bit longer?" the young male dancer queried, an uncharacteristically whiny quality to his voice.

Stella eyed Tyler as she helped him to lower from Kara's shoulder. "Do you see all the sweat on this leotard?"

Tyler let out a dry laugh. "I get it. I'm just not ready to go back to the group home yet," he admitted quietly, the melancholy sense that he had about him which typically disappeared while he performed, quickly returning.

"I figured as much," Stella said, as she walked toward the boy, closing the space between them. "What's going on little man?" she questioned, placing a gentle hand on his shoulder. "Talk to me," the instructor insisted quietly, looking him straight in the eye.

Looking down at his feet, Tyler quickly broke eye contact. "Nothing," he mumbled. "It's stupid."

Stella shook her head vehemently. "No, no, no. I'm not lettin' ya dismiss this, little dude," she insisted. "Besides, anything that gives you more motivation to dance can't be stupid. Now, tell me what's going on before I tickle it out of you."

"It's really not–" Tyler began.

"I warned you," Stella said before quickly and teasingly stroking the little boy's belly.

The tiny male dancer broke out into a bout of laughter.

"Okay, okay," he said after a moment, his face still red from giggling. "It's just that I don't want to go back to the group home. Betsy is making scrambled eggs and bacon for dinner tonight. Her eggs are disgusting and usually come out more liquid than scrambled," he said, cringing at the mere thought. "And, last time I ate her bacon, I chipped a tooth," he explained, pointing to the damaged bicuspid as he opened his mouth.

Laughing, the dance instructor nodded. "I've been there, little man. For all of Madam Sterling's amazing talents, she couldn't cook to save her life. Best advice I can give you is to avoid the bacon and put hot sauce on the eggs."

"Really?"

Stella shook her head. "Trust me, it'll change your life."

Well, would you look at that? Kara thought, watching the exchange between them. *I have never seen Tyler laugh so much, let alone ask an adult for advice. He respects her and she seems to like him*, the little girl realized as she got an idea.

"Ya know, Tyler, if you really don't want to brave Betsy's eggs again, you can hang out here for a while," she said nonchalantly.

"For real?" Tyler questioned, his eyes widened in disbelief.

"Sure. Derrick's always saying we need to hang out more if we want to be better dance partners. Hang here for a while tonight and we'll watch a movie or something," she suggested, her voice still casual.

Shifting his weight from one side to the other, Tyler considered her recommendation. "Can we eat junk food while we watch the movie?" he questioned after a moment.

Kara giggled. "Isn't that a given?"

With that, the kids bid Stella goodbye and bolted out of the studio.

Chapter 8

"Race ya to the snacks?" Giggling, Kara sped ahead of Tyler before he could answer.

"Cheater, cheater, pumpkin eater," Tyler called out as he sprinted to catch up.

"Whoa, whoa, slow down kiddos," warned a 6-foot-tall, 200-pound man with short black hair adorned with bright orange tips and a short goatee, intercepting the princess as she burst into the kitchen just behind Tyler. "You should never run when you're so close to knives."

Tyler grinned. "Yes, I win! Bring on the movie night goodies."

"Yeah, yeah, yeah. Chill out," Kara told Tyler before turning her attention to the man in front of them, who she realized she didn't recognize. "Who are you and what're you doing in my kitchen?"

The man laughed, his shoulders shaking slightly as he looked down at the little girl. "You must be the princess I've heard so much about," he said, extending his hand out toward her. "I'm Antonio Cacciatore, but most people call me Tony. I'm the new chef here at the castle. Can I whip anything up for ya, kiddos? I can cook anything, but I'm best known for my pastas and desserts."

Eyebrows knitted in confusion, Kara shook her head. "But Derrick loves to cook. Why would he hire a chef?"

Accepting the chef's extended hand, Tyler shook it, "I'm Tyler, but most people call me Ty, friend and official dance partner to the princess. I think what she means to say is that it's nice to meet you, Tony. Oh, and thanks for offering to cook us some grub, but we're just here for snacks."

"Fair enough," Tony chuckled. "It's nice to meet you too, little man. And, to answer your question, princess: the king told me he decided to hire me because your mother is having a difficult pregnancy and he wanted to free up more time to devote to her," he explained nonchalantly.

What does he mean by 'difficult pregnancy?' Kara wondered. *Misty seems fine lately. Why does Derrick need to devote more time to her when he spends so much time—*

Are you okay, your highness?" Tony questioned, interrupting Kara's thoughts.

Blinking, the princess smiled. "Yes, I'm okay. Call me Kara and please forgive my rudeness," she said sweetly.

"No worries, little lady," Tony assured her. "It's great to meet you as well."

"Good, now that introductions are out of the way let's get down to business," Tyler said. "Did Derrick tell you where they keep the snacks?" he probed, smiling excitedly.

I've never seen Tyler like this, Kara realized as she spotted his smile. *It's nice to see him so happy and lighthearted for once,* she sighed. *I wish he could find such happiness forever.*

"I'm not sure what snacks you're referring to," Tony said, feigning innocence.

"C'mon, Tony, don't play dumb. If you don't show us movie-night-worthy snacks soon, the princess is gonna have you beheaded, right Kara?" the young royal's friend threatened jokingly.

I wonder if Tony has a girlfriend? He seems like he--"

"Earth to Kara," Tyler waved a hand in front of the princess's face, stunning the pint-sized majestic out of her thoughts yet again.

"Oh, yeah… sorry," the princess flashed Tony a mischievous grin. "Bring on movie-night-worthy sustenance or you'll pay," she warned, her voice colored with amusement.

"What qualifies a snack as being 'movie-night-worthy'?" Tony queried, his expression full of enjoyment.

Kara rolled her eyes. "Like you don't know," she countered swiftly. I'm sure Derrick gave you the 4-1-1 and told you that the queen comes in and out of this kitchen like 20 times a day. I know she's gotta have a stash of sugary goodness nearby. So, like Tyler said, show us the goods."

The fun-loving chef let out a roar of laughter. "Okay, okay you two, I give up," he held his hands up for a moment as if signaling surrender. "I'll show you where the queen goes for snacks, but just this once, and please don't go too crazy. If there is a noticeable difference in goodies then I'll have to deal with the queen's pregnancy-crazed wrath or, worse yet, lose this awesome new gig," Tony explained as he led them to an elevator in the very back of the kitchen.

"Oh my gosh!" Kara shouted as the three of them piled into the lift. "I've asked Derrick and Misty where this elevator leads so many times and they've never answered. They either change the subject or tell me not to worry about it. Where are we going?" she asked, her voice full of eager excitement. "Where does this elevator go?"

"Just wait and see," the friendly culinary artist answered as he pressed the button to take them to their destination.

"Oh, my goodness!" Kara exclaimed as the elevator opened to reveal a room filled with shelves of decadent chocolate boxes, goumet lollipops, delicious truffles, soft baked cookies, and every other confection ever imagined on one side; with gorgeous, bountiful arrangements of every flower from common, yet delicate, Daisies to rare, exotic Blue Angel Trumpets on the other. "What is this place?" the princess asked as she scanned her surroundings, her voice laced with a mixture of disbelief and excitement.

"I'll tell you what it is, it's heaven right here in Starrycrest," Tyler said happily as he ran straight for the chocolate treats.

Tony laughed and looked at the princess. "Do you remember Thomas and Maurice?"

"Sure… they're our friends, the florist and the chocolatier that Misty told to combine shops."

Nodding, he continued, "Right. Well, their business is doing so well that even in the larger shop they can't keep up with demand. Your mother arranged to let them move their shop here to the castle until they find an even larger space, in exchange for them agreeing to donate 20 percent of their profits to the group home for the next three months," he explained.

"Wow… why didn't Misty tell me any of this?" the young royal wondered aloud.

Glancing in the direction of Tyler, the larger-than-life man let out a chorus of robust laughter. "She probably thought you and your friends would eat into the profits of Maurice and Thomas," he joked.

Following Tony's gaze, the princess saw that Tyler had already taken double his body weight in treats from the shelves.

"Think ya got enough treats there, Ty? No one is supposed to notice that we've been here, remember?"

Tyler shrugged, "Gotta load up for the movie."

The chef nodded in agreement. "Ty's right princess," he bent down to her level and smiled genuinely. "Take whatever your little heart desires, but it has to be our little secret because I told your mother and father that I wouldn't tell ya about this place," he whispered sweetly.

"Are you sure?" the princess questioned fretfully. "You could–" Tyler rushed back to his comrade, arms still overflowing with sweets. "What Kara means to say is," he said quickly. "Thanks a million, Tony… you rock."

With that, the pint-sized royal collected her favorite sweets and the friends went off to enjoy a film with enough snacks to last three days.

***

"Whoa... this place is awesome," Tyler said, looking from one end of the theater to the other wide-eyed. "I've never seen a screen that big," he confessed, his eyes transfixed on the focal point of the room. Kara giggled. "I know. It's crazy, isn't it? It's actually bigger than the screens at Starrycrest Theater," she explained proudly. "Derrick designed the whole thing. The chairs are his favorite part."

Tyler eyed the chairs warily. Although each looked immaculate having not even a single piece of popcorn wedged in its crevices, the overall appearance was nothing more than that of classic red theater chairs. "What makes 'em so special?" he questioned, still eyeing the chairs. "See for yourself," the princess encouraged, motioning toward a chair in the front row. "Seems like a regular chair to me," the young boy said, sounding bemused a moment after he sat down. Laughing, Kara hit two buttons that Tyler hadn't noticed on the armrest of the chair. "How about now?" she questioned. Seconds after, the chair simultaneously reclined and began massaging Tyler's back. "Oh," he flashed a cheesy smile. "I could get used to this. What should we watch?" "Not sure," Kara shrugged. "Let's pick something from our film library."

Wide-eyed, Tyler reluctantly stood up from the fancy theater chair. "How many films does it take to fill a library?"

Chuckling, Kara led him up a ramp to the back of the theater where the projector and film reels were stored.

***

This is ridiculous, I should've known we weren't going to be able to agree on a film. We've been here an eternity, the princess sighed. "For crying out loud, Ty. Just pick a movie."

Letting out a huff, the boy shot Kara a look, "Give me a break. I wouldn't even have agreed to watch a movie here if I'd known that 95 percent of the film selection consisted of romantic comedies." The pint-sized royal rolled her eyes. "Fine. Let's just see what's on television, shall we?" she questioned rhetorically, picking up a remote that was stored next to the projector. "Oh look," Kara stopped flipping through the channels after a moment. "*Dare to Dance* is on," she declared excitedly, referring to a competition begun by Zoe Hempster, a ballerina who had become famous after flawlessly starring in Starrycrest Dance Company's performance of *Swan Lake* at the last minute after both the company's principal dancer and her understudy had fallen ill. She had awed everyone in the kingdom, despite not having time to rehearse and decided to capitalize on her fame by creating the show which featured dance battles between her and other dancers in Starrycrest and surrounding kingdoms. "Oh my goodness! Zoe just did like 20 pirouettes in a row and doesn't even look like she's dizzy. Isn't that nuts?" Realizing that Tyler had not said a word since she turned on the show, Kara turned to see that all color had drained from his face. "What's up?" she asked, her voice full of alarm. "You look like you've seen a ghost." "I kinda have. Zoe is my mother," he whispered, still looking at the big screen television and not the young royal. Throwing her head back, the princess laughed. "Very funny, Ty," she said sarcastically while tearing open a package of peanut butter fudge. Reluctantly removing his tear-filled eyes from the screen, the young boy looked down at his feet. "I wouldn't lie about something like this, Kara. I mean, c'mon, I have her eyes. Just look at them." Kara nearly choked on a piece of fudge the moment she saw Tyler's olive-green eyes staring back at her on the big screen. "Oh my gosh! How did you find her and why didn't you tell me?"

Tyler shrugged. "You've had a lot going on over the last couple of years," he pointed out, his voice meek and quiet.

Have I really been so focused on myself that I missed something as big as Tyler finding his biological mother? The little girl wondered as an incredible sense of sadness washed over her. At that moment, Derrick's voice invaded her thoughts. *'You need to realize that there is more to being a princess than glitz and glamour sweetheart. Your title comes with responsibility as well. It's your duty to help Misty and I make Starrycrest a better place.'* Is this what Derrick's been talking about? Have I gotten so caught up in the royal life that I have forgotten about my friends? she scolded herself inwardly as moisture built up behind her eyes.

Fidgeting in the chair next to her, fear flashed through Tyler's eyes. "Oh, Jeez. Kill the waterworks. I didn't mean to upset ya."

Wiping a tear from her right cheek, the tiny majestic turned to face Tyler. "Just because I am royal now doesn't mean that I don't care about my friends. I am so sorry if I made you think otherwise. Tell me what has been going on with you," she pleaded.

"I've always known that Zoe is my biological mother because I was dropped off at the group home with a picture of her and a letter explaining that she couldn't keep me because she was going to be a prima ballerina." Tyler's voice was timid and nonchalant, but Kara could hear the pain behind his words. It was the same pain she still felt during the rare moments that she spoke about how her biological parents hadn't wanted her due to her Spina Bifida and, more recently, the pain she felt when she wondered whether Misty and Derrick would really want her around after the babies were born.

"I feel your pain, Ty."

Nodding, he continued, his voice a bit meeker than moments before, "As soon as I was old enough to understand what ballet was, I started taking classes and actually went with one of my classes to see *Swan Lake*," he explained.

"Oh my gosh!" Kara's eyes widened in surprise. "How was it to actually meet her?"

"Terrifying and thrilling at the same time," Tyler admitted, color instantly filling his cheeks. "She knew who I was right away and actually took me aside to show me some dance moves."

The pint-sized royal's eyes went wide and brightened with excitement. "Wow, that sounds awesome!" she exclaimed.

Nodding, Tyler went on. "It was. Zoe was amazing, until I told her I hadn't been adopted yet," the little boy said, his timid voice full of melancholy. "Her whole attitude changed then. She made it clear that she can't be my mother because her dance career is in its prime. She did offer to give me a recommendation to include in a dance school application in the future, though."

The princess's excitement deflated quicker than air from a popped balloon. *Poor Tyler! It hurts enough to know a parent gave you up once, but to be rejected a second time? He must feel so awful,* she realized. After a long moment, tears welled up behind the small regal's eyes and she said the only thing she could think to say, "I am so sorry, Ty."

The boy shrugged. "Don't be sorry. I don't need her anyway."

Nodding, the princess agreed. "Personally, I think someone like Stella would be a great mother for you," she suggested nonchalantly.

Flashing a mischievous grin, Tyler eyed her. "Someone like Stella or Stella?" he questioned pointedly.

"Huh?"

"C'mon, don't act all innocent," the spiky-haired boy chuckled. "I noticed you watching us in the studio today and whatever plan you have up your sleeve, it ain't gonna work."

"I don't know what you're talking about," Kara said, feigning innocence.

Laughing, Tyler nodded. "Sure you don't. I've known you long enough to know when you're scheming, but it's not gonna work."

"Just enjoy your candy and leave the rest to me," the princess assured him in a voice she typically reserved for public events.

Tyler really does deserve happiness, Kara realized as the two continued to eat candy and chat about their upcoming performance. *And I am going to help him find it,* the princess decided before turning her attention back to the big screen, happy that she and Tyler were both content for the moment.

Chapter 9

"Why does this stupid solo have to be so difficult?" Kara whined. "I've tried this a dozen times. I'm never going to get it right."

"Don't despair, little lady. You're doing great," Stella smiled. "Remember to move your body ever so slightly as you come around that fourth candy cane otherwise it will fall and start a–"

"AHH!" Kara leaned forward quickly to avoid getting squished by a giant Christmas tree prop.

"…chain reaction," Stella said, finishing her prior sentence, as she watched the remaining props fall to the ground.

"Ugh!" Looking down at her feet, the princess shook her head. "I'm never going to get this right. It's just too hard," she said solemnly as a tear rolled down her right cheek.

Sighing, the dance instructor stared her down. "Look at me," she said, her voice calm yet stern.

The pint-sized royal did as instructed but remained silent.

"Do you think any dancer worth his or her weight in pointe shoes performs perfectly at every rehearsal?" she asked pointedly.

Letting out a huff, Kara rolled her eyes. "Of course not, but we've been rehearsing for a while now. I should've had it down a long time ago. There is only three weeks left before the third annual

Starrycrest anniversary celebration. I'll never be ready," she said, her voice colored with panic.

This is never going to work. I am going to make an idiot out of myself and completely embarrass Derrick and Misty. They may even send me back to the group home, the princess fretted, her heart racing, as she gave into her deepest worries.

"Enough of this," Stella said, her voice firmer than it had been just minutes prior. "Take a deep breath in through your nose and let it out through your mouth," she demanded, irritation etched into her features.

Uh oh, she looks really mad. I better do whatever she says before she wants to send me away too. Shaking her head, the princess dismissed her thoughts and took a breath. *Wow. Breathing really does help.* She realized after performing the recommended technique a few more times.

"Feel better?" the dance instructor questioned after a moment.

Kara nodded. "I'm sorry for freaking out. I just want everything to be perfect for the performance."

Stella smiled. "Believe me, little lady, I completely understand." Tilting her head, the dance instructor grinned wider at the little girl. "Do ya know why I've had you practice twice as much as the other starlets?"

"I'm the Sugar Plum Fairy and I have a solo," the young majestic answered as though the reason for her extra practice was painfully obvious.

The dance teacher chuckled. "Yes, there's that, but the other reason… The real reason is because I believe what your father says about you being the best dancer in Starrycrest."

Kara felt herself blush at the revelation that Derrick had shared such an opinion publicly. "He told you that?" she asked, her voice meek and quiet.

"Yes indeed," Stella smiled sweetly. "He told me because he believes in you. We both believe in you but, most importantly, you gotta believe in yourself."

The princess looked down at her feet again. *Ugh. There's that stupid clubfoot again.* "I don't understand how I could possibly be the best dancer in Starrycrest when I can't even wear proper pointe shoes," she said solemnly.

"Well, like I said, that's the issue right there. To be the best dancer you can be, you must believe you have the capacity to be the best."

"How can I do that? How do I make myself believe in my capabilities when I can't even dance a simple figure eight?"

The dance teacher's smile widened. "Practice makes perfect, so stop all this bellyaching and get back at it, little lady."

She's right. I gotta practice and become amazing if I want to impress Misty and Derrick, the princess decided as she settled into position.

"Ya ready for another go?" Stella asked after setting the props again.

The pint-sized royal took another deep breath. "I got this," she said quietly.

"That's the spirit," Stella encouraged. "Remember, slow and steady around the… candy canes," the dance teacher winced as the props tumbled to the floor yet again. "Don't worry, little lady, you'll get it," she assured. "Like I said, practice makes perfect."

"I know. I know," Kara shook her head. "I need to practice and believe in myself." *I need to believe in my plan too if it's going to come together,* the princess smiled at Stella. "You're awfully wise, ya know," she said sweetly.

Eyebrows furrowed, Stella looked at her, perplexed. "Ya do remember I have pink hair, right?" she queried, her voice colored with amusement.

Kara let out a chuckle, exposing her beloved dimples. "That doesn't mean you can't be wise. You are. Lots of people with colored hair are. Tony, the new chef here at the castle, has bright orange hair and he is one of the wisest people I know. He told Tyler and me not to get too close to knives the other day." *Oh my gosh… I sound so silly. This is never gonna work.* The princess smiled, ignoring her thoughts. "Have you met him? You should really meet him," she urged, still smiling.

"Yeah, he sounds like an orange-haired Einstein," Stella joked as she helped the princess to transfer from the Dance Dazzler to her manual chair. "Stop the match-making and go do your homework or somethin'. We'll practice more tomorrow, okay?"

"Sounds like a plan," the princess said, firmly fastening her seatbelt. *I'm gonna need a much more creative plan if I even have a prayer of making this work,* Kara realized as she made her way out of the dance studio and into the castle proper.

***

"Hi, Misty. Hey, Derrick," Kara said by way of greeting as she entered the castle dining room.

"Hi, sweetheart, how was your day?" Misty asked as they sat down to a dinner of buttermilk pancakes, thick-cut bacon, and scrambled eggs that evening.

The curly-haired little girl smiled. "Pretty good. I'm getting excited for my solo but rehearsing the same thing every day is getting a bit old," she admitted before taking a bite of her eggs.

"I know what you mean," Misty sighed. "If I have to handle one more personal audience involving competing businesses, I'm going to scream. Why can't everyone just get along? We're all from the same kingdom for cryin' out loud."

Thank goodness Tony is as good at making breakfast as he is everything else. Kara mused as she enjoyed a bite of eggs.

Derrick, who had been preoccupied with feeding the furry and feathered members of the family, sat next to his wife and reached for her hand. "Sweetie, contrary to what you might think, this kingdom is not perfect. Please let me handle personal audiences until you have the babies. You need to relax… especially now."

Kara looked from Misty to Derrick and back, her crystal-blue eyes filled with apprehension. "What's going on?" she asked worriedly. "Is there something wrong with you and the babies?"

Derrick shook his head. "No, no, sweetheart. Misty is doing a great job of taking care of herself and the babies." Smiling at his wife, he squeezed her hand gently then looked back to his daughter. "Everyone is fine. I'm just being protective," he said sweetly.

The princess smiled. "Being protective is good," she nodded, biting into a pancake. .

"Indeed, it is," Misty agreed, smiling brightly.

"Derrick has always protected you," Kara commented before trying her bacon. "Is that how you knew you guys were a good match?" she asked sweetly.

Tyler would love this bacon, Kara mused as she recalled the time that he and Ben arm wrestled over the last piece of bacon at the group home even though it was burnt to a crisp. Maybe I should be extra nice and bring Ty some bacon. I might not be able to find him a family, but I can at least give him some good food, she decided.

"Yes, I suppose his protective nature is part of the reason," the queen nodded. "Why do you ask?" she responded thoughtfully.

"This isn't about a boy, is it?" Derrick asked nervously before Kara could answer.

Oh, great now if I ask Misty about saving some bacon for Tyler, she and Derrick are going to think I have a crush on him or something. Sticking her tongue out in disgust, the pint-sized royal shook her head. "Eww… no. Boys gross me out." *I guess I'll have to sneak the bacon,* she sighed.

The queen giggled sweetly. "Then why did you ask sweetheart?" Her tone was kind and gentle.

I can never tell them about my plan, the princess decided quickly. *But, like Derrick always says, 'a princess should never lie.'* "I'm thinking of doing a little matchmaking," she admitted quietly, after a moment.

"I don't think that's such a good idea sweetie," Derrick cautioned almost automatically.

Misty nodded. "Yes, sweetheart, I have to agree with Derrick on this one. When it comes to matters of the heart, it is never good to meddle," she warned, her voice stern yet quiet.

Rolling her eyes, Kara sighed. "I know. I know," she insisted. "I'm not going to do anything crazy. I'm just trying to help some people be happy. Isn't that what you do during personal audiences? Solve problems and try to make people happy?"

Derrick chuckled, his eyes bright and filled with love for his daughter. He looked to Misty, smiling proudly. "She's got a point, love," he said before taking a bite of his eggs.

The young, expectant mother looked from her husband to her daughter and back. "How did you get to be so wise? Please stop growing up so fast," she said before Kara could respond. "Before you know it, you'll be the one taking over my personal audiences," the queen sighed wistfully, her eyes welling up as if she were going to burst into tears at any moment.

Uh oh. Here comes another mood swing, Kara thought, as she instinctively reached out and placed a hand on Misty's shoulder. "Misty, I'm not even 10 yet. I don't hit double digits for another five months. There's plenty of time before you have to worry about me liking boys or taking over personal audiences. I promise," she squeezed Misty's shoulder reassuringly. "I'm only trying to help two lonely people here in the kingdom not be so lonely. We all have to do our part to help our fellow Starrycrest citizens, don't we?" the princess's voice laced with innocence.

Misty nodded, wiping moisture from her eyes. "Yes, we do, my darling girl. It's very kind of you to help lonely people here in the kingdom," she smiled proudly at her daughter and continued. "Common interest is a good way to help bring people together. If you feel that two fellow citizens could potentially be good friends. Try to determine what common interests they have, but if this really has to do with matchmaking please remember what I said about matters of the heart. The heart is quite delicate and can be broken very easily," Misty explained, her tone still cautious.

Misty looked to Derrick, grinning at him as he finished the last of his pancakes "Do you have anything you'd like to add?"

The king studied his wife and partner for a moment, his expression thoughtful. "No sweetheart, you are–" he paused, looked down at her belly, and smiled brightly. "And will continue to be a great mother and you handled the question beautifully."

"Aww… You are so sweet," Misty declared, her eyes once again becoming moist.

Now's my chance, Kara thought, quickly putting a few pieces of bacon in a napkin and sticking it in the pocket of her dress while Derrick gave Misty a gentle kiss.

Before the loving couple could notice anything out of the ordinary. Kara hung her head and made a show of faux gagging. "You two are definitely a match made in heaven," she giggled. *How am I going to find out what Tony and Stella's common interests are?* She wondered as she watched Derrick sweetly kiss Misty's hand from across the table. *I don't know much about Tony and Stella yet, but if they are anything like Misty and Derrick, then they'll be a perfect match.* She hoped that her plan would work as beautifully as she imagined.

***

"First thing's first," the princess declared as she walked into the dance studio for her next rehearsal. "Who are you?" she queried a moment later, her voice quiet and coated in innocence.

"What do you mean who am I?" the dance instructor shouted, feigning outrage at the question. "I'm Stella Dixon," the quirky, pink-haired woman grinned, standing flawlessly in fourth position, feet pointed in different directions one in front of the other; her right arm rounded in front of her and her left arm open to the side. She extended both arms and bent her knees, executing a seamless plié, then she brought her arms together while rising up on the ball of her left foot into a perfect demi-pointe. Bending her right leg so that her foot touched her left knee, performing a textbook passé, Stella then zipped flawlessly through three consecutive turns before landing with her legs parallel to one another and back in fourth position. "The most awesome dance instructor to ever grace this land," she announced, a confident smile stretching from ear to ear.

Kara nodded. . "Only the best can teach the best," the princess giggled, her adored dimples brightening her whole expression for a moment before she turned serious. "But, who are you?" The young girl's eyebrows furrowed as she continued. "You make me talk about myself and my life, but you hardly ever speak about yourself. How's that fair?"

The spiky-haired woman shot her a look. "Are you tryin' to get out of rehearsal, little lady?"

"I'm serious," the pint-sized royal persisted. "Who are you? How did you get into dancing?"

Stella smiled wistfully. "As I was telling you and Ty the other day, the amazing Madam Sterling was one of my many extraordinary kiddo keepers back in the day. Smile widening, the dance instructor stared off into the distance lost in thought. "The woman was so passionate about dance it was beyond contagious. We'd twirl around her house until it felt like my toes could snap off at any second," she explained, her voice quiet and reminiscent. She taught me about every famous ballet out there from *Cinderella* to *Swan Lake*. Dance was our life up until… well, up until the very end," the spiky, pink-haired woman said, her voice laced with a sadness that only a profound loss can create.

"I'm sorry," the young royal said, sensing Stella's melancholy. "I didn't mean to upset you."

Waving a dismissive hand, the dance instructor forced a smile. "No worries, little lady. Let's rehearse. Are you ready to get into the Dance Dazzler?" She distractedly walked toward the giant Christmas present and candy cane props and began positioning them, so the princess could dance a figure eight.

The young royal sighed. "Okay, okay, we'll rehearse under one condition. You come to dinner tonight and tell me more about kiddo keepers and Madam Sterling."

Stella chuckled. "So, you're saying the only way you'll rehearse is if I come to the castle for a free meal this evening?"

"Precisely," the princess grinned from ear to ear, exposing her precious dimples again.

The dance teacher contemplated her answer for a moment. "Well, this little suggestion of yours seems like a red flag, but I learned long ago to never turn down a free meal so get to it, little lady, so we can eat," Stella joked, swiftly lifting Kara into the Dance Dazzler.

This plan is so going to work and it's going to be awesome, the princess mused as she carefully weaved around a candy cane in an effort to perfect her Sugar Plum Fairy solo before the two of them left the dance studio to have dinner in the castle proper.

***

Smiling brightly, Kara entered the castle dining room with Stella in tow. "Hey guys, how's it going?"

Derrick, who was busy setting the dining room table, glanced up at the little girl and smiled. "Hi , how was rehearsal?"

"It was good," she smiled innocently. "So good, in fact, that I brought the instructor home for dinner, is that okay?"

"Of course, it is. The more the merrier, right everyone?" Misty questioned, her voice chipper as she entered the room. "In fact, Tyler and all of your grandparents took me up on a dinner invitation for tonight as well."

A chorus of agreement erupted as the queen pulled up to her spot across from Derrick at the dining room table.

"Oh my," Stella said, her eyes wide as she spotted the queen's growing belly. "You're…" she paused, nervously biting her nails as she searched for the right word.

"Huge," the pregnant royal offered, still sounding cheerful.

The spiky, pink-haired woman shook her head. "Please forgive me your majesty, I didn't mean to be rude, I was just so stunned."

The elegant royal smiled sweetly. "Oh, please, call me Misty. It's fine. People are often taken aback when they see a giant incubator with feet." Laughing, she looked from Stella to Kara and back. "Please sit, the chicken parmesan is going to get cold."

"Yay! Stella, you're going to love this dinner," Kara said excitedly as she pulled up at the table next to Derrick. "Tony says this is his specialty," she explained, smiling mischievously at Stella. "I personally think all of his food is good though. I mean, c'mon, how can he not be a good chef with a last name like Cacciatore?" she questioned rhetorically.

Misty looked at the little girl. "Sweetheart, how about you introduce Stella to people who are actually here?" "Oh, sorry," Kara scanned her surroundings, glancing at everyone in the dining room. "Everybody, this is my dance instructor Stella, she is helping the starlets with our upcoming performance of *The Nutcracker*." Smiling at the eccentric woman next to her, Kara continued, pointing to her right, "These are Derrick's parents, Archibald and Marguerite." She winked at Archibald then looked to her left. "This is Reginald and Eliza, Misty's parents. And, of course, ya know Tyler and those two knuckleheads," giggling, she looked to Misty and Derrick.

Eliza sighed. "Kara sweetheart, why won't you refer to us as your grandparents or Misty and Derrick as your parents? Can't you at least try to love the way you dance? It's been over two years since they adopted you and we love you so very much," she explained, her eyes moist as she looked thoughtfully at the little girl.

Ugh, Kara bit her lip to keep from groaning. *There's nothing like being hit with two of my favorite questions at one dinner*, Kara mused sarcastically, fidgeting uncomfortably in her chair as she contemplated her response. After a long moment, she forced herself to smile and answered. "I love you too, Eliza. I love all of you very much," the pint-sized royal assured, her voice quickly filling with anxiety. "It's just–"

Clearing her throat, Stella came to the princess's rescue. "As a former orphan myself, I can tell ya just how precious terms like Mom, Dad, Grandma and Grandpa truly are." She glanced at Misty's mother. "With all due respect your majesty, ya really shouldn't push the use of such terms. Kara will be comfortable with them in her own time."

Tyler took a bite of his chicken parmesan then flashed a grin. "I'm with Stella on this one."

"Yeah," Kara agreed. "What Stella said."

Archibald nodded and glanced at the dance instructor. "Stella, what've you two been working on in rehearsal that has allowed you to get to know my granddaughter so well?"

The spiky, pink-haired woman took a sip of water and cleared her throat before answering. "Well, like the little lady said, we've been spendin' a lot of time together rehearsing for *The Nutcracker* and I guess ya could say we discovered that we're kindred spirits."

"Definitely," the little, curly-haired girl said after swallowing a bite of salad. "We've been doing as much talking as rehearsing. The other day, Stella told Tyler and me all about the Kiddo Keeper Program in Eclipston. We should really try to start something like it here in Starrycrest."

Shaking his head, Archibald looked the toe-headed girl straight in the eye. "Don't be silly, sweetheart. Starrycrest Group Home is a part of our family history. It's here to stay, forever, right son?" he asked, flashing a smile at Derrick.

"Yes father," the ruler of the realm assured, his voice kind and quiet. "The group home is running smoothly and will be for years to come."

The moment those words left the king's mouth, the pleasant atmosphere of the dining room became uncomfortable and awkward.

"But why, Derrick?" the princess queried, her voice coated with more anger than worry. "If something like the kiddo keeper program was established here in Starrycrest then it would give families an opportunity to get to know kids who really need them. Isn't that right, Tyler?" the young majestic looked to her friend for support. "How many times have I told you that you'd have no problem finding a family if people just had a better chance to get to know you?"

"'Bout a hundred million," the youngest of the dinner guests answered, exposing a mouth full of marinara covered penne noodles.

"Right," Kara nodded. "So, wouldn't you like the chance to live with a family and get to know 'em before they adopt you?"

Looking from his plate of half-eaten chicken parmesan to the princess and back, Tyler answered, "I'd stay with anybody as long as the grub was half as good as this," he said, shoveling more chicken into his mouth. "Betsy's chicken smells like feet and it doesn't taste much better."

"See?" Kara giggled. "There'd be many benefits to starting a kiddo keeper program in Starrycrest."

After finishing a bite of salad, the king of Starrycrest looked thoughtfully at the little girl.

"Sweetheart, I know this is difficult for you to understand, but the Starrycrest Group Home is never going to close. Please drop the subject so everyone can enjoy their dinner," he said in the calm yet authoritative voice he typically used when addressing citizens of the kingdom.

"I can't believe you're being so stubborn," the princess shook her head. "This isn't one of your personal audiences, Derrick. If you won't even consider something that could help so many children in Starrycrest, then you are not who I thought you were," she insisted firmly.

Staring at the princess hard, Derrick gave her the kind of disapproving look that only fathers can, turning the mood in the room from awkward to very tense. "Kara, please–"

"No," the young royal persisted. "A kiddo keeper program would do wonders here in Starrycrest. I know you don't believe me, so I'll show you…Tyler and I are going to stay with Stella for a while," she announced defiantly.

***

This isn't how I wanted to introduce my idea, but I have to set Derrick straight, Kara decided as she waited for the stunned majestic to respond.

After a long moment, he and Stella eyed her and simultaneously asked, "Excuse me, what did you just say?"

"Tyler and I are going to stay with Stella for a while," the princess repeated confidently. "What're you babbling about?" the princess's comrade asked, after taking a bite of salad. "And when is this family gonna stop volun–" Smiling innocently, the young royal swiftly elbowed her friend in the side. "Ow," Tyler shouted. "No need to get violent. Like I said, I'll stay anywhere as long as there's good food." Flashing a crooked smile, the young boy looked to Stella. "You're awful quiet. Is it cool if the princess and I crash with ya?" "Ya gonna have to excuse me for bein' a little short on words, bud. I'm not used to people just invitin' themselves over to my house, particularly if they plan to stay awhile."

"This issue goes far beyond the princess's lack of manners," Archibald declared. "I cannot believe this ludicrous idea is even being entertained. Reginald, please help me talk some sense into these kids."

Reginald scoffed. "You and I both know how stubborn these two are. Apparently, they've passed that trait onto the next generation."

"Archibald, darling, this is a matter between the three of them. We should let them handle it," Marguerite suggested.

"Yes, we should let Derrick and Misty handle it," Eliza agreed.

"Nonsense, this is about the Denison legacy. We must take charge," Archibald insisted.

Sighing, Kara ignored her feuding grandparents, avoided Misty and Derrick's frustrated expressions and looked straight to her dance instructor. "I'm sorry, Stella. I know I should've asked you about this before, but I was worried you'd talk me out of it."

"So, ya ambush me instead?" –

"Stella, you benefited from the kiddo keeper program in your home kingdom. You, of all people, should understand what a similar program could do for this kingdom. Help me show them," she pleaded.

"C'mon, Stella. you and I both know that if ya don't agree to this, Kara will be all sad and moody, we won't get anywhere in rehearsal, and our performance of *The Nutcracker* will be doomed. You don't want that, do you?" Tyler questioned pointedly.

"Well, when you put it like that, how can I not agree?" Stella relented. "I suppose if you and Tyler have per--" "That's enough," Derrick shouted, standing up at the table. "These two are children," he said with authority. "My father is right. We can't le…" the king stopped yelling the moment his wife placed her hand over his hand.

"Sweetheart, can we talk in private for a moment please?" she asked, her voice shy and quiet.

Looking from Misty to Kara, Derrick sighed. "Okay, but we are nowhere near finished with this discussion." Letting out a breath, Derrick looked from his parents to Misty's parents and back. "Mother, Father, Eliza, Reginald, I sincerely apologize, but I must ask that you depart for the evening and allow Misty and myself to handle this little situation on our own."

Throwing his head back, Archibald scoffed, "Son, like I said before, this is more than a family matter. This is about the Denison family legacy."

"Yes, father," Derrick nodded. "I'm well aware of that and will handle things appropriately. I only ask that you give me privacy while I do so."

"The boy is right," Reginald agreed. "If he can handle a pregnant Misty and reign over the kingdom, he can handle a little family problem. Let's give them privacy."

"Oh, all right," Archibald lamented, his voice angry and hesitant.

With that, the two former kings and their tearful, yet obedient, wives said their goodbyes and left the castle.

***

The moment that Kara, Tyler, and Stella were left alone in the dining room, the little girl turned to the dance instructor and smiled. "What do ya say? Can Tyler and I stay with you for a while?" she asked eagerly. The eccentric woman bit her lip. "Well," she hesitantly began after a moment. "I think I understand where you are going with this idea and, while I agree that having a kiddo-keeper-like program in Starrycrest is a great idea, will you be okay with not having a Personal Assistant readily available for a little while? My house is small. It's going to be tight quarters with just the three of us, but I was thinkin' maybe one of them could come in an out just to help ya every once in a while. What do ya think?"

The princess waved a dismissive hand. "Oh, that's all right. I had to fend for myself a lot before Misty brought me here to the castle. I'll be just fine."

"Well, in that case, there is one little snafu in your plan," Stella admitted before taking a bite of her chicken parmesan. *Uh oh, even after all Tyler and I have said to convince Stella, she's not going to go for it, and my plan will be ruined*, the tiny royal worried. "What's that?" she asked, her voice coated with anxiety. "My grub is not very good," the spiky-haired woman explained half-jokingly. "I don't cook so having house guests tends to be a problem for me unless they are big fans of peanut butter and jelly," she chuckled. The young royal waved a dismissive hand again. "Oh, that's no biggie. Just leave the food to me," Kara reassured. "Leave it to you?" Tyler questioned. "Uh, last I checked you aren't a cook either. How ya gonna handle the food?"

Sitting up a bit straighter in her wheelchair, the princess smiled mischievously. "I don't cook, but I know people who do." *This plan is becoming more and more genius,* she realized, already feeling much happier than she had been just moments before. *I only hope it works.*

Almost as if on cue, Derrick and Misty returned to the dining room. Looking pointedly at the little girl, the queen spoke, her voice thick and laced with sadness. "Kara, I have loved you since the moment I laid eyes on you. You are as dear to me as the two babies growing inside of me," she explained, her voice on the verge of breaking as tears filled her eyes.

The pint-sized royal frowned, put her hand on her adoptive mother's shoulder, and squeezed gently. "I'm sorry. Please don't get teary-eyed. It's not good for you and the babies."

"Sweetheart, right now it is not myself nor the babies I am concerned about. It's you," she admitted quietly as tears rolled down her cheeks. "That's why I've convinced Derrick to let you do as you wish against our better judgement, but only under two conditions." she sniffled and looked to her husband.

Oh my gosh, Kara mused excitedly. *I can't believe they are actually going for it. Everything is going to work out great. I'll make Derrick see how great a kiddo keeper program would be for the kingdom in no time.*

Smiling sweetly, the princess nodded. "Name them."

"Firstly, you must understand that this is temporary. You are my and Derrick's daughter for better or for worse. We are not at all happy about this charade of yours, but we're going to allow it because we know you'll be safe and we think that a little time away will be good for you. That being said, we want you home the night before *The Nutcracker* performance. Is that understood?"

The little girl nodded her head in agreement again.

"Good. Secondly, if you're hurt or become ill for any reason, you are to call us and come home immediately."

"Nothing will happen. This whole arrangement is going to be good for our family and the kingdom. You'll see," Kara assured.

"We'll have to agree to disagree on that, sweetheart. I called Betsy and told her about this little charade. She was intrigued and agreed to go along with it, as long as Tyler keeps attending school and doesn't cause any trouble. You guys can go and pick up his things after you pack up yours. Now, if you'll excuse me, I'm not feeling so good." Shaking her head, Misty wiped her tear-stained cheek and turned away.

Looking from his wife to Kara and back, Derrick sighed and turned to follow Misty.

"Derrick, wait," Stella called out just before he left the dining room.

The ruler of the realm reluctantly turned to face his friend.

"I just want you to know that I had no idea Kara was going to …"

Holding up his hand to stop her, Derrick shook his head. "Stella, it's okay, I know that Kara, and Kara alone, is responsible for this scheme and its outcome. I am just glad that someone else who knows how special she is can care for her during this tense time."

Stella nodded. "Yes, of course, both children will be well cared for," she flashed a smile, but Derrick didn't return the gesture.

Kara nodded. "Yes, she'll take great care of us and, look at it this way, all of this extra time with my dance instructor is sure to make our performance of *The Nutcracker* absolutely amazing."

Sighing again, Derrick frowned. "Yes, well, I'm beginning to see that some things in life are far more important than dancing. Now, if we're done here, I really should go check on your mother," he said, his voice solemn and quiet.

I hate that he looks so sad. I've got to make this plan work so that all this pain is worth it, she

nodded again, more determined than ever as she followed Stella and Tyler out of the dining room.

Chapter 10

"Yikes," Kara said, her voice full of anxiety as she, Stella, and Tyler approached the house that the dance instructor considered home. The single-story house was a far cry from the castle with its leaky gutters, drainage-stained brick, and half-rotted roof, but it was the three-inch step just below the threshold that worried the princess most. *I definitely didn't think this through.* Taking a deep breath, she pushed her chair up the step as hard as she could, only to be thwarted by the tiny anti-tip wheels in the back. After a moment, she sighed. "I can't get my chair up the step," she said, her voice coated with defeat.

"I'm so sorry, Kara. I didn't even think about the step." Stella looked from the princess to the house and back as if contemplating what to do next.

"Maybe if Tyler helps then we can lift you up over the step or maybe–"

"Are you crazy? There ain't no need to lift her up. How the heck did you survive this long without a man around?" Tyler wondered out loud.

Throwing her head back, Kara laughed. "You're not a man yet."

"Yes, I am!" Tyler protested.

"If you're a man then I'm–"

"Quiet!" Stella shouted, instantly gaining the attention of both quibbling dancers. "Whether Tyler is a man or not, I am in charge of both of you for the time being, is that understood?"

The children sighed, nodding simultaneously.

"Good. Now, Tyler, I need ideas to help get Kara into the house. What ya got?"

"Give me a minute. I'll come up with somethin'," he assured before running off to scour the surrounding area.

Sighing, Kara wheeled her chair under the lone tree in the yard to wait for her dance partner. "Weeping willows are my favorite type of tree. This one is very beautiful," she studied the tree while locking the brakes of her wheelchair into place.

"Thank you, little lady," Stella flashed a smile. "The weeping willow tree is one reason why I bought the house."

Stella went on to explain that Madam Sterling also had an appreciation for droopy yet gorgeous trees. Kara tried to listen, but despite her effort, she soon found herself eyeing the front step once again. *How is it that something so small and harmless looking can cause such a big problem for me? How am I supposed to make a positive impact on the kingdom when I can't even get over a three-inch step?* As minutes ticked by, the little girl's anxiety increased, making her heart pound inside her chest. *What the heck was I thinking?* she wondered. *This is all such a stupid idea.*

"What's goin' on in that head of yours, little lady?" Stella questioned after a couple of more minutes, finally freeing the princess from her thoughts. "I can practically see the wheels spinnin.'"

"It hasn't even been an hour since we left the castle and my plan is already doomed," Kara whined. "I don't know what I was thinking. Maybe this was a mistake. I'm so dumb," she murmured.

Shaking her head, Stella disagreed, "Oh, puh-lease girlie, the only thing that's dumb around here is your attitude. Aren't you tryin' to make a point and improve this kingdom? Why are you givin' up so easily?"

"C'mon, Stella, how am I supposed to change the entire kingdom when I can't even master my solo or conquer a single step?"

The eccentric, pink-haired woman opened her mouth to answer, but closed it as Tyler approached, holding two light brown shutters. "Have a little faith, will ya? I've been gone like ten minutes."

Stella held up a hand, stopping the little girl before she could retort.

"What're you doing with those?" the pink-haired woman asked, pointing to one of the brown shutters.

"I found these shutters on the side of the house. They are a bit tore up, but I figure they will work," Tyler explained.

Stella shrugged. "It's worth a shot," she said. "Who knows? Maybe that's why they got torn off during that bad storm a couple weeks ago."

Kara looked from Tyler to Stella and back, eyebrows wrinkled in confusion. "I don't understand. How are shutters going to help us?"

Tyler kneeled in front of the small step and put the shutters down, side-by-side, off the edge of the step, creating a makeshift ramp.

"Wow!" Kara exclaimed.

Tyler grinned. "Simple, right? Give it a shot."

After flashing a nervous smile, Kara wordlessly positioned herself in front of the rough-and-ready ramp and pushed forward.

"Well, it's not the sturdiest ramp, but it'll do," the princess said after making it up to the front porch. "Thanks, Ty."

"Yeah, thanks, bud," Stella praised. "Awesome save."

Cheeks slightly red, Tyler shrugged, dismissing the compliment. "Yeah, yeah, yeah, can we go in? It's getting cold out here."

***

"Welcome to my humble abode," Stella declared, opening the front door. "It's certainly no castle, but–"

"Don't be silly. Your home is lovely and we appreciate you letting us stay with you, don't we, Ty?" The princess asked, wheeling in behind him.

After taking a moment to scan his surroundings, the boy flashed a grin and looked from Kara to Stella and back. "It's about time I benefit from one of your crazy plans."

"Whatever," Kara rolled her eyes. "I am awesome and my plan is awesome. You'll see," she insisted, her voice laced with assurance.

Throwing his head back, Tyler laughed. "I'm not holdin' my–"

Stella interrupted, eyeing the children at the same time. "Crazy or not, you both are here with me for the next two weeks so, first thing's first, we are going to go over some ground rules."

Tyler laughed again. "I'm sure you ain't got nothing on Miss Betsy when it comes to rules."

Nodding in agreement, Kara giggled. "Yeah, we know the drill. Go to school, keep up our grades, stay out of trouble, and be home a half-hour before lights out."

"Yeah. All of that is fine and dandy, but you're in my house now so you're going to follow my rules," the eccentric woman insisted. "Firstly, you are to be up, dressed, and ready to go to school by 7:45 each morning. Secondly, you are to return by 3p.m. sharp and go with me to the castle for rehearsal. Thirdly, you are both to be present for family dinner each evening following rehearsal. Lastly, there will be no gallivanting around the kingdom at all hours of the night. I am to know where you are at all times and, regardless of your plans, you are to be home and in bed by 9 p.m. Is that understood?" she laid down the rules.

"Jeez," Tyler groaned. "Account for our every minute why don't ya?"

Elbowing her friend and dance partner, Kara whispered. "Shush. She didn't mention weekends."

Stella chuckled. "Oh, rest assured that your weekends will be filled with rehearsal and family time as well. Being part of a family takes effort and I am goin' to do my best to have you kiddos learn that."

Tyler sighed. "C'mon, we just got here. Why ya gotta be so dramatic?" he questioned, his voice coated in annoyance. "She's not being dramatic. Being a part of a family can be hard," Kara agreed. "Yeah, yeah, yeah, can you please just tell us where we are going to sleep?"

Folding her arms across her chest, Stella eyed him. "Anyone ever tell you that patience is a virtue, kid?" Tyler groaned again. "Sorry. It's just this bag's gettin' heavy." Stella nodded. "It's okay, bud. I can show you to your room but–" Pausing, the dance instructor walked down the hallway and motioned the kids to follow. Stopping in front of a door, she addressed them. "I thought you may want to put your stuff in here for a bit." She smiled and opened a door revealing a wall covered in mirror tiles, a tile floor, and ballet barres.

"Oh my God!" Tyler exclaimed. "You've been holding out on us. Why didn't you tell us that you have your own studio?" Stella chuckled. "How do ya think I became such a good dancer? Practice has to become as natural as breathing if you want to become an excellent dancer." Despite the words coming from Stella's mouth, Kara heard Derrick's voice the moment they hit her ears. *Derrick says that all the time. Or he used to before dance became his second priority.* As that thought crossed her mind, the young girl's eyes filled with tears.

"Uh oh, what's wrong little lady? Are you already having second thoughts about stayin' here?"

Shaking her head, Kara wiped the single tear that had fallen down her cheek. "No, I am just feeling a little overwhelmed," she admitted quietly.

Stella nodded. "I see. And what do dancers do when we're overwhelmed?"

The little girl shrugged her shoulders.

"We dance it out," Stella declared as though the answer were the most obvious thing in the world.

With that, the three friends danced out their feelings until Stella tucked Kara and Tyler into their beds for the evening.

***

"Fire!… Fire!… Fire!" *What the heck?* Kara wondered as the smell of burnt bacon assaulted her nostrils. A moment later, the distant shrill, robotic voice of the smoke detector registered. "Oh, my gosh!" she breathed. Pulling her wheelchair slightly closer to her bed, she locked the brakes, quickly transferred into it, and raced down the hallway.

Stunned by the sound of Tyler's laughter. Kara stopped at the kitchen doorway. *Either this is a dream or I fell and hit my head*, the little girl mused as her dance partner continued to laugh while putting out a small fire on the stove. "Are you guys okay?" she questioned after a moment. "What's going on in here?"

"This knucklehead told me he knew how to cook bacon," Stella explained, her eyes bright with mischief.

Eyebrows furrowed, Kara shot Stella a look. "You actually believed him?" she asked, her eyes widened in disbelief.

The eccentric woman shrugged. "What can I say? It's early and he's very convincin'."

"I convinced you because it's true. Bacon is one of the few things I can cook. I can't help it that your oven is ancient," Tyler protested, his voice thick with conviction.

141

Kara looked from the char-filled frying pan to her dance partner and back. "If you can cook bacon yourself then why were you so grateful when I brought you a few measly pieces from the castle?" she questioned pointedly.

"I, uh, learned how to cook it just recently," Tyler murmured, shifting his weight from one foot to the other.

Throwing her head back, the little girl scoffed. "Yeah, sure… say whatever you gotta say to make yourself feel better dude."

"Whatever *princess*," He retorted. "At least I'm not wearing footie pajamas with only one footie."

The reminder that her usually covered clubfoot was exposed made heat rise into Kara's cheeks. "Oh, yeah, well--"

"Enough," Stella shouted, effectively grabbing the attention of both children. "Have some toast and get ready for school. *The Nutcracker* is less than two weeks away. We've got a big rehearsal ahead of us this afternoon," she reminded them after a moment.

Coming back to the castle this soon is going to be so awkward, Kara sighed, pushing her wheelchair up to a small table in the center of the kitchen. Accepting a slice of toast from Stella, she bit into it. "Ouch!" the little girl exclaimed. Dropping the toast, she touched her two front teeth as if making sure they were still intact. "That's as hard as a rock."

Stella's shoulders slumped a little. "Sorry, little lady. I told ya I don't cook much."

"Yeah, get off Stella's back. She warned us," Tyler argued as he took the seat next to her. "Besides, didn't you tell us to let you handle the food situation?" he queried pointedly.

Kara nodded. "Yes, and I am definitely going to. Otherwise, one of us might break a tooth." She looked at Stella. "No offense. We really appreciate you letting us stay here, right Ty?"

The young boy nodded his head in agreement. "'Course we do, but what's your plan to keep us from starving?" he probed anxiously. *If only he knew my entire plan*, Kara mused. *He'd be nervous about much more than starving. Still, this is best for him and the entire kingdom. He, Derrick, and everyone else will understand eventually,* she decided. "A princess never reveals her secrets," she joked.

Groaning, Tyler eyed her. "Must you always pull the royal card?"

Sitting up straighter in her wheelchair, Kara flashed a proud smile. "Like it or not, Tyler, I'll always be a princess."

Tyler scoffed, throwing his head back, "Not if Misty and Derrick decide that they love those precious babies more than you."

"That's enough!" Stella shouted. "That was uncalled for. Apologize to her right now," she eyed Tyler, her demeanor and voice suddenly very maternal.

Jeez, that was harsh even for Tyler. If this is what it's like to have siblings maybe I am not cut out for it.

Fidgeting slightly in his chair, Tyler stared down at his feet. "Sorry," he mumbled.

Letting out a sigh of frustration, Stella eyed Tyler. "Anyone ever tell you they can't understand ya when you mumble?" she asked pointedly. "Apologize like you mean it," she insisted.

Tyler groaned again and looked to Kara. After a moment, he spoke – his voice sincere – but still slightly hesitant. "Saying that wasn't cool. I'm sorry. Will ya forgive me?"

Kara nodded slowly despite his words cycling repeatedly through her mind, causing questions that had plagued her for months to resurface. *Will Derrick and Misty love the babies more than me?* A lump formed in her throat as that thought crossed her mind and she swallowed hard to push it down. Before she could do anything to stop it, another thought crashed into her consciousness. *What will happen to me if they do?* Unable to bear where her thoughts were heading, Kara took a breath and shook her head to clear her mind. A single tear escaped from her right eye before she could do so.

Tyler's eyes widened as he spotted it. "Hey, are you okay?" he questioned, his voice fretful. "I didn't mean to make you cry. I really am sorry."

Wiping the tear from her cheek, Kara nodded again.

"I'm fine. I was just thinking you might be right," she admitted, her voice meek and quiet.

"Yeah, well, even if I am, at least you had parents for a little while," he said solemnly.

Rolling her eyes, Stella looked from Tyler to Kara and back. "For cryin' out loud, would you two stop feelin' sorry for yourselves and get ready for school?"

Glancing up at the ballet slipper-shaped clock above the stove, Kara gasped. "I don't have a Personal Assistant here to help me. How am I supposed to get ready in 35 minutes?"

"Ya should've thought about that before you two started arguin.' You told me when I agreed to this arrangement that you'd be okay without your assistants so hurry up and get ready," Stella urged. "We've got a long day ahead." *This is definitely going to be an interesting couple of weeks,* Kara realized as she raced off to get ready for the day.

***

"Uh oh," Kara whispered to Tyler as he slipped into the seat next to her after entering Starrycrest Schoolhouse. "Ms. Ryder has that look in her eyes this morning. Five coins says she's about to introduce a big project."

Tyler eyed the teacher for a moment and noticed that she was practically gulping down a cup of coffee. "Are you nuts?" he asked. "She's half asleep. There is no way we're going to learn anything new today. I'll definitely take that bet."

The two briefly shook hands and then turned their attention to Ms. Ryder, who was clearing her throat to gain the attention of the class.

"Good morning children," she declared after a moment. "I thought I'd start today off by introducing the history project you'll be working on for the next couple of weeks."

Kara flashed a satisfied grin in Tyler's direction and then turned her attention back to the teacher.

"Each of you will be expected to choose a historical figure who has had an impact on Starrycrest, the former kingdoms of Mooncrest and Starryton, or a surrounding kingdom and give a five- minute report about that historical figure and their impact in front of the class. The historic figure can be alive or dead but must have had a significant impact on this or a nearby kingdom. Does anyone have any questions?"

As her classmates peppered Ms. Ryder with queries, Kara pondered who she should report on. *People are probably expecting me to give my report on Misty or Trovella, but if there is one thing I've never been, it's predictable. Maybe I should do my report on Reginald or Archibald instead.* A moment later, she dismissed the idea. *Nah, I love them, but a fight between them caused a division in the kingdom. I'd rather my report be about someone who has a positive impact. Derrick's always saying that, as the royal family in the kingdom, it's our responsibility to spread positivity.* She smiled, remembering how much he enjoyed telling her about the way his great grandfather taught him the importance of having a positive attitude toward life. *Oh my gosh! That's it. I'll do my report on Derrick's great grandfather. It'll be perfect.*

The princess's head pounded changing the course of her thoughts in that moment.

I should've taken some Tylenol before leaving Stella's house this morning. My head practically has its own heartbeat, Kara mused as she cupped her forehead into her hands.

"Are you okay, princess?" Ms. Ryder questioned, her usually nasally voice coated with concern. "You don't seem like yourself today."

Hesitantly lifting her head up, Kara glanced at the teacher and managed a half smile. "I'm okay Ms. Ryder. I just have a little headache today," she assured nonchalantly.

Ms. Ryder nodded. "I'll call Nurse Charlotte and tell her you're coming. We can't have our princess sick," she said kindly.

Sitting up straighter in her wheelchair, Kara shook her head vehemently. "No, no, no. That's really not necessary," she assured. "I am fine. I need to stay and work on my report about my favorite historical figure. I promise you; it's going to be amazing."

Ms. Ryder chuckled. "How can I say no to that?" she questioned rhetorically. "Tell me immediately if you start feeling any worse," the teacher cautioned before walking toward her desk.

Kara nodded. "I will. I promise." The pint-sized royal managed to widen her grin despite feeling as though someone were hammering a nail into her head. *Oh, thank goodness,* she let out a deep breath as the teacher turned her attention to paperwork on her desk. *There is absolutely no way I can go home yet,* Kara realized. *If Tyler is right, then I might not have much time as princess to make a difference in the kingdom.* The mere thought of no longer being princess brought tears to the little girl's eyes and made her feel nauseous. *I can't lose everything,* she told herself. *No orphan I know of has ever been lucky enough to get a family and gain the power to make a difference in the kingdom. I won't waste it.* Overwhelmed by her racing thoughts, Kara began to cry harder. Clutching her stomach, she took a couple of deep breaths. *Pull yourself together. The pregnancy makes Misty nauseous all the time. If she can run the realm while nauseous then I can definitely make it through my day. I really hope she and the babies are doing okay.* At that moment, Kara was struck by how much she missed Misty after such a short amount of time. *Misty seemed so upset when I left. I wish I could help her understand what I am trying to do,* sighing, she turned slightly in her chair and grabbed Maxwell Denison's biography from the backpack she kept on the back. *I told Archibald that I'd read this eventually. Now is as good a time as any,* she decided. Within minutes, despite her headache, as Kara read the biography, she became enthralled. Derrick had told her that his beloved great grandfather had polio and was a strong advocate for people with disabilities, but he hadn't told her that Maxwell was an orphan. *Why didn't Derrick or anyone else ever tell me?* she wondered as she continued reading. Tears continued to fall from her beautiful blue eyes as she read that Maxwell was forced to live in an infirmary with other kids with disabilities at age six, after his family had given him up because he'd contracted polio. The princess hurt not only for Maxwell, but for herself. She knew the pain of feeling unwanted all too well. *Oh my gosh, this is so sad. I can't believe someone known for being one of the kindest rulers the kingdom ever had experienced such pain.* Closing the book, she wiped her eyes. *My plan must work. I cannot let another child in this kingdom feel the pain of being unwanted. I just can't. I won't stand for it,* she decided, more determined than ever to make her plan successful for herself, for Tyler, and, most importantly, for the entire kingdom of Starrycrest.

Chapter 11

"Whoa… easy on that spin little lady. You're about to cause another–" Loud thuds echoed through the dance studio as the candy cane and Christmas present-shaped props used in the princess's solo fell to the floor, interrupting Stella's thought.

"Chain reaction," Kara finished, her voice meek and defeated as tears escaped from her eyes.

"Hey there, little lady, it's just a couple of fallen props. There is no reason to cry. I'm just going to find someone to hel–"

Shaking her head, Kara wiped moisture from her eyes. "This isn't about the props," she sniffled.

Grabbing a stool, Stella positioned herself in front of Kara. "Talk to me," she urged. "What's goin' on with ya?"

Kara shook her head. "I don't want to talk about it," she admitted sheepishly, her eyes still full of moisture.

Hanging her head, Stella sighed. "Fine, I'll guess…" A silence settled between them as Stella studied her intently. *I'm in for it now,* Kara mused. *If Stella stares at me much longer, she is going to bore a hole through my forehead.* After contemplating for another moment, Stella finally broke her stare and spoke. "You look a little pale. Do you feel sick?" She placed a hand to the little girl's forehead.

The princess shook her head vehemently, shirking Stella's hand away. *I can't let her know that I haven't felt well today,* Kara decided. *She'll make me come home for sure. I guess I better own up to at least part of the plan.* "I am just really overwhelmed. I know I need to focus on the performance, but I just can't get the kiddo keeper program out of my head. I really need to talk to Misty and Derrick about it again," she explained.

"Are ya sure that's such a good idea, little lady? It didn't go over so well last time."

Wiping the last of the moisture from her eyes, Kara let out a breath. "I know, but I don't have much time. I have to do what I can to help the orphans of the kingdom now."

Stella eyed the little girl, her eyebrows showing her confusion. "What are ya babbling about? You're not even ten years old yet. There's plenty of time to leave your mark on the kingdom."

Kara sighed inwardly. *If I tell Stella that I think I might not be princess for much longer she'll just tell me I'm crazy and try to make me feel better. I am going to have to tug at her heartstrings for this to work,* she reasoned. After allowing her eyes to fill up with all the emotions she'd been feeling for the past few days, Kara looked Stella straight in the eye. "C'mon Stella, you of all people should understand my sense of urgency when it comes to helping kids in need. The orphans of Starrycrest all have a right to find families. I think a kiddo keeper program is the best way to give them a chance to do that. Don't you agree?" the princess asked, her voice laced with conviction.

The dance instructor groaned, "Ya know I do, but it's–"

"No buts," Kara declared cutting her off. "Let's go find Derrick and Misty." Leaning forward slightly, the princess headed off to do just that.

"Kara... wait," Stella called out. "The Dance Dazzler isn't meant to be off of–"

At that moment, a distant male voice distracted Stella. "Whoa there, princess," the voice cautioned as she burst into the castle family room. "Where ya headed in such a hurry in that fancy chair?"

"Yeah, why the rush?" Stella reiterated as she caught up with the princess. "Is there a fire I don't know about?" she joked.

"Hi, Tony," the princess said hurriedly after realizing that the newly-appointed chef was the person who had stopped her in her tracks. "I'm just trying to catch Misty and Derrick before they sit down to dinner," she explained as she struggled to look past the large man and into the more family-friendly of the dining rooms in the castle.

Shoulders slightly slumped, the culinary artist frowned at the tiny royal. "I'm sorry to tell ya this kiddo, but the king and queen had obligations in Eclipston this evening. They left hours ago."

Letting out a breath, the princess felt her eyes fill up with moisture yet again. "What kind of obligations?" she questioned. "Is it even safe for Misty to travel? Is she okay? Are the babies all right?" The living room was a large space outfitted with a dark purple sofa and matching loveseat made from what Derrick and Misty believed was the softest suede in the kingdom.

The dark purple roses that adorned the space not only helped to make it beautiful, but also left a rich yet floral aroma in the room. The sweet scent usually had a calming effect on the tiny royalbut, in that moment, it did nothing to help her. As the princess's questions hung in the air unanswered, she became lightheaded and felt as though all the air had been sucked out of her lungs. Despite this, she couldn't stop tears from streaming down her cheeks. Without even realizing it, the princess had worked herself into a frenzy and was soon bawling.

***

Why can't I stop crying? This is ridiculous, Kara told herself as tears continued to stream down her face. *I am the one who left the castle. Why do I feel so alone?* she wondered angrily. *I wish I could just talk to Misty and Derrick and make them understand. Why does this have to be so difficult?* She buried her face into her hands and continued to weep.

Lifting the princess from the Dance Dazzler as though she were as light as a feather, Tony comforted her. "Don't cry," he soothed, pulling her into a hug. "I'm sure the queen is fine. His Majesty wouldn't let anything happen to her."

Kara nodded against Tony's shoulder. "I know," she sniffled. "It's just that I wanted to talk to them about something very important and now I can't. I've been gone a day and they've already forgotten about me," she cried, fresh tears spilling onto her cheek.

"Aww, sweetheart, that could never happen," Tony soothed, squeezing her tighter. "No one in this castle could ever forget about you."

Pulling slightly away from his chest, the princess looked him straight in the eye. "How can you be so sure?" she sniffled. "You've only been here a few days."

Tilting his head to the right, the kind chef looked at her pensively, as if contemplating the answer.

Stella, who'd been listening to the conversation, took advantage of the silence and joined in. "I've only known you for a couple of months little lady and I can say, without a doubt, that I could never forget ya."

"See?" Tony insisted. "You're unforgettable." Gently wiping the tears from her eyes, he hugged the princess again. "Why don't you tell me and this lovely lady." Pausing briefly, the kind chef flashed a smile, tilted his head toward Stella, and then continued. "All about what you wanted to discuss with your parents while I pack up the meals you asked for," he suggested.

Kara flashed a slight grin. "Okay, but can ya please put me down first?"

Chuckling, Tony carefully placed the little girl back into the Dance Dazzler.

Kara looked at Tony, her smile brighter than moments before. "This is my friend and dance instructor, Stella Dixon," Still grinning, the little girl addressed her dance teacher. "Stella, this is Tony Cacciatore, the official castle chef."

"AKA, your answer to our food shortage," Stella joked.

"Food shortage?" Tony questioned, his eyebrows furrowed in confusion.

Glancing at Stella, Kara saw that her cheeks were slightly pink and that her eyes were fixed on a spot on the floor.

Clearing her throat, the little girl took the opportunity to tell Tony about the kiddo keeper program in Eclipston. She then went on to explain how she and Tyler were staying with Stella, who, while a very talented dancer, had no cooking skills whatsoever.

"Wait a minute, are you and Tyler staying with her to show your parents that a kiddo keeper program would work well in this kingdom?"

Jeez, he caught on quick, Kara mused. *I hope he doesn't catch on to the rest of my plan*, she thought as she nodded vehemently.

Shaking his head in disbelief, Tony chuckled good-naturedly. "You are really somethin' princess."

Kara's smile widened. "Thank you, but I can't take all of the credit. Stella gave me the idea."

"I wouldn't go as far as to say I gave you the idea," Stella said, finally joining the conversation. "I told her about a similar program in the kingdom I'm from and the next thing I knew I had two house guests."

Tony nodded. "Trust me, miss, I haven't worked in the castle long but, from what I hear, ya are not the first to find yourself caught in the middle of one of our princess's crazy schemes. I'm just glad that this latest one has given me the opportunity to make my famous pot roast sliders."

"Huh?" Stella questioned, confusion etched through her features.

"The princess contacted me during her lunch break today and asked that I pack up some lunch meat sandwiches for her and her friends, but I decided to pack up something a bit heartier. Kids need food that sticks to their bones, so I whipped up some pot roast sliders," he explained.

"Pot roast, hmm? I don't really have much of a taste for veggies," the dance teacher admitted, her cheeks still slightly pink.

"Yeah neither do I," Kara agreed.

"Oh well, don't despair ladies. I used a grandma Anita's Pot Roast recipe. The only vegetable in those puppies is pepperoncini so, as long as you're the kind of girls who enjoy hearty, spicy food, I guarantee you'll love 'em."

Kara smiled. "I hope you're right. We could definitely use some hearty food. Stella and Tyler tried to cook some bacon this morning, but there was nothing hearty about it. It was just plain hard," she explained.

Stella let out a nervous laugh. "Oh c'mon, it wasn't that bad," she argued. You're gonna make Tony think I'm starvin' you kiddos or some–"

"You two are supposed to be rehearsing and instead I find you here talking to this goon about food?" Tyler interrupted, wide-eyed as he walked in the living space. "Unbelievable," he muttered angrily.

Rolling her eyes, Kara groaned at him, "Don't be so dramatic. We were going to come get you in a minute. Tony was just telling us about his pot roast sliders."

Tyler let out a huff. "Can we stop talkin' about food and start eating it? I finished my homework without a snack and now my stomach is rumblin' like crazy," he said, his voice as dramatic as it had been moments before.

"Uh oh," Tony shook his head. "I can't have any rumbling tummies on my watch. What are ya in the mood for little man?"

"I'd kill for a cheeseburger and a—"

Stella held up a hand. "Whoa, not so fast there, bud." Turning her attention toward Tony, she shook her head. We can't ask you to cook for us. We'll just head back to my house and have PB&J or somethin'. C'mon kiddos," she urged her voice full of anxiety as she ushered them out of the living room.

"Don't be silly, a growing boy needs a substantial dinner," Tony urged, stepping in front of them to block their exit. "I couldn't in good conscience let you leave with the plan to make these young, impressionable, innocent children such a sparse dinner. Like I said, kiddos need food that sticks to their bones," he insisted. The light-hearted quality of his voice did nothing to hide the nervousness the chef felt at that moment.

Eyeing the burly, spiky-haired culinary professional, Stella let out a curt laugh. "You're talkin' like PB&J is a meal fit for prisoners or somethin'. I practically grew up on it and I turned out fine. These kiddos will too," she assured him.

Wow, Stella's not Budging one little bit, Kara realized. *I thought I sensed a vibe between them, but this may be a bit harder than I thought. I better help Tony fast,* the princess decided. "I wouldn't be so sure about that," she said quickly. "The queen is very worried about how many people in the kingdom have developed a peanut allergy. I think she'd ban it if she could."

"What?" Stella questioned in disbelief. "No disrespect to the queen, but she's plumb crazy if she bans the goodness that is peanut butter."

Tony laughed. "I couldn't agree more, but I still think these kiddos deserve better than a peanut butter and jelly sandwich. For instance, peanut butter works far better in a pie than it does in a sandwich," he suggested, winking at the children.

"Oh, I'd give my right arm for a slice of peanut butter pie right now," Tyler commented eagerly.

"Remember Tony's chicken parm? If his peanut butter pie is half as good as that then it must be delicious," Kara urged.

Smiling, Tony winked at the princess. "Thanks for the vote of confidence, little one. I gotta admit that I can't take credit for the chicken parmesan because I used my grandma Anita's recipe, but my peanut butter pie is a completely original creation. Every aspect of it, from the peanut butter sandwich cookie crust to the homemade whipped cream topping screams Tony Cacciatore," he explained proudly.

"You actually make your own whipped cream?" Stella asked, her voice coated in surprise.

The larger-than-life chef nodded. "Of course. Ya gotta make your own. The canned stuff is gross and full of preservatives. It just so happens that I have a peanut butter pie cooling in the kitchen as we speak. It'd go great with a couple of cheeseburgers. I could whip 'em up in no time. What d'ya say?" he suggested, his voice almost as enthusiastic as Tyler's had been earlier.

Kara opened her mouth to try to convince Stella to stay but closed it as Tyler opened his.

"Please let us stay. I'll dance, do extra homework, do chores. I'll do anything. Just please don't keep us from the deliciousness that is cheeseburgers," he pleaded.

"Oh, all right," Stella lamented. "But, you two have gotta rehearse more after we eat," she insisted.

Tony sure is happy, Kara thought as she spotted him smiling dreamily at Stella. *This may not be so difficult after all,* she mused. *If only convincing Derrick and Misty that Starrycrest needs a kiddo keeper program were this easy,* she sighed. *I can't believe how much I already miss them. It'll be weird eating in the castle without them here,* she realized. *And what if they come home and see us eating dinner together? I want to make the point that a kiddo keeper program would help the kingdom, but I hate the idea of rubbing this situation in their faces. I better do something quick,* she decided before addressing her friends.

"Uh, guys, I'm looking forward to a cheeseburger too," the princess held her growling stomach. "But, to be honest, I feel a little weird eating here at the castle with Misty and Derrick gone," she admitted meekly.

"C'mon," Tyler groaned. "It's not like they are gonna give a crap if Tony makes us some burgers. Heck, they'd probably prefer that over letting us starve," he said pointedly.

Stella chuckled. "No one is gonna starve, bud, but I gotta admit, Kara has a valid point. I feel a little strange eating here while the king and queen are out and about."

Rolling his eyes, Tyler let out a huff. "So, what're we gonna do?"

Kara opened her mouth to answer, but stopped short when Tony jumped in.

"Well, I'd invite y'all to eat in the staff quarters, but we're bumping elbows as it is." He looked to Stella and flashed a smile.

"But I wouldn't mind grabbing the ingredients and cooking 'em at your place," he paused, hesitant, as heat rose up into his cheeks, shading them a deep crimson. "That is if a beautiful woman like yourself doesn't mind me takin' over your kitchen," he finished after a moment.

Kara eyed Stella as her cheeks also turned bright red. The spiky, pink-haired woman let out a nervous giggle. "That could be arranged but, fair warning, my whole house could probably fit in the castle foyer."

Nodding, Tony flashed her another smile. "Sounds like my kind of place. Let's get goin'."

With that, the foursome gathered ingredients needed for the much-anticipated cheeseburgers, as well as the amazingly smelling pie, and headed to Stella's house for supper.

***

This is déjà vu if I've ever experienced it, Kara mused, as the clang of forks against plates was the only sound to fill Stella's tiny kitchen for the first few minutes as the small group of friends sat down to dinner.

After finishing a little more than half of his burger, Tony braved speaking. "Normally, when people are enjoying my food, I ask how it is but y'all are quiet so I know it's good," he said proudly.

Tyler nodded. "Best cheeseburger I've ever eaten," he assured, revealing the mashed ground beef in his mouth.

"Eww!" Kara exclaimed. "You shouldn't talk with your mouth full. That's gross," she said matter-of-factly before taking a bite of her cheeseburger.

"Oh, c'mon Kara, loosen up a little. You're not in the castle anymore," Tyler retorted.

The princess opened her mouth to argue but closed it when Tony jumped to her defense.

"Regardless of where you are, when you're in the presence of a lady, you should act like a gentleman," the chef advised the little boy.

"I couldn't have said it better myself," Stella agreed.

Nodding, the culinary artist finished the last of his cheeseburger and stood up from the table, quickly busying himself with cleaning as the others finished their meal. "As soon as I was old enough to understand, my old man taught me how to properly treat a lady," Tony explained, smiling as he wiped down the light pink laminate countertop, which took up almost the entire left side of the small kitchen.

"Oh, you don't have to do that," Stella told him after finishing the last bite of her burger. "You cooked. At least let me handle the cleanin' up."

Shaking his head, Tony protested. "After the long day you've had, trying to wrangle these two knuckleheads." Pausing, he flashed a mischievous grin at the princess and Tyler. "That ain't gonna happen."

The pink, spiky-haired woman sighed after a moment. "Oh, all right. At least say you'll sit down and have some dessert with us. The kiddos can clean up later."

Tony's smile brightened. "Peanut butter pie and more time with a pretty lady? You don't gotta twist my arm," still grinning he sat down across from her.

Kara smiled as Stella blushed at the compliment. *This may work out better than I imagined,* she mused happily as Tyler placed a slice of peanut butter pie adorned with chocolate shavings and fresh whipped cream in front of her.

"Thanks Tyler. Have you decided yet who you're going to do your report on?" she asked before taking a bite of the indulgent dessert.

Taking a seat across from her, Tyler shrugged. "Nah, I'll figure it out in a few days. I work better under pressure," he admitted before taking a bite of his own slice of pie.

Stella chuckled. "I'm glad you don't have the same attitude regardin' dancing, bud. We'd be in some trouble."

Tony nodded in agreement. "Word of advice kiddos: procrastination is never the answer. Time will always catch up with ya in the end. Take it from a guy who is gettin' used to working against a royal clock. Pregnancy makes things real tricky. I can't fix peanut butter and pickle sandwiches fast enough these days."

While Tony's comment made the princess's dinner companions laugh, it had the opposite effect on her. Just thinking about Misty made Kara miss her. *Great. Not only did I break Misty's heart when I left, I distracted the person who has been helping to handle her pregnancy cravings? How could I be so selfish?* she wondered. Swallowing a lump in her throat the princess tried to prevent her emotions from surfacing.

"You okay there, princess?" Tony questioned, his voice coated in concern.

Uh oh. I better steer the conversation to a safer subject, Kara told herself. Quickly wiping at the tears prickling at her eyes, the young royal nodded. "Yeah, I'm fine," she assured nonchalantly. "I don't procrastinate. I know who I am going to do my report on," she explained.

"That's great, little lady!" Stella exclaimed. "Tell us who you chose; maybe it'll get Tyler's creative juices flowing," she suggested.

"Maxwell Denison," Kara declared, her voice brimming with pride.

The tiny majestic experienced another moment of déjà vu as Stella choked on her pie, instantly reminding her of the night Derrick had choked on a piece of chicken after hearing about Misty's pregnancy. The only difference was that Stella didn't have to brace against the table to save herself, because Tony sprang into action. Standing behind Stella, he wrapped his arm around her waist and formed a fist with his right hand. Grabbing onto the fist he'd formed with the opposite hand, he pushed against her belly, performing six abdominal thrusts until the pie was dislodged from her throat.

"Holy crap!" Tyler exclaimed. "I'd never seen someone choke like that before. I thought your eyes were gonna pop out of your head."

Kara nodded vehemently. "Your face is as red as a tomato."

Eyeing both kids, Tony gritted his teeth. "Calm down and get the lady some water, will ya please?"

Standing on tiptoe, Tyler reached into the cabinet above the stove, grabbed a glass, filled it with water, and quickly handed it off to Stella's savior. "Here ya go," he said, his voice laced with anxiety.

Without being prompted any further, the spiky, pink-haired woman grabbed the glass from Tony and took a drink.

"Thank you," she managed to croak out after a moment.

"You okay, darlin'?" Tony questioned, his forehead wrinkled with concern.

"Did I hear right?" she queried nervously. "The princess is doin' her report on Maxwell Denison. The Maxwell Denison who…" Stella trailed off, hesitant to finish her thought.

Nodding in confirmation, Tony showed that he had connected the dots just as quickly as the dance teacher.

"'Fraid so," he said knowingly.

"Okay. What do you guys know about Maxwell that I don't?" Kara asked pointedly, looking from Stella to Tony and back.

"Yeah, fess up guys," Tyler urged. Why are ya actin' so weird?"

"I'm not sure what you're talkin' about," Stella said feigning innocence.

"Me neither," Tony agreed. "No weirdness here. Just helping a pretty lady."

The princess opened her mouth to argue, but shut it as Tyler jumped in.

"Cute," he quipped sarcastically. "Now, can you guys get real and tell us what's goin' on?"

"Fine," Stella lamented, turning to look at the princess. "All I'll say is you should do your research and maybe talk to Betsy."

"Betsy? What does Betsy have to do with any of this?" Kara questioned wonderingly.

"Just do your research," the eccentric woman reiterated.

"I will," Kara assured. "Like I said, I don't wait 'till the last minute to do my homework," she flashed a smile, but it failed to reach her eyes. *What does Stella mean by "ask Betsy?"* The princess wondered. *What do the adults in my life know that I don't and why did it make Stella choke on a piece of pie?* Questions bounced in the little girl's mind until the loud clang of dishes startled her back to the present, spotting Tyler standing in front of the sink covered in suds.

"Jeez Tyler, what are you doing over there? Washing the dishes or breaking them?"

Rolling his eyes, the boy sighed. "I can't help it if the dishes slip right out of my hands. I was supposed to have help cleanin', but you're over there daydreaming and those two are flirtin' it up," he pointed his head toward their adult dinner companions who were sitting at the table chatting.

They're so in their own little world that they didn't even notice Tyler's comment, Kara mused excitedly. "Leave them alone," she whispered through gritted teeth. "I'll give you a hand." *Uh oh, this should be interesting,* the little girl realized as she rolled up to the sink and discovered she couldn't reach it.

"You wash and I'll dry," she suggested after a moment. "Just remember to scrub thoroughly and be careful with each dish."

Rolling his eyes at Kara yet again, Tyler handed her a towel. "Whatever. Less talking. More drying."

Over the next half hour, the kids worked together to clean the dishes, wipe down the stove and counter, as well as straighten up the kitchen. A seemingly oblivious Stella and Tony continued talking amongst themselves while she showed him around the house.

"What's with those two?" Tyler asked as Stella and Tony walked by the children and into the dance studio. "It's like they don't even know we're here."

Kara smiled. "Isn't it great? I think they're really starting to like each other."

"Yeah… whatever," Tyler shrugged. "I'm gonna go dance."

"Ty, no, we should leave them alone," the little girl called out, following him down the hall to the dance studio.

Ignoring Kara, Tyler opened the door to the dance studio, to reveal Tony and Stella standing just inches apart from one another. *Are they about to kiss? Is my plan actually working?* Kara wondered.

"Are we going to rehearse tonight or what?" Tyler asked.

Jumping at the sound of his voice, Stella stepped back, putting space between herself and Tony. "Oh, hey bud. Yeah. We're goin' to rehearse. What time is it?"

"It's 8 o'clock already. You guys have been gabbin' for a long time," the boy complained.

Hitting him in the shoulder, the princess protested, "It hasn't been that long."

"Ow," Tyler exclaimed, rubbing his shoulder.

"That's enough, you two," Tony cautioned. "If it's really that late, I need to get going," he said, his voice slightly hesitant. "But if ya ladies don't mind, I'd like to talk to Tyler about something first."

"If it's okay with Ty, it's okay by me," Kara said.

"Same here," Stella agreed, smiling from ear to ear. "Thank you again for supper."

"The pleasure was all mine," Tony assured her. "I hope we can see each other again soon."

"I'm definitely goin' to need some help wrangling these two over the next couple of weeks so I think that can be arranged," she joked.

Throwing his head back, Tony laughed then looked to Tyler. "Speaking of wrangling, let's you and I talk outside little man."

Nodding, Tyler followed the burly chef outside while Stella and Kara discussed the little girl's solo.

The spiky-haired boy returned moments later. "Lookin' good, partner," he praised as Kara flawlessly performed first through fifth positions with her arms.

The princess grinned. "Thank you, but don't think that flattery is going to get you out of telling us what that was all about."

"Huh?"

Stella chuckled. "Don't play innocent, bud. You're no good at it. What's up with Tony pulling you aside? What did you guys talk about?"

Tyler shrugged, "Oh, ya know, just guy stuff."

"Oh, c'mon, can't you at least give us a little hint?" Kara queried, her voice laced with a mixture of frustration and annoyance.

Eyes darting nervously around the room, Tyler avoided the curious gaze of his dance partner and the wonder-filled eyes of their instructor. His lips broke into a mischievous smile as he spotted a phonograph in the far right-hand corner of the room. Running to the oak-encased turntable, Tyler filled the tiny room with melodic sounds. "Are we going to rehearse or what?" he questioned pointedly.

Sighing, Kara lamented, "Fine. We'll let you off this time, but it's not going to happen again, is it Stella?"

"You got that right," the pink-haired woman answered. "We'll rehearse, but first who's up for a little freestyle?" she asked, grinning from ear to ear as she twirled enthusiastically from one end of the tiny room to the other.

With that, Stella and the children danced happily until she tucked them into their beds for the night.

***

Brinngg...brrinngg...brringg.... *How the heck is it morning already?* Kara groaned as she rolled over and hit the alarm clock on the side of her bed, silencing it.

6:00 a.m. comes way too early, but a girl's gotta do what a girl's gotta do, she decided as she pulled her chair closer to bed, locked the brakes, pushed the footrest aide, crawled into the seat, grabbed onto the backrest to pull herself up, turned around, locked the footrests into place and planted her feet into them, effectively transferring herself.

I am so tired, Kara thought, grabbing one of the dresses from her suitcase at the end of the bed. *I really was spoiled by life in the castle,* she realized as she brushed her teeth and spit into a cup when finished because she couldn't reach the bathroom sink. *Maybe if I had tried to be more independent before, instead of relying so much on others, I'd be faster now and wouldn't have to wake up at the crack of dawn so that I have enough time to make myself look presentable. I can't go back now, but I'll make sure things are different from here on out no matter what happens*, she decided.

After using a moist towelette to wash her face, she removed her pajama top and replaced it with her dress. *I'm so glad that Misty showed me that a girl doesn't have to wear tight clothes to be fashionable. It makes getting dressed so much easier. Now for the really hard part,* she sighed. Pushing herself up on her feet, Kara positioned herself so that she was halfway standing up in her chair, removed her bottoms, and replaced them with tights.

"Ow," *I really wish my clubfoot would just disappear*, she groaned inwardly as her tights got caught as they did almost every morning. After untangling her foot, Kara stood halfway up in her chair again and pulled up her tights.

Sitting back down in her chair, she took a brush to her curls and looked at herself in the mirror. *Still a little unruly, but it will have to do*, she decided before finally venturing out to the kitchen. "It's about time you came out princess," Tyler quipped as she positioned herself at the table. "The rest of us need to use the bathroom too, ya know."

Letting out a breath, Kara laid her head on the table and closed her eyes. "I am sorry," she mumbled. "I'm just so tired."

"Are you sure that being sleepy is your only problem, little lady? You look a little pale," Stella commented as she sat at the table across from the little girl.

Uh oh, I better put on a smile or she'll make me call Misty and Derrick. I miss them, but I'm not ready to go home yet, she decided as she opened her eyes, lifted her head, and flashed a smile at the pink-haired woman. "I'm fine," she assured nonchalantly. "I'm just worn out. Even with all our royal duties, life is not nearly this busy at the castle. I am to go to school, keep my grades up, and help with the animals, but otherwise things are pretty laid back."

"Well, we don't all have the luxury of being royal little one. You really lucked out," Stella pointed out.

Nodding, Kara agreed. "Yeah, but I didn't luck out just because I became royal. I lucked out because I found my forever family. I want other orphans in the kingdom to experience that joy. I don't get why Misty and Derrick can't understand that."

"Well, little lady, all I can say is that you need to have courage, discipline, and patience in all areas of your life not just dance. In short, you need to be brave and learn to love and live the way you dance."

"I really wish people would stop saying that to me," the little girl groaned. "I love the way I dance and always have!" she exclaimed.

Chuckling, the pink-haired woman shook her head. "That's not exactly what love the way you dance means in this case, girlie."

"Well, then what does it mean?" the princess questioned, her voice a mixture of frustration and persistence.

"Don't worry, you'll learn someday," the eccentric caretaker assured her.

"Speakin' of learning, are you two gonna keep chattin' or are we goin' to go to school?" Tyler inserted himself into the conversation as he approached.

"Chill out," Kara exclaimed. "I'm almost ready. I just need to pack up some sliders for lunch."

Stella shook her head. "Sorry, girlie, we ate the last of 'em for supper last night. You're gonna have to eat lunch at school."

"Does that mean we're stuck with peanut butter sandwiches for dinner tonight?" Tyler whined.

"There is nothing wrong with peanut butter," Stella insisted. "But, if you must know, I saw Tony at the castle yesterday and invited him over for dinner tonight."

"Wait, *you* invited him?" Kara questioned, pointedly.

"Yeah. So what?" Stella's forehead wrinkled in confusion. "We need to eat, don't we?"

"We sure do," Tyler agreed.

"You like him," Kara teased.

"Sure, he's nice and he can cook."

Shaking her head, the princess disagreed. "No, I mean you *like* him," she explained.

"I do not," the eccentric woman protested, her cheeks instantly as pink as her hair. "What're we in… the third grade?"

The children simultaneously burst into laughter. "Uh, yeah, we are," Tyler confirmed, his eyes light with amusement.

"I mean, I know you're in the third grade. I meant–" The dance instructor paused contemplating what to say next. "Well, I don't know what I meant," she admitted after a moment. "Just get to school. Both of you. I'll see you later for rehearsal. Don't be late," she cautioned.

Still smiling, Kara nodded. "See ya later," she assured. *Things are going so well. My plan is going to work. I can feel it in my bones,* she mused as she followed Tyler to school, feeling more confident than she had since her idea first popped into her head.

Chapter 12

Oh my gosh. If I didn't know any better, I'd say my skull was literally splitting open, Kara could barely hold up her pounding head and struggled to concentrate as Ms. Ryder explained long division with remainders in a way that made it sound as appealing as elevator music. Looking up at the clock, the little girl groaned inwardly. *How is it the teacher's only been giving this lesson for 30 minutes? I swear it feels like she's been at this for three hours.*

Tyler glanced at the princess from his seat next to her. "You okay, partner?" he whispered. "You look real pale."

Nodding, she mouthed, "Headache."

Ripping a piece of paper from his notebook, Tyler quickly scribbled a note and passed it to her. *If I get caught with this, I'm so calling Tyler out,* Kara decided as she swiftly opened the note and glanced at it. The note simply read: shunt???

Oh no, why would Tyler even put worries about my shunt out into the universe? she groaned. I haven't thought about my shunt since… well, since the last time. Shaking her head, Kara dismissed her thoughts and attempted to focus on the long division lesson. However, her mind had different ideas. As much as she tried to resist it, the princess soon found herself trapped in memories. In minutes she was no longer the spunky, nine-year-old princess, but instead a terrified five-year-old orphan sitting in Mooncrest group home with the other girls combing baby dolls' hair while Tyler, Ben, and the other boys built a train track.

"Betsy, my tummy hurts," Kara whined, holding her stomach as she approached the caretaker's office.

Letting out a breath, Betsy got up from her desk and kneeled in front of the little girl. She studied the child for a moment then placed a hand to her forehead. "Well, you don't feel warm. Why don't you go lay down and I'll bring you some lemon-lime soda to settle your tummy, okay?"

Nodding, Kara did as she was told.

"Lay on your side, bring your knees to your tummy, and take small sips of this," Betsy instructed a few minutes later, her usually stern voice kind and quiet as she held a drink out to the little girl.

Shaking her head, Kara frowned. "My tummy still hurts. I think I'm going to be–" Stopping cold, Kara retched, quickly moving her hand to her mouth and swallowing to keep from seeing her last meal once again.

"Ben, grab me a…" Betsy began.

In that second, despite Kara's best efforts, her stomach contracted violently, sending the leftover chili she'd eaten for lunch from her mouth to Betsy's blouse in seconds.

"Eww," Tyler exclaimed as he and the other orphans gathered around Betsy and Kara.

Sighing and still covered in vomit, the caretaker turned her attention to the boy. "Don't worry, Tyler. Kara and I are fine," she assured. "She just has a little stomach bug. Go play." She looked at the other children. "Go play. Everyone, go play," she urged. "Keep a safe distance from Kara to make sure you don't catch this bug."

Throwing his head back, Tyler laughed. "Yay, you can't bug me," he taunted, sticking his tongue out at Kara before running after the other children.

"Tyler, be nice," Betsy called out before turning her attention back to the sick little girl.

"I'm so sorry, Betsy," Kara said, her voice weak and quiet.

Betsy shook her head. "You don't have to be sorry, little one. Although, I do recall saying that once the chili was gone, I didn't want to see it for a month," she joked.

Kara responded with a quiet giggle, exposing her dimples.

The typically stern caretaker flashed a smile. "There are the dimples everyone loves," Betsy gently poked the dimple in the girl's right cheek. "I'm going to go change and get a cool wash–"

"Who is the caretaker of this shoddy establishment?" a 300-pound man whose face was redder than a strawberry on a hot summer day shouted as he burst into the group home without knocking.

"Hold that thought, little one," Betsy said before rushing to address the angry gentleman. "I am, sir. I am quite busy at the moment, so I'm going to have to ask you to lower your voice, calm yourself, and tell me why you burst into my group home."

"Yeah, I can see how busy you are." The man laughed curtly, eyeing the vomit running down the front of her blouse. "You're obviously in way over your head."

Looking the man straight in the eye, Betsy let out a huff. "Sir, I will have you know that I have successfully been the caretaker of this group home for the past ten years. What is this about?"

Standing up taller, the man looked down at Betsy as though he were trying to ensure his dominance over her. "I'll tell you what this is about. I'm George Mills, father to this little weasel, otherwise known as George Jr.," he explained as he stepped aside to reveal a teenager with his green eyes and pointed chin that looked like he could throw up at any moment. "He and Felicia Hunter have been dating for a couple months now and this afternoon I caught them getting handsy and talking about running away to Rubiesville," he chuckled angrily at the mere thought then continued. "I will not have my son running away. Keep a short leash on Felicia and the rest of these pathetic little leeches or I swear I'll report you and have you replaced in a second flat," he threatened, his voice laced with pure anger.

Shaking her head, Betsy protested. "How dare you come in here and insult these children, Mr. Mills. I understand that you're angry with Felicia, but that doesn't give you the right to storm in here and insult me or the—"

"Betsy," Kara yelled out weakly, cutting her off.

"One second, Kara. I'll be right there," the caretaker called out, her attention still on George.

Uh oh, why is the room spinning? The little girl struggled to concentrate on the glass of lemon-lime soda next to her bed. *What's happening to me?* She wondered as her entire body began to shake uncontrollably and everything around her went black.

"Kara, what's wrong?" Tyler asked. After a long moment with no response, Tyler looked to the children's caretaker. "Miss Betsy, why is Kara shaking?" he asked, his eyebrows wrinkled with worry.

Sighing, Betsy looked to the boy. "I don't know, Tyler. I need one more minute with Mr. Mills, okay?"

"Okay, but she might fall out of bed," Tyler answered nonchalantly.

"Wait, what?" Betsy queried rhetorically before turning her attention to the little girl's bed. "Oh, my goodness. She's seizing. Mr. Mills called the infirmary, now!"

***

Beep... beep... beep. Startled awake by a distant yet persistent sound, Kara wiped the sleep from her eyes. A moment later, the fact that the five-year-old girl was lying in a larger bed than usual registered. Quickly scanning her surroundings, she noticed that the bright, cheerful drawings featuring unicorns, kittens, fish, and other cuddly, fantastical animals she and her friends had created for the group home were not on the walls. "W-where am I?" she asked, her tiny, sweet voice coated in anxiety. When her question was followed by nothing but an eerie silence, the little girl realized that she was alone and her heart sped up inside her chest. Overwhelmed by the unknown and the sadness of being alone, she began to cry.

A few minutes later, a red-haired, blue-eyed woman wearing scrubs came into the room. "I thought I heard some noise in here. Why the tears, sweet pea?"

"I don't know where I am," Kara admitted sheepishly as tears continued to fall from her eyes. "And I am all alone."

"You're not alone. I am here now. The name's, Suzie by the way. I work as a nurse here at the Mooncrest infirmary."

"I'm Kara. How did I end up here?" Sniffling, she wiped her eyes and looked to the nurse wonderingly.

Looking away from Kara, Suzie mumbled under her breath, "Why do we nurses always have to do all the dirty work?"

The little curly-haired girl's eyebrows knitted in confusion. "Huh?"

Cheeks slightly red, Suzie waved a dismissive hand and sat down on the edge of the little girl's bed. "A very nice man, Dr. Tylerson, has been taking great care of you since your caretaker, Betsy Burno, brought you to the infirmary.

"Huh?" Kara asked, eyebrows furrowed in confusion for the second time in moments. "Why did Betsy want me to see a doctor?"

Sighing again, Suzie studied the young patient, her expression thoughtful. "Kara, sweetie, has anyone ever explained to you what Spina Bifida is?"

Kara rolled her eyes as though the answer were the most obvious thing in the world. "I have Spina Bifida because my spine didn't form right when I was a baby."

Nodding the nurse smiled. "That's right. Has anyone ever spoken with you about the problems that Spina Bifida can cause?"

"Duh." Kara chuckled. "I'm not a baby. I'm five, she pointed out proudly.

Giggling, Suzie nodded. "Okay, Miss Smarty-Pants. Tell me about how Spina Bifida affects you."

"Well, I can't feel my legs," Kara said. "That makes it hard to stand and walk so I use that chair," she explained, pointing to her pink manual wheelchair parked in the corner opposite her bed. "And I have to take medicine to help empty my tummy. Miss Betsy says it's because my tummy muscles and my brain don't get along."

Suzie frowned. "Bummer."

Shrugging her shoulders, the little girl dismissed the thought. "The real bummer is that I have a clubfoot and can't wear pretty pointe shoes," she whined.

"I see." Suzie nodded again as she contemplated what to say next. "Did Miss Betsy ever tell you that your spine and brain don't get along either?" she queried after a moment.

Kara shook her head. "Why don't they get along? Don't they like each other?" she asked, her voice coated in childhood innocence.

Letting out another quiet sigh, Suzie grabbed Kara's hand and squeezed it. "No sweetie, in your case, your brain and your spine don't get along well at all. Your spine didn't form right when you were really little, so the space between them doesn't close like it does for most people. You see, everyone's spine has fluid inside." Tilting her head to the right, Suzie tried to think of a more kid-friendly term. "The fluid is kind of like water," she continued. "Our bodies use it to keep the brain and spine safe, but we only need a little bit. Too much water on the brain can confuse it and make people sick. Your spine and brain don't get along, so sometimes too much water drips from the space between them into your brain, which can make you not feel so good. Do you understand?"

Kara nodded. "Yeah. I think so. My brain and spine aren't friends. I'm wondering about one thing though."

"What's that sweet pea?"

"How can the space between my brain and spine be closed so I don't get sick again?"

"Well, listen to you, smarty-pants. I guess you do get it. That's a great question. When you were a baby, your doctor put a tube called a shunt into the space between your spine and brain to keep too much water from getting into your brain and making you feel yucky. You've grown a lot since you were a baby, so your shunt had to be replaced," Suzie hesitated for a moment then continued. "You'll need a shunt your whole life, sweet pea, so you need to learn the signs of shunt trouble."

"Okay, but shouldn't we wait until Betsy picks me up? She should know too," Kara urged.

Suzie smiled and opened her mouth to answer, but closed it as the caretaker knocked on the door, as if on cue and poked her head in. "That's right little one. I want to know how to keep you safe. We all do."

"We?" Suzie questioned.

"Come on in children," Betsy called out.

With that, Tyler, Ben, Felicia, and the other children living in the orphanage came into the infirmary room and Suzie told them about every sign of shunt malfunction from staring spells to seizures before they took Kara home.

***

A loud thud startled Kara, bringing her back to the present. Glancing to her right, she saw that Tyler had purposely knocked a book onto the floor to gain her attention.

Uh oh, I totally spaced. Kara realized as she mouthed "thank you" to her dance partner.

"Princess, did you hear the assignment?" Ms. Ryder questioned.

Looking down at her hands, Kara shook her head reluctantly. "I'm sorry, Ms. Ryder, will you repeat the assignment please?"

"Everyone is to continue researching whomever they've chosen for their history report until the day is over. I don't know how far along you are, but I suggested everyone put together a list of main discussion points to get the ball rolling. That list is due by tomorrow morning."

Kara nodded and hurriedly pulled Maxwell Denison's biography from her backpack. "Yes, ma'am."

As Ms. Ryder turned her attention to the dirty chalkboard at the front of the room, Kara attempted to read about her great, great grandfather's teenage years. Within minutes, despite the princess's best effort to concentrate on the book from Archibald, her stomach started somersaulting as if she were on a never-ending rollercoaster and Tyler's note went racing through her mind. *No, it can't be,* she insisted. The headaches and stomachache are just a coincidence. *All the stress of the performance and everything else is catching up with me. I just need to focus and everything will be fine,* she decided, focusing once again on Maxwell Denison's biography. *Derrick's great grandpa lived a sad life,* Kara realized as she read about how Maxwell was never adopted and struggled for years until, finally, he found an apprenticeship as a cobbler. *How the heck did a struggling cobbler become king?* Kara wondered, as she went on to read about how he fell in love with Elyse Ellison, once a principal dancer at Starrycrest Theater, who had come into his shop in search of pointe shoes and subsequently doubled his business.

Tears filled Kara's eyes as the book went on to describe how the then royal family all passed away because of a horrific carriage crash, while en route to their vacation cottage. *That's awful. First, Maxwell was never adopted and then he had to watch the family who gave him up die? That's so unfair.* Wiping the moisture from her eyes, the tiny royal pulled a notebook from her backpack and proceeded to jot down a few discussion points.

Tyler glanced at her again, his eyebrows wrinkled in confusion. "Why do you look like a baby who just had her blanket taken away?" he whispered jokingly. "It's only a history report. Toughen up, *princess.*"

"Shut up, Tyler," she retorted. Turning her attention back to the biography, Kara saw that she still had about two-thirds of it left to read. *This is going to take forever*, she sighed. *I wish I could just talk to Derrick to find out more about Maxwell's life, but I just can't face him yet. I must focus on truly making a difference before the babies come.* Glancing at the date on the chalkboard she saw that the baby's due date was just a few short months away. *I'm running out of time,* she realized. The thought of no longer being princess made Kara's heart practically catapult out of her chest. Taking a breath, she went back to reading and tried to calm herself.

That's probably the only time that DNA ever helped an orphan, Kara mused after reading that Maxwell only became king after taking a blood test to prove that reigning over the land was his birthright after the royal family died. *If only birthright were not the only factor used to determine who can reign over the kingdom,* she thought wistfully. Laughing to herself, she dismissed the idea. *Of course, it all comes down to birthright, what else would it come down to?* she mused. *My plan is dumb anyway. Even if it works and I convince Derrick and Misty that Starrycrest needs a kiddo keeper program, I have no idea how I'm going to convince the rest of the king–*

"Hey *princess,* I know you think you're special and all, but this little thing called the lunch bell just rang and usually when that happens us common folk go get something to eat. Ya comin'?"

"The world doesn't revolve around food and dance, Ty. I have way more important things to worry about."

Eyes widened in disbelief, the spiky-haired boy stared at her. "Who are you and what have you done with Kara Denison?"

"Haha, very funny, Ty," Kara retorted sarcastically. "Get real."

"Oh, trust me. I am," the boy insisted. You better not let Stella hear you say that dance is anything but the most important thing ever. I don't get why you're letting this assignment get to you anyway. It's just a stupid history report."

"Maybe to you. But, for me, it's different. I'm doing a report on Derrick's great grandfather for cryin' out loud. That's a lot of pressure."

Rolling his eyes, Tyler dismissed the idea, "Oh c'mon, you've got it easy. There are so many people you can talk to about him. You can go to Derrick, Archibald, or even Betsy."

Kara's eyebrows furrowed in confusion. "Betsy's not related to Maxwell. Why would I talk to her?"

Tyler shrugged. "Heck if I know. Stella's the one who suggested it, remember?"

Kara's eyes widened in disbelief as a smile stretched across her lips. "Oh my gosh! Ty, you're a genius!" She exclaimed

"Uh, have you forgotten Stella's rules? We're supposed to stay in school," Tyler reminded her.

I know, but this is way more important, trust me. Cover for me and I'll owe you one," the princess insisted."

With that, she breezed past Tyler, giving him no time to object.

Chapter 13

I can't believe I didn't think to approach Betsy before. She's always said that the group home is her kingdom and she knows the place better than anyone. I should've done this a long time ago, Kara realized as a new hope ignited deep in her chest. *Here's to hoping she has the answers I need.* Taking a deep breath, the curly-haired girl knocked on the door of the building she'd once believed would be her forever home.

"Young lady, what're doing here? Shouldn't you be in school ?" the elderly caretaker asked, eyebrows arched with suspicion as she answered the door.

The tiny majestic flashed a nervous smile, her cheeks turning slightly red. "I haven't visited in a while. I just thought I'd come by and see how you're doing," she explained innocently.

"You came by just to see how I'm doing?" the gray-haired woman questioned, her eyebrows arched even higher than moments before.

"Yeah, I figured this would be a good time because the older kids are at school and the little ones are taking their afternoon nap, am I right?"

Nodding hesitantly, Betsy confirmed her assumption. "Yes, but I'm busy nonetheless and I'm not buyin' this causal little visit of yours. Come into my office and tell me what's really going on," Betsy stepped aside, giving the little girl room to enter.

Wasting no time at all, Betsy led Kara to her office and took a seat at her desk. "Does this have anything to do with your little kiddo keeper-related scheme?" she queried before Kara could even pull up across from her.

Whoa, I forgot how intense Betsy can be sometimes. If looks could kill, I'd be six feet under right now, Kara mused. "I don't know what you're talking about," the little girl answered, faking innocence. "I'm here because I'm doing a report on Maxwell Denison. It turns out he was an orphan." Pausing, she smiled before adding, "You're practically a walking encyclopedia when it comes to the past and present orphans of the kingdom. What can you tell me about Maxwell?"

Chuckling, Betsy leaned forward, so she and Kara were nose to nose. "I appreciate the not-so-subtle sucking up, but you're not going to get off that easy, young lady."

"What do you mean?" Kara queried, her voice still coated in innocence.

"Just how much research have you done on Derrick's great grandfather?"

Kara shrugged. "Not much," she admitted. His biography is really long and I'm running out of time, so I thought it'd be easier to talk to people who knew him or knew of him." Heat rose up in the young girl's cheeks as she rushed to defend herself. Taking a deep breath to calm herself, she continued. "When I mentioned doing my report on Maxwell, Stella choked on a piece of pie and insisted I talk to you about it."

"Oh, she did, did she?" the elderly caretaker questioned, her voice edged with irritation.

Kara nodded vehemently. "Please just tell me what you and Stella know that I don't," she pleaded.

"Well, after Maxwell proved he was a member of the royal bloodline, he began his reign by founding this very group home to ensure that no child in the kingdom would be alone and without a home ever again," the caretaker explained after a moment.

"Wow, really?" Kara's bright blue eyes widened. "I didn't realize this place was that old. What was it like back when it was first opened?"

Betsy chuckled. "I'm certainly not old enough to be your great, great grandmother, young lady. I wasn't here when this place first opened so I don't know what it was like back then, but I do know that this place meant so much to Maxwell that he made the time to be caretaker while he was king."

Kara's eyes grew even wider than they were a moment prior. "This place must have really meant a lot to him," she murmured.Nodding, Betsy agreed. "It meant a great deal to him. Next to his family, this group home was the most important thing in his life. He put this place and the children who lived here ahead of his royal duties, his passion for making shoes, and everything else. Eventually, Maxwell decided to make his trusted friend, Henry Miles, Misty's great grandfather, his second in command. For years, the families worked together to ensure the safety and happiness of the kingdom until–" The caretaker paused for a moment and then continued, "Well, you know what happened next."

Kara nodded. "Yeah, but I don't understand. If the Denisons are true royalty, how did Misty's family end up with their own kingdom?"

"Wahh, wahh, wahh," a distant cry stole the elderly caretaker's attention.

Jumping up from her chair, Betsy poked her head out of the office door to investigate the source of the sound. A moment later, she turned back to the princess. "I have to go and you should really get back to school."

"But this is important," Kara protested.

"Take these," the caretaker suggested, pushing two books as big as any book the little girl had ever seen toward her.

Accepting the literature reluctantly, Kara placed the books on her knees and sighed.

Great, I come to Betsy to get out of reading and she gives me more reading to do. That's just my luck, the little girl grumbled as she left the group home and hesitantly made her way back to the schoolhouse .

***

"You look a little pale today, little lady," Stella commented as Kara rounded a giant Christmas gift prop in the Dance Dazzler while practicing her solo in the castle studio.

Uh oh, I gotta play it cool, Kara decided, quickly pasting on a fake smile. *As much as I miss Misty and Derrick, I can't come home yet. Not until I have more answers.*

"Earth to Kara," the dance instructor called out as she waved a hand in the little girl's face, interrupting her thoughts.

"Oh, sorry. I'm okay. It's just that I've had a long day. I'm tired and hungry," the princess explained, covering her mouth to stifle a yawn.

Tyler, who'd been sitting in the corner of the studio doing his homework while Kara rehearsed, perked up. "Me too. I'm so hungry I'd eat some of that burnt bacon from the other day if you had it."

Shaking her head, Stella laughed. I can't risk any chipped chompers on my watch. "Let's get going so we can see what Tony's cooked up for supper tonight."

"Sounds good," Kara agreed as Stella transferred her from the Dance Dazzler to her wheelchair. "Speaking of Tony, have you two talked much lately?"

Stella's cheeks flushed instantly at the mention of the kind, handsome chef.

"Not much," she said wistfully. "I have my hands full with you two and he says that working for the queen has been –" Stella stopped short of finishing her sentence. Clearing her throat, she looked away from the little girl and down her feet. "Well, uh, let's just say things have been hectic here at the castle lately," she stammered.

Kara blinked. "Hectic, what do you mean 'hectic'?" she asked, her voice coated with alarm. "Are Misty, Derrick, and the babies all right?"

"Of course, little lady. I'm sure your family is fine. Tony was mentionin' the other day that as the pregnancy progresses Misty's cravings become more intense. I guess she's been keepin' him pretty busy," Stella explained. The words came out in a rush, but her voice was casual. Even though the dance instructor's voice held no trepidation, her eyes were full of apprehension. *Stella knows more than she's letting on,* Kara realized. *But, what? She just said that my family is fine and Derrick promised to let me know if anything happened. They wouldn't lie to me, would they?* She wondered. Kara's stomach began to churn as that question entered her mind. Taking a deep breath, she pushed through her nerves and decided to try to get more answers. She opened her mouth to do so but closed it when Tyler spoke.

"If life at the castle is as crazy as you say it is right now then I'm sure Tony will be happy to get out of here and feed us tonight, can we get goin' before my stomach growls enough to make me gnaw off my left arm please?" he insisted.

I guess I'll have to dig for more information later, Kara decided as they made their way out of the studio and to Stella's house.

***

I was so right about Stella and Tony liking each other. He's looking at her the way Derrick looks at Misty. Like she's the most beautiful woman he's ever seen, Kara realized as they approached Stella's home and found Tony outside, flashing a bright smile.

"Hey beautiful," he greeted, kissing her sweetly on the cheek. "I've missed you."

"Ditto," Stella said, her cheeks nearly as pink as her hair.

"Eww," Tyler's face twisted in feigned disgust. "Get a hold of yourself, man. There are kids here," he joked.

"Sorry, bud. I just can't help myself around this pretty lady," Tony flashed a smile at Stella then looked back to the boy. "You'll learn someday."

"Gross," the spiky-haired boy stuck his tongue out in distaste. "Can we go inside and eat please?

"Yes, let's eat," Kara agreed, placing a hand to her stomach. "My tummy is all rumbly. What did you bring for supper?"

Letting out a huff, Stella eyed the children. "Where are your manners? Do you kids ever think about anything other than food?"

"It's not our fault we're so hungry," Tyler protested. You're the one who is practically a drill sergeant in the dance studio."

Clearing her throat, Stella focused all her attention on the boy. "Not the point, bud. Isn't there somethin' you want to say to Tony?"

"Oh, yeah… uh, sorry man. It's good to see you."

Kara nodded. "Yeah, Tony it's great to see you as always. Please forgive me for thinking with my stomach instead of my head."

Tony waved a dismissive hand. "No worries, kiddos. You're talkin' to a chef. I understand what it's like to think with your stomach. Believe me. Right now, my stomach is craving the baked ziti and garlic bread I prepared for us, so let's get inside."

Why did he have to make something that reminds me of Misty and Derrick? the pint-sized royal wondered as she took a bite of ziti, which she knew was one of their favorite meals. *I miss them more than I ever thought I would*, she realized. *I can't believe they haven't been at the castle for any of our rehearsals. I bet Tony will tell me what's going on.*

Determined to get answers, she opened her mouth to question Tony, but stopped herself as he turned to Tyler.

"So, bud, have you decided who you're goin' to do your history report on yet?" he queried before chomping into a piece of garlic bread.

Tyler nodded. "I've been researchin' Madam Sterling. She seems like she was an awesome person."

Flashing a smile, Tony shook his head in agreement. "As someone who knew her personally, I can confidently say that she was pretty much the coolest person ever."

Stopping short of biting into a fork full of salad, Stella's mouth dropped open. "Wait, you knew Madam Sterling?"

"Sure did. I was in her care for a short while. My dad and my mother's parents fought for custody of me after my mom died," Tony divulged before taking a bite of ziti.

Stella's gaze softened but stayed focused on Tony. "I'm sorry to hear about your mother. You couldn't have been in better care during such a difficult time in your life though."

"Very true," Tony nodded. "I've always been so grateful for Eclipston's Kiddo Keeper Program. How long were you in her care?"

"I was with her for six years before she passed," Stella explained, her tone solemn and quiet.

Tony hung his head. "I heard that she passed about seven years after my grandparents got custody, but I didn't want to believe it." Reaching across the table for her hand, Tony squeezed it gently. "I'm sorry that you witnessed the loss of such a great woman, but I'm sure she appreciated havin' you with her in the end."

"Thanks. It's crazy to think that if you'd stayed with her for just a year longer, we would've met."

Grinning mischievously, Tony shook his head. "It's good we didn't meet back then because I never would've been able to resist pursuing you and Madam Sterling would've never let that fly."

Nodding, Stella cackled. "I can only imagine how many pirouettes she would have made you do as punishment."

Tony chuckled, his eyes bright with amusement. "It wouldn't have been as bad as the time I was tossing a ball around with my buddies and broke the window of her dance studio. Let's just say I thought the pirouettes would never end."

"Madam Sterling sounds like she was real tough," Tyler said before taking a bit of garlic bread.

"The toughest," Tony agreed.

"Yeah, but she was also the best," Stella pointed out after finishing her salad. "A wonderful dancer, a great cook, and a loving mother."

"Don't forget an awesome negotiator," Tony added.

"Tell me more about her," Tyler urged. "What did she like most about dance?"

Kara observed her dinner companions as they continued to discuss Madam Sterling. *This is working out better than I ever imagined it would,* she realized as she watched them. *They look good together. It's almost like they're meant to be a family.* While that thought and the fact that her plan was coming together should've made Kara happy, it did the exact opposite. *I wonder if people think that Misty, Derrick, and I look like a family when we're together.*

We are a family. The best family. With that realization came another. *I belong with Misty and Derrick and I want to go home.* She opened her mouth to express her thoughts, but bit her tongue at the last second, stopping herself. *I got into all of this with a purpose and I can't go home until I fulfill it.* In that moment, the gravity of her plan to convince Derrick that the kingdom needed a kiddo keeper program hit her and her stomach began somersaulting again.

"I don't feel so good," she admitted sheepishly before backing away from the table and gaining the attention of her friends.

"Uh oh," Tyler exclaimed. "You look kinda green. Are you about to hurl?"

"Ty, bud, never use the word hurl or any of its synonyms at the dinner table. Especially when you're having dinner with a pretty lady," Tony advised.

"Yeah, hush," Stella urged before turning her attention to Kara.

"What's wrong, little lady? Should we call your parents?" Stella's voice was coated with urgency.

Taking a deep breath, Kara pushed through the nausea. "I'm not gonna yack. I just have a bit of a stomachache."

Tony frowned. "I hope it wasn't the ziti."

Placing a hand to the little girl's forehead, Stella's eyebrows wrinkled with worry. "You're a tad warm. Are you sure we shouldn't call your parents?"

Uh oh, I better come up with an excuse fast. As she pondered what to say next, Derrick's voice popped into her head. *When all else fails, dance.* "There's no need to call Derrick and Misty," she assured. "I'm fine. It's just a stomachache. It's probably just 'cause I'm a little nervous about the performance," she explained meekly.

Tony nodded. "That makes sense. Madam Sterling always said that a dancer wasn't a true performer until they cared enough to get a little nervous beforehand."

"Well, in that case, I must be the truest dancer around because I'm terrified," Kara admitted.

"Madam Sterling did always say that, didn't she?" Stella said sounding nostalgic. "I'll tell you what, little lady," she said after a moment. "I'll give you the night off from rehearsal so you can get some rest, but if you're still feeling under the weather tomorrow then we gotta call your parents, okay?"

Kara nodded. "Thank you. I'm sure I'll feel better tomorrow."

With that, she excused herself from the table and went to bed for the night hoping to dream about the family she missed so much.

Chapter 14

*C*lap, clap, clap! *What the heck is that noise?* Kara wondered as a loud hammering sound startled her awake.

Wiping sleep from her eyes, she looked out the window and saw that Tony was hanging a new shutter onto the front of the house while Tyler painted another a beautiful sky blue.

Scooting her wheelchair closer to her bed, she locked the brakes and carefully transferred into it. *Whoa, my head has found its heartbeat again*, Kara acknowledged. *Today should be interesting,* she realized, hesitantly making her way into the kitchen.

"Morning, little lady, all that clatter wake you up too?" Stella asked by way of greeting.

Nodding, Kara glanced up at the clock, her eyes widening in disbelief when she saw that it was not yet 7:30 a.m. "Who does any kind of home improvement this early? Don't they realize it's Saturday?"

Stella, who was sitting at the kitchen table sipping a cup of coffee, smiled dreamily.

"I guess this is what they were conspirin' about when Tony pulled Tyler aside the other day. They have a whole list of projects that they wanna finish over the weekend," she explained, her smile stretched from ear to ear. "I think it's sweet."

Rolling her eyes, Kara groaned, "It would be sweeter in the afternoon."

"Someone woke up on the wrong side of the bed," Stella joked before finishing the last of her coffee.

After putting her mug in the sink, Stella turned her attention back to the little girl. "All kiddin' aside, how are you feelin' today?" she queried, her voice reflecting the concern she'd had the night before.

As if on cue, Kara's head began pounding once again, reminding the little girl that she was not her usual self. Sitting up a bit straighter in her chair, the young royal forced a smile. "I'm fine. I feel like a new person," she managed, pretending to be excited. Fidgeting slightly in her wheelchair, the little girl struggled to relax as Stella eyed her suspiciously. *Play it cool*, she cautioned herself. *That's not a complete lie. Headaches do bring out a new side of you. Just keep smiling.*

"Great, so you'll come out to help me and the boys then?" Stella suggested, an edge of doubt to her voice, even though she seemed as excited as the little girl had pretended to be a moment before.

"Well, um, I, uh, I'm not very outdoorsy," Kara admitted after a moment.

Stella laughed. "Yeah, well, neither am I and I'm sure as heck not a handywoman, but that ain't stopping me. Aren't you the one who, when you guys first got here, told Tyler that being part of a family is hard work?" Stella asked pointedly.

Hearing Stella refer to all of them as family should have made Kara happy but instead it infuriated her. *This isn't my family. It's yours. I have to fight for my family and Starrycrest as a whole. I don't have time to fix up your house too.* Biting her bottom lip, the little girl kept herself from voicing her thoughts. As she considered what to say instead, Derrick's voice popped into her head. *Stay grounded, sweetheart. Always remember that royalty is as much a responsibility as a privilege. You'll always be special in your own right, but you must understand that being royal does not make you better or more important than anyone else.* Sighing, Kara lamented, "Okay, I'll come out and help after I get dressed."

"I'm lovin' the enthusiasm, little lady," Stella joked, heading outside to help the boys herself.

I never thought I'd miss Marie, Ashleigh, and the other castle personal assistants this much. I should really do something special for them when I get back to the castle, she decided as she struggled to pull a shirt over her head. A wave of nausea hit the princess as she stood halfway up in her chair and pulled on a pair of sweatpants. Taking a deep breath, she tried to alleviate it. When that did nothing, she looked at herself in the mirror. *Oh, my goodness, I look worse than I ever did after fighting for time in the restroom at the group home*, she mused. *If I go outside like this, Stella will definitely send me home.* Knowing it was going to take more than a fake smile to get past the eccentric dance instructor this time, she ran a brush through her unruly curls and pondered what to do. The solution hit her just as quickly as the wave of nausea moments before. *I'll use my homework as an excuse. Stella will have to let me out of helping the boys then. School comes first, right?* Quickly losing confidence in her plan, she headed outside before she could talk herself out of it.

"Hey there, little lady, you ready to get your hands dirty?" Stella asked as Kara made her way down the makeshift ramp Tyler created. Scanning her surroundings, the curly-haired girl saw that Tony was hanging the new shutters while Tyler measured wood in preparation for making a permanent, safer ramp and Stella busily planted some sunflowers in front of the hedges.

"You guys look like you've got this under control. Since I turned in so early last night, I've got some homework to catch up on so I'm gonna go to the library," she explained before racing down the ramp.

"Hold on there, little lady," Stella cautioned, stepping in the little girl's path. "We talked about this. I thought you were gonna help us today."

"I-I was. I mean, I-I am, but I s-should really finish my homework," she stammered. *Jeez, since when do I stutter? Maybe it's good there's a chance I won't be a princess for much longer. I'd never be able to handle personal audiences.* That thought, as fleeting as it was, brought tears to her eyes in an instant. *The last thing you need to do is cry. Pull it together*, she told herself, swiftly wiping the tears in hopes that no one would notice. A quick glance from Tyler showed that he'd spotted the tears despite her efforts. The alarm in his eyes revealed his concern. *Oh great. Ty is gonna tell Stella that I'm sick. That's it. I'm going home. It's over.*

"C'mon Stella, you, Tony, and I got this handled. Let Kara go do her homework," Tyler urged. "Besides, somethin' tells me she's not near as ready to give her history report as I am," he teased.

Kara opened her mouth to object but closed it when she realized that Tyler was actually coming to her defense. Nodding vigorously, she confirmed the boy's suspicion. "Sadly, Tyler's right for once. I still have a lot of work to do," she admitted.

"Okay, but why do you have to go to the library? Why can't you just study here?"

After hanging the last of the shutters, Tony turned his attention to the pink-haired woman . "Stel, hun, don't ya think the sawin' and hammering might be a bit distractin'? Let the girl go study. School comes first, right?"

Sighing, Stella relented, "Okay, okay. I give up. Go study. Just be back in time to rehearse this evening, all right?"

"Of course. I wouldn't miss it," Kara assured. "Thanks so much, guys. See you later," she called out before letting out a sigh of relief and heading toward the kingdom's library.

I forgot how much I love this place, Kara realized as she entered the red brick building that housed Starrycrest Library. It was one of the oldest, tallest structures in the kingdom, second only to the castle. The massive space was filled with row after row of books with spines facing outward to indicate whether they were historical anthologies, informative encyclopedias, or literary classics. Kara instinctively went to the children's section, housed in the far-right corner of the building. Although the little girl hadn't been there in over two years, it felt familiar to her. Prior to being adopted, she'd often come to this corner of the library to seek refuge. Transforming time and time again from an orphan to a pirate exploring the high seas, an all-mighty dragon slayer on a quest to save her land from certain doom, or, her favorite, a fair maiden who defies an evil sorcerer to rescue her family, all thanks to the books she'd read there. *The castle library is awesome, but nothing beats this place,* she realized as the smell of paper and leather binding helped to take the edge off her pounding headache.

"Princess, is that you?" a petite woman with bright amber eyes and long red hair queried as she approached.

"Karen, oh my gosh, it's good to see you," the little girl exclaimed as she recognized her favorite librarian.

"It's good to see you too," the librarian agreed, pulling the little girl into a hug. "It's been too long. How are you? How is our beloved queen?"

Grabbing onto the wheels of her chair, Kara rolled back slightly, putting space between herself and the librarian. It had been a while since anyone had asked her about Misty and she wasn't sure how to respond. Derrick's voice once again popped into her head as she contemplated how to answer. *Sweetheart, when in doubt, honesty is the best policy.* "We're all as busy as ever preparing for the babies and the upcoming Starrycrest anniversary celebration, but we're all doing well," she answered after a moment.

"Oh, I'm so glad to hear that. Your mom usually comes here to get the latest novel by the Bonnet sisters and to see if it is appropriate for the royal library, but she's missed the release of the last two. Would you like to take them to her?" the librarian questioned sweetly.

Uh, oh, how should I handle this? the princess wondered. *I hope my face doesn't show how freaked out I am. I guess I should just keep being honest,* she decided. "I'm just here to find a quiet spot and catch up on some homework, but I'll definitely remind her about the books," Kara flashed a smile as she attempted to reassure Karen.

"I'll get out of your hair then. Be sure to let me know if you need anything," the red-haired woman urged before pulling her into another hug.

As the librarian let her go and walked away, Kara's mind began to wander. *Misty loves the Bonnet sisters. I've seen her read some of their books in like two days. Something's definitely wrong if she hasn't read their last two books. I've gotta think of a way to convince the kingthat we need a kiddo keeper program so I can get home and figure out what's going on,* she decided as she began to read one of the books Betsy had given her. As she turned the yellowing pages of the book, a musty smell wafted into her nostrils, making her nauseous yet again. Sighing, she slammed the book shut. *This book smells older than it is and it's pretty darn old. Fingers crossed the next one doesn't make me upchuck,* Kara mused, grabbing the second book Betsy had given her from her bag. *So much for a newer book,* the curly-haired little girl coughed as she opened it and a puff of dust flew into her face. *This isn't a book. It's a journal. It's Maxwell's journal. This is just what I need,* she realized. Smiling, she exposed her beloved dimples and thumbed through the pages reading entry after entry detailing the struggles and adventures of Maxwell's life. She read everything from the scared scribblings of a six-year-old who had just been diagnosed with polio to the grateful thoughts of a cobbler turned king. She laughed, got teary eyed, and even became angry after reading a few of them. Within minutes, she was hooked. Although she'd intended to read the journal in its entirety, she stopped the moment the following entry astounded her:

> *Well, it's official. I signed my first royal decree today. I should be happy, but instead as I sit and write this, I find myself disheartened. You see, today I founded the Starrycrest Group Home to give the orphans of the kingdom somewhere to stay. Being an orphan myself, I have a unique understanding of just how important it is to have a roof over your head. Moreover, I know that having a safe place to live does not lessen the emptiness only known by those who don't have a family to care for and love them. I did what I could to*

help them today as I always will, but the truth is I'm a perfectly imperfect man who makes a lot of mistakes. As a king, I probably shouldn't admit that, but this journal has always been home to my biggest dreams as well as my darkest fears. That's not about to change just because my birthright was finally recognized. I fear that I made a mistake today. I fear that because I gave the orphans somewhere to stay, they will become less visible to families in the kingdom and be less likely to get adopted. Time will tell, I suppose. Then again, by Starrycrest law, a royal decree cannot be overturned unless extraordinary circumstances arise. Extraordinary circumstances are just a fancy way of saying: "unless a better solution for the problem solved by the royal decree is found." While my giving the orphans of Starrycrest a place to live is a big step, my greatest hope is that someday the decree I made today will be overturned and all the orphaned children in this kingdom will find a forever family. Seems too good to be true, does it not? I suppose that is why it's a dream.

Oh my gosh! This is amazing! It's the answer I've been looking for. I gotta go tell Derrick and Misty. Practically bursting with excitement, the princess gathered her things and raced toward the circulation desk. "Karen, I changed my mind, I think I'm going to go ahead and take those books by the Bonnet sisters to Misty." Kara fidgeted in her wheelchair as she waited, struggling to contain her excitement.

The kind librarian flashed a smile. "Great, I actually have them right here," she grabbed two novels from the corner of the desk and offered them to the little girl. With that, Kara accepted the books and practically flew out of the library and toward the castle, feeling happier and more confident than she had in weeks.

***

The princess's confidence diminished when she was about halfway to the castle and noticed horseshoe-shaped prints on the ground. *Uh oh, these don't look like any footprints I've ever seen and I know that there are no horses that big in the kingdom which means they must be*—she shook her head, too scared to even finish the thought. Despite the tiny royal's best efforts to prevent fear from entering her consciousness, her arms suddenly felt so heavy that she struggled to push her chair. *Pull it together*, she groaned, following the tracks even though her every instinct told her to turn around and go the other way. *Why would the footprints stop here?* Kara wondered, her eyes widened in horror as the tracks led her straight to Starrycrest Square. *Apparently, I am not the only one concerned by this,* she realized as she noticed Tom, a senior member of the royal guard studying the tracks.

"Tom, do these footprints belong to you-know-who?" she whispered urgently.

"Oh, my goodness!" The elderly man exclaimed, instinctively taking a step back from her. "Princess, what are you doing here? You shouldn't be here right now. Head to the castle, you'll be safe there."

"So, these are Victrollia's footprints then?"

Even though the princess was still whispering, Tom's blue-gray eyes instantly clouded with fear. "Shh, don't say her name out loud," he cautioned. "I don't want to frighten anyone else."

"Really, Tom? If you don't want anyone to be scared, you might want to do something about all the giant footprint around here. How is everyone so calm about this anyway?" The young majestic suddenly became aware of her surroundings beyond the footprints she'd followed. Her eyebrows scrunched in confusion as she looked from one end of the square to other and saw that none of her fellow citizens seemed the least bit afraid.

"The guard announced about an hour ago that the footprints are part of a simulation used to help us sharpen our troll tracking skills. I'm surprised you didn't hear it."

"I was reading in the library. I guess I got really engrossed in my books. Besides, even if I had heard the announcement, I wouldn't have bought it for a minute. What's really going on, Tom?"

"With all due respect, princess. You already know too much. I don't feel comfortable--"

"I'm not leaving the square until you tell me the truth, Tom. I'll stay out here all night if I have to," Kara insisted, locking her wheelchair into place.

Letting out a breath, the older man relented. "Okay, Okay, you're right. These are Victrollia's tracks," he confirmed, his voice the quietest of whispers. "They start at the outskirts and stop here, but we haven't managed to locate her anywhere."

The little girl's eyebrows scrunched in bewilderment for the second time in minutes. "That doesn't make sense, how did she get in and out of the square without anyone noticing? If these tracks are any indication, she's huge."

"Honestly, princess, your guess is as good as mine," Tom admitted after a moment. "The other members of the guard and I are wondering if she's planted the tracks as a distraction before some sort of sneak attack."

"So, what's the plan?" she asked, fretful even though she was still whispering.

"I've called in reinforcements. Members of the royal guards of neighboring kingdoms will be here any day to help us. Once we have the extra men, I'm confident we'll find her and thwart whatever she's planning in no time," he assured her. Even though the elder had said he was confident, his slightly shaky voice made him sound anything but.

If an experienced member of the royal guard like Tom is spooked by Victrollia, then she must be a bigger threat than I thought, Kara realized as a knot formed in the pit of her stomach. *I'd feel better if Tom and the rest of the royal guard had an idea of what Victrollia is planning to do. Isn't it their job to know that kind of thing?* She wondered.

"Princess, if you're okay, I really should go sweep the kingdom again to make sure there are no additional signs of you-knowwho," he explained, stunning the little girl from her thoughts.

"Yes, I'm fine," she fidgeted in her chair as she fibbed to the older man. Hoping he didn't know her well enough to notice, she continued. "Good luck, Tom. Please be careful and keep my family posted."

Nodding, he agreed. "I will. Promise me you'll do your best to stay safe and not tell anyone what I told you?"

"I promise," the tiny royal assured him, flashing the weakest of smiles.

I guess Misty, Derrick, and I are going to have more to talk about than I thought, she realized as she unlocked the brakes of her chair and headed toward the castle, feeling a lot less zealous about the visit than she had when she'd left library.

***

"Hi Fred. Hello Edna, are you joining Misty and Derrick for dinner tonight?" she asked by way of greeting upon entering the castle and seeing the elderly couple that her family had befriended a couple years earlier sitting on a loveseat in the living room. "I've decided to come home and have supper as well."

Edna, a fragile, petite woman with soulful hazel eyes and a sweet smile looked up from some knitting she'd been working between her fingers. "Kara, sweetheart, it's so good to see you. What would you like for dinner?" she queried, her voice kind and quiet.

The princess looked from Edna to Fred and back. "Hmm?"

"Didn't your parents tell you that you are stuck with us tonight, cutie?" Fred questioned.

"Misty set it up with me weeks ago. She said she and Derrick needed to run some errands this evening and the staff would all be away at a childcare class that her and Derrick's parents fought—" The elderly woman bit her bottom lip as her cheeks turned slightly pink. Clearing her throat, she corrected herself, "I mean, worked with experts for weeks to develop," she explained. *An evening to themselves? I haven't seen them in forever. How can they need an evening to themselves? Does this have something to do with Victrollia? Did they go to another kingdom to get help?* The little girl wondered as she tucked some of her unruly blonde ringlets behind her ear. *Oh my gosh! No one has told them I've been staying with Stella*, she suddenly realized as pink rose into her cheeks. *This is so awkward.* In that moment, the tiny royal wanted nothing more than to know what was really going on with Derrick and Misty, but she was so confused and uncomfortable that a quiet, "Oh," was all she could manage.

"Don't worry, sweetheart," Edna assured. "I'm sure it has nothing to do with you. They are probably just tired. Misty told us about how she's having twins. I can only imagine," she said absentmindedly. "The three of you must be so excited."

Kara nodded and managed a half-smile despite how quickly the exhilaration she'd felt after discovering Maxwell's journal had faded.

I was excited until I realized these babies were going to take my place, the princess thought as the half-smile fell from her face. Fred jumped in, quickly sensing her uneasiness.

"So, about dinner, what do ya say we get a pizza?"

"Throw in some cinnamon sticks and you got yourself a deal, but I need to call a friend first," Kara smiled, exposing her dimples.

Fred chuckled. "You drive a hard bargain, sweetheart, but I can handle that." The elderly man flashed a smile. "You make your call. I'll take care of ordering the food," he assured before leaving the room to do just that.

After gaining Stella's permission to stay for supper, Kara turned her attention to the elderly woman who was still knitting. "Edna, what are you making?" she queried, parking her wheelchair next to the loveseat "You seem to be working really hard on it."

The elderly woman smiled proudly. "Thank you. I am trying my best. I'm knitting some booties for your future little siblings and I want to make sure they are perfect."

Oh my gosh! Can't anyone around here think about anything other than babies? she wondered. Biting her lip, she kept herself from voicing her thoughts and instead changed the subject. "What kind of trouble have you and Fred gotten into lately?" she joked.

"Sweetie, coming to visit you is the most exciting thing we've done in a month. We're just two old fuddy-duddies," the older woman laughed, exposing crow's feet around her eyes.

"Speak for yourself, little lady. I went fishing the other day," Fred declared as he came back into the room and sat next to his wife.

"Oh yes, how could I ever forget about your scintillating afternoons of fishing?" Edna asked, her voice dripped with sarcasm.

The princess giggled, once again exposing her beloved dimples. "Are you as good a fisherman as Derrick? He brings home a catch of the day nearly every time he goes fishing."

Fred scratched his temple. "Well, ya know, sweet pea, fishin' isn't always about what you catch. Sometimes it's more about having time to reflect."

Rolling her eyes, his wife retorted, "You're retired. You can reflect as much as you want." Chuckling, Edna went back to her knitting.

"She's got a point," Kara giggled.

"Yeah, yeah, yeah. Laugh it up you two. I'm going to wait for the pizza guy."

"So, what makes you most excited about being a big sister?" Edna questioned, her voice full of happiness as she changed the subject back to babies.

Ugh. If I didn't know any better, I'd say Edna has pregnancy brain just like Misty, the princess thought. Forcing a smile, she did her best to remember what it felt like before she worried so much about the impending new additions taking her place and answered, "The idea of having more family sounds nice."

The elderly woman sighed wistfully. "Yes, it does," she murmured quietly.

Leaning toward Edna, the princess closed the space between them and enveloped her into a hug. "You and Fred will always be a part of our family," she assured sweetly.

"And you and your family will always be a part of ours." Smiling, the surrogate grandmother returned the gesture, squeezing her tightly. "Isn't that right, dear?" she asked as Fred returned with pizza in hand.

"Yes, whatever you say, sweetheart. Let's eat," he urged, leading them into the informal dining room.

"Can I tell you guys a secret?" Kara asked after the three sat down at the table in the center of the room.

Fred shrugged, smirking slightly. "You can tell me, but for all of the wonderful qualities my wife has, she can't keep a secret to save her life."

Glaring at him over her glasses, Edna flashed a mischievous smile. "Don't be so sure about that, dear. I've kept a thing or two from you over the years."

Eyes wide, the elderly man's smirk widened. "Like what, pray tell?"

The elderly woman shook her head. "No, no, no. I'm too smart to fall for that," she giggled. "Besides, Kara has something to tell us." She looked at the little girl, "You can tell us anything sweetie. What's on your mind?"

"I'm going to be the Sugar Plum Fairy in the Starrycrest Starlets performance of The Nutcracker this year and I am going to dance in a hands-free wheelchair called the Dance Dazzler," she declared, her voice brimming with pride.

"That's great sweetheart. We'll definitely be there," Edna said, her voice colored with happy excitement.

"Yes, we'll be in the front row, but why are ya keepin' it a secret?" Fred questioned, his left eyebrow arched in confusion.

"Derrick and Misty know about my solo, but not about the Dance Dazzler. I'm going to surprise them with what I can do in it," the princess explained, her voice full of delight.

The young girl's surrogate grandma smiled from ear to ear. "That's so wonderful sweetheart. I only hope your future siblings love to dance half as much as you do."

Why is everyone around here so baby obsessed? Kara wondered as she bit into a piece of pepperoni pizza.

Nodding, the old man agreed. "The babies are bound to look mighty good in those little dance leonards."

At that moment, the princess could no longer hold her tongue. "Leotards. The outfits are called leotards. And the babies can't wear them. They can't dance. They can't steal that too," she shouted, tears streaming down her face, as she rushed to her bedroom.

***

"May I come in?" Edna asked in a meek, fretful tone as she knocked on the door of the princess's room.

"Yes," Kara replied, tears continuing to spill from her eyes as she stroked Dex's ears softly. *I can't believe I just did that. Edna and Fred didn't deserve that. I just don't know what to do.*

"What should I do, Dex? What should I do?" she questioned absent-mindedly as she continued stroking his ears.

A moment later, as if on que, Dex looked to Edna, who hesitantly walked into the room. Following the gaze of her canine friend, Kara saw tears spilling from the elderly woman's eyes. *I can't believe I made her cry. This is just awful*, she realized as fresh tears streamed down her cheeks. "I'm so sorry, Edna. Running off like that wasn't right. I didn't mean to upset you," the young royal sniffled, her voice thick with sadness. "I'll apologize to Fred too," she assured.

Reaching out, Edna placed a hand on her shoulder and squeezed gently. "It's okay, sweetheart. I'm not concerned about apologies. I am worried about you. What's going on with you?"

Taking a deep breath, Kara wiped her tears, and answered, her voice hesitant. "Dancing has always been something special for Misty, Derrick, and me. I know a lot of things are going to change when the babies come, but I don't want that to change."

Pulling her in close, the elderly woman let Kara rest her head on her shoulder. "Oh, honey, it won't," she stroked the young royal's blonde ringlets, which had become matted with tears, as she spoke.

"I'm sure that dance will always be something that bonds you and your parents."

The princess looked up at Edna, her big blue eyes still moist. "B-but things have already started changing. How can I make sure that we always have dance?" she asked pleadingly, as tears escaped her eyes yet again, and spilled onto the lavender sweater of the older woman holding her.

Edna softly dabbed the little girl's left cheek as though she didn't want to damage the dimple that often graced it. After a long moment she spoke, "Sweetheart, life is what you make it. If you want dancing to be special, make it special."

The young royal lifted her head, eyebrows furrowed. "What do ya mean?"

Looking Kara straight in the eye, the older woman spoke softly and deliberately. "You should remind your parents of the special part that dance plays in your bond with them. Hold a private performance for them or something. I can tell you that, without a doubt, they would love it."

The princess's eyes brightened as the elderly woman's suggestion registered. "Oh my gosh, Edna you're a genius. I'll invite Misty and Derrick to a dress rehearsal."

Kissing the little girl's forehead gently, Edna smiled. "I'm not a genius, sweetheart. I'm just a wise old woman."

Kara nodded. "You are very smart."

The elderly woman's smile widened. "What do you say we go finish our supper?"

"Yeah, we better hurry," the princess agreed. "Fred has probably eaten all of the cinnamon sticks by now," she giggled.

"Oh, without a doubt," Edna chuckled.

With that, the two headed back to the dining room, Dex and his trusted sidekick, Cliff, in tow, along with a very welcomed chorale of laughter.

Chapter 15

ifting Tyler is getting easier. I might actually be able to pull this off, Kara mused while rehearsing in the castle studio a couple days later.

"Nice jobs, kiddos," Stella praised. "A little more practice and you'll definitely be performance-ready."

Tyler, who was still sitting on the princess's shoulders, glanced nervously down at the floor. "I wish I felt more confident. I nearly hurl every time I think about dancin' in front of the whole kingdom."

"There will be no upchuckin' from either one of our stars," Stella reassured as she helped Tyler lower from Kara's shoulders. "Or any of our stars for that matter. You're all goin' to do a wonderful job."

"Ya know there's one way we can make sure we're ready," the princess flashed her dance partner a look as Stella transferred her from the Dance Dazzler to her wheelchair.

"Uh oh, what crazy idea are you cookin' up now?" Tyler queried.

Eyeing the spiky-haired boy, Kara stuck her tongue out then turned her attention to Stella. "I was thinking we should have a dress rehearsal with just a few of our closest family and friends in the audience to make sure we're ready before the show."

Tyler's eyes widened in disbelief. "That idea isn't as crazy as I thought it'd be. It just might work."

Smiling from ear to ear, Stella nodded, "I agree. A dance rehearsal is a great idea."

"Thank you." Flashing a smug smile, the tiny royal turned her attention back to her dance partner, "I like to think all of my ideas are great."

Scoffing, the boy shook his head. "Whatever. The dress rehearsal idea may be good, but don't ya think you're getting a little ahead of yourself? Have ya thought about when we're gonna have it or who we're gonna invite?"

"Hold on there, bud," Stella cautioned. "I'm the adult and dance instructor here, remember? I say that we have the dress rehearsal the night before the anniversary celebration, so we don't lose much practice time before goin' up in front of other people. As far as invites go, we should keep it real small, 10 to 15 people at most, so we don't take any excitement away from the anniversary celebration."

The princess smiled from ear to ear, exposing her beloved dimples. "Sounds good," she agreed. "Just leave the invites to me."

"No fair," Tyler complained. "Why do you get to be the one to skip practice and put the word out?"

Sitting up a bit taller in her wheelchair, the curly-haired girl looked to the boy, "Isn't it obvious?" she queried rhetorically. "I'm a princess. I've got royal connections."

Rolling his eyes, Tyler sighed. "Pull the royal card, much?"

"Stop it!" Stella raised her voice, gaining the attention of both young dancers. "Enough bickerin'. If the princess wants to use her royal connections to get the word out about the dress rehearsal that's fine. However…" Pausing, the eccentric dance instructor focused her attention solely on Kara, "…you, little lady, are goin' to have to do so on your own time because I'm not gonna let you miss practice unless you're bleedin' or dyin'. Is that understood?"

"Yes, ma'am." Kara nodded vehemently. "I'm going to go find Misty and Derrick so I can invite them now. How about you guys go find Tony, we all meet back in a little bit, and head back to your house for supper?"

After getting the green light from her dance instructor, Kara practically burst into the castle proper, excited to invite her adoptive parents to the now-confirmed dress rehearsal. *Misty and Derrick are going to love seeing a preview of The Nutcracker. This dress rehearsal will definitely help bring us back together*, she thought happily.

It's close to dinnertime. Where could they be? she wondered after finding both the formal and informal dining rooms empty.

The princess's excitement quickly faded as she made her way through the castle only to realize that Derrick and Misty were nowhere to be found.

They must be out and about yet again, she sighed. *I miss them so much. Don't they miss me? They must miss me. They just have to. I don't know what I'd do if Derrick and Misty decided to send me back to the group home.* Tears flooded the tiny royal's eyes as the thought crossed her mind. *I guess I'll find Tyler and Stella and try again tomorrow,* she sniffled. *No matter what,* she decided as she made her way back to the dance studio, *I can't give up. I must show them…* The sound of footsteps startled Kara, abruptly discontinuing her rumination.

Hi princess, we didn't expect to see ya today. We figured you'd be in Eclipston with your parents. How're ya doin'?" the kingdom's florist questioned as he spotted her.

Uh oh, I can't let them see me cry and start asking questions, the little girl realized as she quickly wiped the tears from her cheeks. "Hey, Thomas, I'm okay. I was just heading to the dance studio. How are you and Maurice doing?" she queried, having noticed the kingdom chocolatier standing beside him.

"We're doing good sweetheart and we're glad to see you, as always, but if ya don't mind my saying so, you look like you could use some chocolate. Why don't you come with us?"

"Whoa, this is awesome!" the princess exclaimed, acting surprised when Maurice and Thomas showed her where their excess inventory was being stored in the castle.

Winking at Kara, the chocolatier chuckled. "Tony told Thomas and I your little secret and it's perfectly fine with us if ya wanna come down and indulge from time to time," he said sweetly.

The princess flashed a sweet smile at the elderly gentlemen. "Thanks guys. Do you have anything new that I can take to a friend's house for dessert tonight?"

Nodding, Thomas smiled. "Sure thing, little lady. What did ya have in mind? Truffles, chocolate-covered fruit, or maybe some homemade fudge? Our newest flavor is cookies 'n cream."

Maurice shook his head and waved a dismissive hand at his business partner. "Don't listen to this clown, sweetie. He's holding out on you."

Eyebrows furrowed, Kara eyed the elderly confection maker. "Huh?"

Smiling, the kind old man scanned the sweet and botanical filled space around them. After a moment, his blue gray eyes lit up and he wordlessly, carefully pulled a red velvet covered heart- shaped box from behind the counter. "We've been working real hard to perfect these chocolates for the Starrycrest anniversary celebration," he explained. "Something tells me that you and your friend might be the perfect people to us whether these goodies are up to par." Pausing, he flashed a mischievous smile, opened the box and asked, "What do ya say, princess?"

Kara's eyes lit up when she saw that the box held miniature peanut butter cups, dark chocolate covered cashews, and plump milk chocolate covered cherries among others. "Oh my gosh! It's a mixture of my, Derrick, and Misty's favorite chocolates," the tiny royal exclaimed. *This is a perfect and delicious way to symbolize unity and help bring our family back together,* the princess realized as she got an idea.

Maurice nodded. "It sure is. We like to call this collection of chocolates our Denison Delectables, why don't you take this box tonight and report back in a couple days on how everything tastes?" he coaxed, smiling at the little girl.

"Thanks guys, but I've got a better idea," the curly-haired majestic let out, the excitement and anticipation she felt quickly seeping into her voice.

"Do tell," the elderly business partners urged simultaneously.

Within minutes, the princess told them about the upcoming dress rehearsal and ordered enough Denison Delectables to send to those invited to the special performance.

People are going to be so excited when they receive their dance rehearsal invites, Kara mused as she bid her elderly friends goodbye. I knew my royal connections would come through. *Now, I just have to hope that my familial connections come through as well,* the tiny royal realized as she made her way back to the dance studio.

***

These candies all smell so good. I only wish I was at the castle enjoying them with Derrick and Misty, Kara sighed as she and Tiphany sat at Stella's kitchen table a few days later addressing boxes of Denison Delectables to the few people they and the other starlets wished to have attend their dress rehearsal.

"Uh, I know you love Fred and Edna and all, but unless you plan on staying with Stella forever, shouldn't you be addressing one of those to your parents?" Tiphany asked as the princess addressed a box of chocolates to her surrogate grandparents.

Shaking her head, Kara disagreed, "Thanks girl, but there's no need to worry. I already took three chocolate boxes and an invitation to the castle for Misty and Derrick. Tony says the pregnancy has given her quiet the sweet to–"

"Oh, yeah!" Tyler exclaimed as he walked into the kitchen cutting her off. "I'm starvin'," he declared, grabbing a handful of dark chocolate covered cashews and tossing them into his mouth.

"Ty, don't!" Kara shouted. "These chocolate boxes are for dress rehearsal invites."

"You mean to tell me that you gave Misty three boxes and I can't even have a handful? I know she's the queen and your mom and all, but c'mon, that just ain't right," Tyler whined.

Rolling her eyes, Kara scoffed at her dance partner, "Oh, stop your bellyachin' I left a chocolate box on the counter just for you. I'll switch that one for the box you stole from and you can just go on stuffing your face."

Tyler's eyes brightened with excitement. "Awesome. Just don't tell Stella I'm about to ruin my dinner," he urged, before stuffing three miniature peanut butter cups into his mouth and flashing a toothy smile at the girls.

"Eww!" the girls exclaimed. "Either swallow that and help us with these invites or go be gross somewhat else!" Kara commanded.

Eyeing the boxed chocolates that littered the kitchen table, Tyler shook his head. "No way. You and Tiph can have your girlie time. I'm hittin' the studio."

"Boys are so annoying," Tiphany groaned as Tyler left the room. "I don't know how you've been able to have him as your dance partner, much less lived with him for so long."

Kara shrugged. "Ty's not so bad, as long as he's not tired or hungry," she explained, continuing to address chocolate boxes.

Chuckling, Tiphany nodded. "That sounds about right. I guess it's good that he's preparing you."

Confused, Kara eyed Tiphany, eyebrows wrinkled. "Huh?"

"Girlie, did you forget that you could have a brother or two in a few months?"

Unless Derrick and Misty decide to replace me with the babies and leave me without any family at all. At least if both babies are boys, they'll have a reason to want a daughter, she realized. Who am I kidding? They don't care if their babies are boys or girls. They've been distracted for weeks and don't even know the babies' gender. Heck, they weren't even home when I dropped off the Denison Delectables.

"Kara… Kara… where are you?" Tiphany stunned her from her thoughts.

"Sorry, Tiph, what did you just say?" she asked after a moment.

"The doorbell just rang, girl. Stella says there is someone here to see you," the princess's fellow starlet explained.

Kara eyebrows wrinkled in confusion again as she made her way to the front door. Her confusion quickly turned to worry when she saw one of the most trusted personal assistants on the castle staff standing in the doorway. "Marie, what are you doing here? Is everything okay? Are Misty and the babies all right? Did something happen?"

Stella, who was standing beside the tiny royal, placed a hand on her shoulder. "Take a deep breath and let the woman speak," she advised, giving the young girl's shoulder a gentle squeeze.

"Everything is fine your highness. Your parents and everyone else at the castle miss you terribly. The castle just isn't the same without you, but everyone is fine. I'm just here because your parents are busy this evening, but her majesty couldn't bear the thought of you waiting for a response to your invitation. I'm under strict orders to give you this," she explained, pulling a small box from her pocket and holding it out toward the little girl. "Her Majesty told me to be sure to tell you that she and Derrick are very excited to see you."

After accepting a hug and saying goodbye to Marie, Kara enthusiastically tore open her gift only to find an even smaller purple velvet box and a note written on a piece of Misty's personal stationary.

Sweetheart, Derrick and I stumbled upon these the other day and decided to get them for you because even the most beautiful dancers need a little luck. We cannot wait to see you and promise to be in the front row at the dress rehearsal cheering you on. Love Misty.

It's working. The dress rehearsal is already bringing Derrick, Misty, and I back together, Kara realized as she smiled down at the note. The princess's grin widened as she opened the small velvet box to find diamond studded four leaf clover-shaped earrings.

"Oh, my gosh! These are the prettiest earrings I've ever seen," Kara proudly put the diamond jewelry in her ears. *And the best part is this shows that Derrick and Misty still love me. I can't wait for them to go to the dress rehearsal. They'll be so proud that there is no way they could forget me or replace me. Things might be okay after all,* she realized.

With that, the tiny royal made her way into Stella's kitchen to show Tiphany her new earrings, feeling happier and more confident than she had in days.

***

Oh, my gosh, they look flawless. Not one wrong move and they are smiling beautifully. I am about to go out there and look like such an amateur. Biting her lower lip, Kara peeked from backstage at the other starlets performing *The March of the Nutcracker*. As the princess continued to watch them, her face grew hot and her stomach tightened. She glanced from the other starlets to out in the audience and saw Fred, Edna, and Tyler smiling from their front row seats. *Oh no, why aren't Misty and Derrick with them? What if they don't get to see me dance? What if all of this was for nothing?* The young royal held her stomach. *I wish I hadn't eaten those chicken tenders for lunch. I think I'm about to see them again.*

"What are you doing? You're up next," Stella whispered as she came up behind the princess.

Jumping slightly, the princess moved her hand from her stomach to her chest. "Oh! Stella, you scared me," Kara whispered.

"What's wrong?" the dance instructor asked, her voice full of apprehension.

"I can't go out there. The other girls are so much better than me. I shouldn't even be the Sugar Plum Fairy," the young royal's anxiety was apparent in not only her whisper, but also her rigid limbs.

Shaking her head, Stella tried to calm the tiny dancer, "Don't give into the nerves little lady. You can do this. You're ready. I believe in you. Your parents believe in you. You're going to be amazing."

Letting out a sad sigh, Kara hung her head. "Misty and Derrick aren't even here," she pointed out.

"I told them the exact time of your solo, little lady. I'm sure they'll be here any second but, regardless of that, you need to be amazing so that everyone here will get the rest of Starrycrest excited about the show before the celebration tomorrow night by talking about this awesome dress rehearsal, got it?"

"I don't know if I can," the little girl said sheepishly, her voice colored by fear.

"You have to. Now is the time," Stella urged in a hushed tone "Go out there and be the best Sugar Plum Fairy you can be."

I can either humiliate myself by trying or by not trying so I'm goin' to try, Kara decided. Taking a deep breath, she pushed away her sickly feelings, leaned forward slowly, and headed out onto the stage. *I can do this. I can do this,* the princess held her breath, leaned her torso slightly to the left to weave around a candy cane and then passed a giant Christmas present. *The candy cane didn't fall. Maybe I'll pull it off this time*, she thought, still holding her breath as she leaned to the left a bit more, weaving past a giant snowflake. *This is it. I can do it*, the pint-sized royal told herself as she weaved past the final candy cane that, in practice, had fallen and caused a chain reaction half a dozen times. *Oh my gosh. I did it... the candy cane didn't fall!* Kara mused as she successfully finished her figure eight and smiled at the audience. *What? Where are Misty and Derrick? Maybe they snuck in the back.* Looking out, she scanned the audience, forcing herself to continue to smile when she realized that neither Misty nor Derrick were anywhere to be found.

***

"I knew you could do it. You were great," Stella praised once Kara was again backstage.

"Misty and Derrick never showed," the young girl said solemnly.

"Aww. That's okay little lady. I'm sure that they have a good reason," the pink-haired dance instructor assured. "And, like I said, they're goin' to hear how awesome the dress rehearsal turned out and be really excited for the anniversary celebration tomorrow."

No, it's not okay. I did all of this for them. Something must have gone terribly wrong for them not to be here. What if something happened to Misty? A wave of nausea hit the princess again as she worried about her adoptive mother. Taking a deep breath, Kara tried to calm herself using the technique Stella had shown her days before. *Misty is fine*, she told herself. *She and Derrick probably got held up at personal audiences or something*, she reasoned, anxiously watching the other starlets perform from backstage. *What am I saying? She'd cancel personal audiences before she'd miss this. Something has got to be terribly wrong.* Worried that time may be of the essence she rushed to the front of the auditorium not even caring that she was still in the Dance Dazzler.

"You were wonderful sweetheart," Edna gushed as the young royal approached their front row seats.

"Definitely the best dancer I've ever seen," Fred nodded in agreement.

"Yeah, don't let it go to your head or anything, but you were pretty good," Tyler complimented, flashing her a crooked smile.

"Yeah, yeah, yeah, thanks," Kara quickly dismissed the praise. "Where are Derrick and Misty?" she asked, her voice full of apprehension. "Why didn't they show? What's wrong? Is Misty okay?"

Looking the little girl straight in the eye, Fred comforted her. "Calm down little lady," he said, his tone composed and sweet. "Your parents are just fine," he assured.

"If my parents are fine then what's going on? Why aren't they here?" she questioned pointedly.

"It's nothing you need to worry about, sweetheart," Edna assured. Your mother is resting and your father thinks it's best that he stay with her, but he promises he'll be at the performance tomorrow night, no matter what." The elderly woman smiled sweetly, but it did nothing to calm the young royal.

Yeah, I've heard that before, she thought as the words Edna had just spoken registered in her mind. "Wait… did you say *he* promised? As in just Derrick? Will someone please tell me what's going on with Misty?" Kara insisted, her face more than a little red with anger.

Edna fidgeted a bit in her seat. "Well, you know, sweetie, Misty's pregnancy has been really difficult for her. Your mother needs her rest. She's going to try her best to be there tomorrow but didn't want to promise."

Oh. My. God. Now Misty isn't coming to the anniversary celebration either? I can't believe this. Not coming to my dress rehearsal is one thing, but not coming to the Starrycrest anniversary celebration is another, the young girl decided as her body stiffened with frustration. Her surrogate grandmother continued talking, but in the wake of her fury, nothing registered. *How could Misty do this?* The princess wondered. *It's one thing to let me down, but how could she possibly let down our entire kingdom? I hope I never have a baby if it changes me as much as the twins have changed Misty. She'd never do this if she wasn't having the babies. I wish she'd never gotten pregnant.* In that moment, the young majestic got an idea. The very thought should have frightened her, but she was far too mad to care about the consequences. *I'm going to take charge of my life just like Misty took charge of hers. I'll show her who really cares about our kingdom and our family*, she decided.

"Earth to the Sugar Plum Fairy," Tyler joked, stunning Kara out of her thoughts. "What're ya thinkin' about?"

Taking a deep breath, Kara tried to calm herself and act casual. "Nothing," she shrugged her shoulders and smiled. "What are you guys up to this evening?" The young dancer forced herself to smile again, hoping she appeared and sounded at least half as nonchalant as she was trying to be.

Looking from Kara to Tyler and back, Fred smiled genuinely. "We were thinkin' of taking you kiddos out to dinner. What do ya say?"

The princess's comrade flashed a crooked smile. "Rain check? It's not like me to turn down free grub, but I got plans to hang with Stella and Tony tonight so I'm gonna get going."

"No worries. We'll just do it some other time then." Edna glanced at the young royal as Tyler left the theater. "What about you? Will you give us the honor of taking the Sugar Plum Fairy out to supper?" she asked, her tone sweet and quiet.

Oh no. I set myself up for that one. What can I say to get out of it? "That's so sweet of you guys, but unfortunately I need to take a rain check too. I promised Misty that I'd give Dex a bath tonight," she mumbled quickly. *Oh my gosh. What did I just say? That sounded so lame. There's no way they are going to fall for it.*

The elderly couple nodded. "Well, if you made a promise to your mother, I supposed we'll just have to wait," Edna said thoughtfully.

"Yes," Fred agreed. "You do what you have to do tonight but be sure to get a good night's rest so you are ready for the celebration tomorrow."

"I will, Fred, I will. I promise," Kara assured him as the small audience began exiting the auditorium. *I can't believe they actually bought that excuse.* Leaning her body forward, the princess rushed to leave before anyone else could attempt to stop her.

"Where are ya going so fast?" Tyler grinned, jumping directly into the princess's path.

Wide-eyed, Kara sat back and stilled herself, bringing the Dance Dazzler to a halt. "Oh my gosh, Tyler, you scared me! What are you doing here? I thought you left."

The young royal's friend shot her a knowing look. "Don't go changin' the subject. Answer my question. Where are you headed so fast?"

"What makes you think I'm going somewhere special?" Kara queried innocently.

"Get real, Kara. You can pull one over on the old folks but not me." Crossing his arms in front of his chest, the boy looked the tiny majestic straight in the eye, "Cut the bull and tell me what the heck you're up to," he insisted.

Uh oh, Ty looks angry. Guess I should just tell him. He knows what a hard time I've been having. He'll understand. "Calm down, I'll tell you, but you've got to promise not to tell anyone."

Tyler let out a huff. "Duh, that goes without saying. Ya know I'm not a snitch. Spill your guts," He coaxed, his voice coated with resolve.

"I'm going to see Victrollia so I can wish that Misty had never gotten pregnant," the princess blurted out quickly.

Tyler's eyes widened in disbelief. "Did a prop fall on you during the performance without anyone seein'?" he asked urgently after a moment.

The princess giggled. "No, of course not. I saw Victrollia's tracks the other day so I'm going to follow them and find her, she explained matter-of-factly.

Tyler eyed her, his brows furrowed. "What are ya babblin' about? Those tracks were part of a simulation the royal guard used to practice troll tracking. Ya know, since the royal guard are the ones who should be looking for her anyway."

Throwing her head back, Kara scoffed. "Whatever, Ty, I can't believe you fell for that announcement. The tracks were real and I'm going to use them to find her. If Misty could find Trovella then I can find Victrollia."

"Give me a break, Kara. Did you go nuts overnight or somethin'? If the royal guard can't find Victrollia, there is no way you'll be able to find her. Besides, you can't use the tracks anyway. They got washed away in last's night's storm."

Kara shook her head. "I don't care. Tracks or no tracks. I'll find her. I have to find her,"

"Why? Why do you want to find Victrollia so badly?" the young dancer queried pointedly. "C'mon, Ty, you know how upset I've been. I gotta do something to fix this so I'm gonna go make a wish."

Tyler let out a curt laugh. "Oh yeah, 'cuz that worked out so well for Misty. Stepping forward, he closed the space between them and looked her straight in the eye. "Wake up, *Princess*! Ya know goin' to see a troll is never a good idea. It could be dangerous for the kingdom," the spiky-haired dancer yelled, his voice becoming louder with every passing second. "I can't let you do this. Misty and Derrick would never approve."

Kara let out an exasperated laugh. "Since when do you care whether or not adults approve of anything? If ya think you can stop me, you're wrong. No one can. I'm taking fate into my own hands," she declared firmly, her voice coated with the authority of her royal status.

I have to do this no matter what Tyler or anyone else says, the princess decided, determined to see Victrollia no matter what. *He'll just have to forgive me.* With that, the princess weaved past her still-protesting friend just as smoothly as she had the giant props on stage and raced out of the theater without looking back.

Chapter 16

"I don't care what Ty says, guys," Kara said as she made her way to the outskirts of the kingdom with Dex and Cliff reluctantly in tow. "We'll find Victrollia without her tracks. I can feel it. I feel in bones. Besides, Misty found Trovella without tracks, right? Ms. Ryder is always saying that history is bound to repeat itself." The moment her teacher's words of wisdom left her mouth, the princess wondered just how much history was repeating itself at that moment. "So, Dex, do you think Misty was this nervous when she travelled to see Trovella?" The little girl giggled as she looked over and saw her canine companion, who had their feathered friend on his back, enthusiastically wagging his tail. "I'm glad to know I'm not the only one," she whispered. *Is that peanut butter cookies I smell?* She wondered as the familiar scent that only the combination of fresh, sugary dough and melted peanut butter can create began wafting through the air minutes later. *A cookie or two would be nice,* she decided as she felt her stomach rumble. "We'll find Victrollia as soon as I figure out where this delicious smell is coming from," she told her comrades as they all followed the aroma. After what felt like an eternity to the young royal, she and her friends came upon a small cottage surrounded by bright pink tulips, beautiful lavender carnations, and vibrant yellow daisies. "Oh my gosh... do you guys see this?" she exclaimed, looking at her pals, wide-eyed. These are all my, Derrick, and Misty's favorite flowers!" *That has to be a good sign,* she thought. *I mean what are the chances that I would find the favorite flower of everyone in my family when none are in season?*

As the princess contemplated this, she realized that the purple door of the cottage was open. Peeking in, her eyes grew wide for the second time in minutes as she realized that the largest plate of peanut butter cookies, she'd ever laid eyes on occupied the dining room table along with a lone glass of milk. Without even thinking, Kara leaned herself forward in the Dance Dazzler, rushed into the cottage, and enthusiastically bit into one of the cookies. Looking at her canine friend, she smiled brightly. "This is so yummy I could eat the whole plate." The tiny majestic was so excited about the dessert she'd stumbled upon that she didn't even notice an astonished Dex frantically wagging his tail beside her or a nervous Cliff fluttering above her head. Before the pint-sized princess knew it, she had finished all but two of the sweets on the platter. *Those cookies were so good. Why aren't Dex and Cliff begging me to share like they normally would*, she wondered. *Oh well, more for me, I guess. I'm going to eat one more and save the last one for later,* she decided as she tucked the cookie into the pocket of her dress. Moments later, after polishing off the glass of milk and second to last cookie, the little girl finally noticed her friends' apprehension. "What's wrong? You guys aren't having second thoughts about going to see Victrollia, are you?"

"Did someone say Victrollia?" a loud yet thick, raspy voice was heard.

"AAAAHHHHHH!" The princess jumped causing both her friends and the Dance Dazzler to shake slightly before turning around to face the source of the interruption.

"I, uh… I did," Kara admitted sheepishly, voice trembling. "I'm trying to find her," she whispered, looking the owner of the voice up and down. The creature before her had hair as silver as her grandmother's oldest jewelry. A nose adorned with the largest, ripest looking wart the majestic had ever seen, and eyes that matched the putrid color of day-old guacamole. It easily outweighed an expectant elephant, had a grimace rivaling that of a wolf ready to pounce on its prey, and had a large, black, diamond-shaped gemstone in the center of its belly.

The being was like none other she had ever laid eyes on, yet there was something very familiar about it. *Oh my gosh... it looks like the trolls on the bag Misty gave me... it's Victrollia!* The princess gasped, unable to hide her sudden nerves, as she faced the domineering treasure troll.

Victrollia nodded, as if she could read the princess's thoughts. "That's right little one," she chuckled, her voice thick and hoarse. "I am the one you seek."

"It's v-very nice to meet you Vict–"

"Tell me why you're here," the troll screeched, leaning over the little girl, revealing that her breath stank like a skunk that had been rolling around in a garbage can filled to the brim with rotten fruits and vegetables for a week.

The princess turned away from the troll, staying in front her feathered and furry friends in an effort to shield all three of them from the disgusting odor. "I-I'm here to make a w-wish," she managed.

Victrollia let out a roar of laughter. "You, of all people, should know that you can't just come to me and make a wish, little one."

"This is a m-matter of k-k-keeping my family together," the young majestic said sheepishly. "I'll p-pay w-whatever the p-price."

"The immensity of your wish shall help determine your price," the troll announced, her voice laced with disdain. "Name it now and be quick about it. I don't have all day."

It's now or never, Kara decided as she glanced at her feathered and furry friends who looked nervous enough to pass out at any second. Staring up at the domineering creature, the princess spoke apprehensively. "I… I wish that M-Misty was not pr-pregnant anymore and that Derrick would understand the importance of starting a kiddo–"

"Speak up," Victrollia shrieked. "Or did you come all this way just for peanut butter cookies?" she croaked, a hint of sarcasm sprinkled in her still disdainful voice.

Ugh… she's right. I didn't come all this way just to be screamed at by some overgrown monster with garbage breath. I gotta get myself together, the princess thought as she took a deep, cleansing breath to calm herself.

Clearing her throat, the young royal sat up a bit taller in her wheelchair and said, "I wish Misty was not pregnant anymore and that Derrick understood the importance of a kiddo keeper program," as if she were making an announcement to the kingdom.

Uh oh, the princess thought as Victrollia's eyes turned from day-old guacamole to a fiery red. "You've come to the right place, dearie. I can grant your wish and make you the one and only apple of your parents' eyes, but it'll cost you."

Focusing on the troll's eyes, Kara ignored her furry and feathered comrades who were each sending her wary glances. "Like I said, I'll pay anything," she assured. "I just want my family back."

"You will have them back in no time dearie, all I require in exchange is your ring," the troll declared, her tone boisterous yet nonchalant.

Leaning back slightly to put space between herself and Victrollia, the princess eyed the evil creature, eyebrows furrowed. "My ring… what do you want with that?"

"I've been looking for smaller jewels to add to my collection," Victrollia explained, her voice cold yet casual. "The stones in your ring are unique and would fit nicely."

Holding out her hand, Kara studied her ring and contemplated Victrollia's proposal. *I can't give up this ring. When Derrick gave it to me, he said it symbolized us being a family forever. Then again, maybe that's why I should give it up. After all, I'm doing all this because I want my forever family back.*

"I don't have all night," Victrollia spat, leaving a bit of green spittle on the princess's cheek. "If you want to be your parents' main focus once again and help the annoying little orphans of your beloved Starrycrest, cough up those jewels dearie! Otherwise, get out of my sight!" the intimidating treasure troll yelled, eyeing the Ruby, Topaz, and Sapphire gems in the ring as though the stones were the source of life itself.

Taking a deep breath, Kara slid the precious piece of jewelry off her finger. "This ring isn't nearly as important as what it symbolizes," the princess said as she held it out to Victrollia. "You can have it as long as you grant my wish and I get my forever family back."

The skunk-breathed monster let out another roar of laughter and snatched the small ring. "Your wish is my command, dearie. Just repeat it while rubbing my gemstone and you'll have your family back in no time," the troll spoke, her voice coated in urgency and anticipation.

Eyeing the gemstone closely for the first time, Kara noticed dust and cobwebs covering it. "Uh, are you sur—" the pint-sized royal began.

"Yes, yes, quickly now," Victrollia insisted, the fire in her eyes intensifying.

Extending her arm toward the troll, Kara hesitantly rubbed the center of the creature's belly, making dust fly into the air. Discontinuing the motion, she instinctively covered her mouth.

The troll shook her head. "Keep going," she insisted. "You must say your wish, while rubbing my gemstone."

"Okay, here goes." Turning her head away from the dust, the princess rubbed Victrollia's belly vehemently and said, "I wish Misty wasn't pregnant anymore and that Starrycrest had a kiddo keeper program." Within seconds, the princess felt the ground shake under the wheels of the Dance Dazzler. "Whoa, what's happening?"

"Just a little magic taking effect, dearie. Nothing to worry about," the giant wart-adorned creature assured, flashing a stain-covered smile at the little girl. "Now let me tell you how this is going to work. You mentioned something about Derrick creating some program in Starrycrest--"

"It's called a kiddo keeper program," the princess interrupted, her voice suddenly full of more anticipation than fear. "It would allow–"

"Do I look like I care?" Victrollia shouted, the fire in her eyes intensifying ten times more than moments before.

In that moment, as the troll towered over her as though she were nothing more than a cockroach that needed to be squashed, Kara felt extremely small and insignificant. "Sorry," she muttered.

"As I was saying, you have 24 hours to convince Derrick and the rest of the kingdom that creating such a program is worth it. If you do, then the other part of your wish will come true. If you don't, then things will remain as they are now and you will have to compete for the affection of your parents for the rest of your life. Is that understood?"

The princess nodded vehemently. "Yes, ma'am," she assured. "Your magic was not wasted. "You will not be disappointed."

"No, dearie, but you might," the troll let another roar of laughter. "Now, get out of my cottage before I change my mind."

"As you wish," Kara quipped, flashing the giant troll a smile before she ran out of the cabin with Dex and Cliff in tow.

***

Letting out a quiet sigh as she approached the castle, Kara looked to her furry and feathered friends and smiled dreamily. "I am so glad to be home boys. Stella's house is nice and all, especially since Tony fixed it up, but I'm excited to sleep in my own bed tonight. I know that 24 hours is gonna fly by, but I have to get some shuteye before I show Derrick and Misty Maxwell's diary." A yawn overtook her as the words escaped from her lips, confirming her exhaustion.

Glancing at her companions again, she noticed that they too were struggling to keep their eyes open. "Aww, looks like you boys could use some sleep too. C'mon let's get you to bed," she urged before leading them to the castle gates, which she was surprised to find unattended and unlocked.

That's odd, she realized. *The gates are never left unguarded, much less open. Derrick and Misty must've given the royal guard the night off or something.* Rolling through the gates, she quickly slid up the ramp and through the front door of the castle. *This place is never completely empty. There's always at least a few staff working. What the heck is going on?* the little girl wondered as she entered the foyer only to find the castle pitch dark. Quickly flipping on a couple of lights, Kara made her way to Misty and Derrick's room only to find not them, but their midwife.

"Tabitha, what're you doing here?"

"AAAAHHH!" the doula screamed, bringing a hand to her chest as terror-filled eyes darted around the room before landing on the little girl. "Oh, my goodness princess, what are you doing here?" she asked, her voice full of the anxiety etched in her expression.

"What do you mean? Where is everybody?" Kara queried, her heart racing as fast as a cheetah in her chest.

"Oh no… no one's warned you." Tabitha's eyes widened in horror as the realization hit her.

"Warned me about what?" the princess questioned, her voice fretful.

"Victrollia is coming," the midwife whispered.

Shaking her head, Kara disagreed. "No, no. That can't be right. I have 24 hours."

"It is," the midwife insisted. "That monster somehow got her grubby hands on some gemstones and now she's coming after your family." Even though the midwife was still whispering, Kara could hear a mixture of anger and terror in her voice.

"W-wait... what?" The young royal's eyes widened in disbelief. "This can't be," she murmured.

"I'm afraid it is," Tabitha persisted. "I must get back to the queen now. I promised his majesty I'd keep her safe. He's headed to Stella's house now to get you. Stay here where you'll be safe. I'll try to–"

"If Derrick's at Stella's house, then that's where I'm going," Kara declared, cutting the midwife off.

Tabitha shook her head. "No, no, you mustn't. It's not safe," she urged, eyes widened in horror as the princess turned away, ignoring her protest.

Safe or not, there is no way I'm gonna let a troll threaten my family, Kara decided before leaning as far forward as could and racing toward Stella's house in the Dance Dazzler with her furry and feathered friends not far behind.

***

Oh, my goodness! How did a tornado form that quickly? Kara wondered as she spotted a giant twister in the distance. As the question entered her mind, a dull ache formed in the pit of her stomach. *This is dark magic, isn't it?*

The sheer terror in the eyes of her canine and winged friends was all the confirmation she needed. *This is the work of Victrollia. This is all my fault*, she realized.

Even though her every instinct told her to run the other way, Kara continued to maneuver the Dance Dazzler through the streets of Starrycrest toward the storm. *Oh no, the tornado is headed right for Starrycrest Square. Most of the kingdom is there right now getting ready for tomorrow's celebration. I never should've gone to that stupid troll. I've put the whole kingdom in danger,* she realized as tears filled her eyes. Knowing she had to do something fast, the little girl wiped away her tears, and sped the rest of the way to Stella's house.

"AAAAAAHHHHH!" Kara bellowed as she approached Stella's house only to find Derrick, Tyler, Tony, Stella, Fred, and Edna trapped in snake covered nets all struggling to stay calm while Victrollia, who stood in the middle of all of them, eyed Derrick as though he were a juicy steak ready to be devoured.

Ugh snakes. Why did it have to be snakes? Kara wondered, her heart beating faster than that of a hummingbird in her chest.

"Hello, dearie, I've been expecting you," Victrollia sneered.

The princess's anger toward the troll gave her the courage to confront the creature, even though she was a hundred times more terrified than she had been at the cottage. "This wasn't our deal Victrollia," Kara shouted. "Let them go!"

Shaking her head, the evil troll let out a chuckle that sounded more like the roar of an angry lion than a laugh. "I never intended to honor our deal. The cookies and milk, the cottage, the flowers. It was all a trap that you fell right into, dearie."

"You Denisons have been getting in the way of us trolls for years. My brilliantly evil cousin, Trovella, sabotaged that stupid cooking contest, my fantastically wicked grandmother, Tromelia, tried to chase you all away by making that idiot, Alistair, ban dance, but you fools somehow managed to persevere. Heck, my wonderfully malevolent great grandmother, Trorista, orchestrated the most tragic carriage crash in history and still couldn't defeat you annoyingly optimistic royals. But soon all of that will change. Soon, you and your precious family and friends will die and the kingdom will be mine!" Victrollia declared, her deep, scratchy voice full of smug arrogance.

Kara's face grew hot, as anger bubbled up inside her, making her stomach tighten and her throat constrict. For the past few weeks, she hadn't let herself completely feel her emotions for fear of breaking down, but, in that moment, she allowed anger to completely consume her in hopes that it would give her the strength needed to defeat the evil troll.

Trolls have messed with my family long enough. I need to channel my inner Misty and destroy her. But how?

"Aww don't be scared, dearie," Victrollia quipped, momentarily exposing her slime-stained teeth. The heartbreak you'll feel when these idiots are poisoned by snakes will be momentary. You and your fancy chair are going to be swallowed up by my terrifically dark twister before you know it."

The evil troll's explanation was followed by another roar of laughter. At that exact moment, the tornado off in the distance, instantly tripled in size, as though it was controlled by her voice.

"Scared? I'm not scared," Kara insisted as the strong winds shifted. Victrollia continued laughing as a chilling gust moved the weeping willow tree from one end of the yard to the other dropping it just inches away from the princess with a loud thud, causing her and the Dance Dazzler to tremble simultaneously.

"Oh yeah, you're not scared at all," Victrollia snarled, her thick and raspy voice brimming with sarcasm. "You're only about to jump out of your skin because you're excited about the snakes," the troll quipped, her fiery red eyes glowing with excited anticipation.

Kara opened her mouth to object, but stopped short when the fire in Victrollia's eyes became so intense, the little girl feared she may be turned to ash in seconds.

"You can't fool me, little one. I've been watching you. I know you're deathly afraid of those creepy, crawly, deviously dark little creatures, the evil troll let out yet another howl of glee, taunting the tiny royal.

Kara's heart was beating so fast by then that she could feel it in her ears. Her face felt so hot that she was certain it was redder than the ripest tomato ever. Her legs continued shaking as a wave nausea that seemed powerful enough to knock both her and the Dance Dazzler over hit her. *Pull it together before you throw up*, she told herself. *Victrollia is just trying to get under your skin. She couldn't have been watching that closely if she doesn't know that Derrick cured me of my fear of snakes. Oh my gosh! That's it!* She realized. *I'm going to use the snakes to beat Victrollia at her own game!*

Knowing she had no time to waste, the princess turned to her furry and feathered comrades and retrieved the peanut butter cookie she'd saved earlier from her pocket. Sniffing excitedly, Dex eyed the sweet confection. "Looks good, doesn't it, guys?" the princess questioned as the black labrador and his winged best friend ogled the sugary sweet, their adorning eyes suddenly as big as saucers.

"I wouldn't bother giving your friends a treat, dearie. They will be dead soon just like the rest of you," Victrollia declared, her voice booming with excitement.

Looking the evil creature straight in the eye, Kara shrugged, feigning confidence. "If they are gonna die soon, what do you care if I give them one last treat?" Kara held the cookie out toward her comrades, allowing them to smell it and salivate a moment longer, before she threw it as far across the yard as she could. Despite feeling as nauseous as ever, Kara had to bite her lip to keep from smiling as Dex and Cliff ran off in hot pursuit.

"Make them stop! Victrollia shouted, rolling her still fiery red eyes at the animals, who were mere moments into a lively round of fetch. "Their happiness is nauseating!"

"Apparently, the snakes don't think so," the princess pointed out. The pint-sized majestic, once again, had to make a conscious effort not to smile as the snakes began to slither away from the nets trapping her loved ones and toward the cookie.

I never thought the sound of snakes gliding away from nets could be such a relief. I can't believe this is working, Kara mused as Victrollia shouted at the wayward serpents, who, surprisingly seemed as enthralled by the game of fetch as they were by its prize.

"No, no, you idiots. Now is not the time to feed. We have a job to finish! "Victrollia shouted, her voice as menacing as ever, despite its nearly deafening volume. Taking advantage of the fact that Victrollia was occupied with the snakes, Kara rushed to the aid of Derrick, who was still struggling to break free of the net that entangled him. Seeing him struggle instantly brought tears to her eyes, and a lump to her throat.

"Kara, sweetheart, I can't get out. She's hexed the nets so we can't free ourselves even with the snakes gone. You're going to have to grab my sword and use it to cut me free," Derrick explained, his voice just above a whisper.

Shaking her head vehemently, the little girl disagreed. "N-no, I can't," she stammered, eyeing the sharp blade warily.

"Yes, you can," Derrick insisted. "I'm right here with you. You can do this," he assured. "Don't let her win."

Derrick's right. Victrollia thinks that this is going to break me and end our family, she realized. *Well, she's got another thing coming.* Taking a deep breath, Kara used the remote clipped to her leotard to put the brakes on the Dance Dazzler, bent down, reached into the net, and hesitantly grabbed the weapon.

"Good. Now cut the rope as fast as you can," Derrick coaxed.

Not wanting to waste another second of precious time, the girl nodded and sawed through the net as quickly as her tiny arms would allow.

"You did it, sweetheart," Derrick praised after untangling himself from the rope trap and enveloped her in a tight embrace. "Now we just have to–"

"Aww… father and daughter reunited. So cute I could barf," Victrollia sniggered sarcastically as she turned her attention back to the princess.

"Go free the others. I'll take care of Victrollia," Derrick whispered urgently, taking his sword from Kara and pointing it toward the devious troll.

Shaking her head defiantly, Kara disagreed. "I got us into a mess, so I'm going to get us out," she insisted.

Derrick shook his head in disbelief as the slightest of smiles formed on his lips. "Like mother, like daughter," he whispered.

Huh? Kara opened her mouth to question him but closed it when Victrollia laughed so loud the ground beneath the Dancer Dazzler shook. *Uh oh, we're in big trouble now,* the princess realized as she spotted the tornado swirling mere feet away from Starrycrest Square.

Terror flashed through Derrick's eyes, as he, too, glanced at the looming twister, but as he turned his attention back to Kara, his voice and gaze exuded confidence. "We're going to get through this, but we must move quickly. We don't have much time. You get the jewels," he urged. "I'll free our friends."

"Your strategizing is really cute, yet utterly pointless," Victrollia declared. "Even if you are all freed from the traps in time, there is no way you'll escape my treacherous twister!"

It all comes down to this, Kara realized. Despite having practiced activating the enchantment with Archibald and Marguerite dozens of times, at that moment, her mouth went dry, her entire body trembled, and her mind went blank.

Chapter 17

Oh my gosh... I'm doomed. We're all doomed. Leave it to me to freeze up when the kingdom really needs me. Some princess I am, Kara mused, quickly becoming as entangled in her thoughts, as she was in fear. *This is all my fault. What am I going to do? Is there anything I can–*

The tiny royal's eyes widened once again when, at that very moment, the fairy song from *A Midsummer Night's Dream* began to play, abruptly interrupting her thoughts. Despite the perilous winds still swirling around her, the familiar, melodic sounds instantly relaxed the little girl and helped her remember the chant.

It's now or never, she decided before taking a deep breath and addressing the troll. "If I only have a few minutes left to live, then dance with me," she declared.

Victrollia scoffed, "That's preposterous! I hate dancing!"

"How can you hate dancing?" Kara asked. "It's so much fun. Just try it. You'll see," she insisted while twirling the Dance Dazzler.

"Yeah, it's fun, join us," Tyler, who Derrick had just freed, encouraged as he performed a perfect assemblé and eagerly rose on tiptoes into relevé.

"Smooth move, kiddos," Derrick praised after Kara flawlessly lifted Tyler onto her shoulder. By the way, I know this isn't the time for small talk, but that chair is amazing. Misty is going to be so jealous," he said before turning his attention back to Victrollia.

"Time's up, tiny danc–" the evil troll began, her insult thwarted as a horrific scream escaped her mouth instead.

Kara once again had to bite her lip to keep from smiling, as Dex reemerged and nipped the back of Victrollia's ankle, causing her to twirl around to investigate the source of the pain.

"Now, sweetheart!" Derrick shouted.

Knowing that her fate and the future of Starrycrest would be decided in mere moments, Kara recited the chant as loudly as she could while continuing to twirl in the Dance Dazzler.

"Royal gemstones have fallen into evil hands. Here and now I chant the dynastic Denison Divination to destroy the darkness over our lands."

"Looks like the beloved Denison ancestors aren't going to come through for you," Victrollia taunted. "Face it, dearie! Your worst fear has been realized and your precious kingdom is about to be mine!"

Oh no! The enchantment didn't work. Derrick and his parents always said if I believed in the Denison family magic then the enchantment would protect us. Why didn't it work? I can't believe that using the enchantment to defeat Victrollia isn't enough proof that I believe in it. What more do our ancestors want? she wondered, her eyes overflowing with tears as the wind shifted and the tornado swirled frantically just above Starrycrest Square. *I've failed, and now everyone is going to pay the ultimate price*, the princess realized.

Tears streaming down her face, she ignored the evil troll who was still taunting her and ran to Derrick's side. "I'm so sorry," she cried. "I tried. I really tried. I am so sorry I let you down," the words came out in a rush as the princess's cries morphed into sobs.

Enveloping the little girl into a protective embrace, Derrick squeezed her tightly. "Sweetheart, I want you to know that I love you and, no matter what happens, you'll always be my little girl," he tightened his embrace around Kara as though he was trying to protect her from the inevitable.

I can't believe that, even after I failed and put the entire kingdom at risk, Derrick is standing here comforting me and telling me he loves me. In that moment, the princess felt so loved and protected that she said the only thing she could. "I love you too, Dad."

Kara's eyes widened for the third time in a matter of moments as the tornado changed course as soon as those words left her mouth, abandoning Starrycrest Square and instead engulfing Victrollia and her snakes before evaporating into thin air in a matter of seconds.

Oh my gosh! We're going to be okay. We're saved! Kara realized as a rainbow appeared where the tornado had been moments before.

Another strong bout of nausea overcame the princess as the gravity of what had just happened hit her.

"I knew you could do it, sweetheart, you were amazing," Derrick praised "We will definitely celebrate later, but right now I must get to the infirmary. Stay with Stella and I'll come get you as soon as I can."

Eyebrows wrinkled in confusion, Kara opened her mouth to question him, but didn't get a chance to before he ran off toward Starrycrest Square.

If Derrick's leaving me after everything that just happened something must be seriously wrong, she decided. Unable to stand the unknown for a second longer, she leaned forward, following him in the Dance Dazzler.

"Whoa, where are you headed to so fast?" Stella bellowed, catching up with the princess moments after Tony who, while looking around to make sure everyone was okay, noticed her attempted departure.

"The infirmary. Derrick won't tell me what's going on, but I know something is wrong. I can feel it."

Shaking her head, Stella disagreed. "No that's not a good idea. Come inside, we'll go to my studio and dance things out a little, okay?"

"Yeah, that sounds like a plan," Tony agreed. "We'll have a dance party, and top things off with some ice cream sundaes."

"Sweet," Tyler exclaimed. "I'm always down for ice cream."

"Mind if the Mrs. and I join ya for the ice cream?" Fred asked, as the elderly couple approached. "We're not supposed to have much sugar but, considerin' what we just lived through, I think we earned an exception."

Wiping her tear-stained cheeks, Edna eyed her husband suspiciously. "Sounds to me like you're just lookin' for an excuse to eat some sweets," she joked. "But, lucky for you, I could really go for some chocolate right now."

"No!" Kara shouted. "My family needs me so I'm going to the infirmary. You guys can come or not, but there is no way I can go off and have ice cream with you when my family needs me. Families stick together, right?"

"Right," Tyler agreed. "As much as you annoy me sometimes, you are my dance partner and the closest thing to family I've got. I'm goin' with ya," he declared. "But you totally owe me some ice cream."

Letting out a sigh, Stella lamented. "Okay, we'll all go, but if Derrick asks it was the little lady's idea."

Not wanting to waste another moment, Kara raced to the infirmary in the Dance Dazzler, her friends not far behind.

***

Woah, the infirmary cleaning crew must have started early tonight, Kara guessed as she practically burst into the infirmary with her friends in tow only to be nauseated by the strong smell of antiseptic.

"Princess, w-what're you doing here?" a familiar voice asked, as she stepped in front of Kara, cutting off her path to the receptionist desk.

"Oh my gosh, that's the nurse who helped me when my shunt had to be replaced. She's so nice. She'll definitely help me. Even though her head had begun pounding in time with her churning stomach, Kara forced a smile and asked Suzie about her parents in hopes that the nurse would have the answers she needed.

"Oh my gosh, Suzie!" she exclaimed. "After the night I've had I am so glad to see a friendly face."

"It's great to see you too, sweetheart, how have you been?" the red-haired nurse smiled as she waited for the princess to answer, but the gesture didn't reach her eyes.

"Good. I've been good but, right now, my friends and I are trying to figure out why our beloved king rushed here to the infirmary. You haven't seen him, have you?" the princess questioned instinctively placing a hand on her still churning stomach.

Shifting her weight from one foot to the other, Suzie looked down at her feet. "I, uh, I, um–," she stammered.

"Suz, all hands on deck in room 104," a blonde-haired nurse shouted as she and two other women in scrubs came rushing down the hallway.

"I'm sorry, I have to go," Suzie frowned then rushed to join the other nurses.

Eyebrows furrowed, Kara watched as the nurses disappeared down the hallway. *Was it just me or was Suzie acting really–*

"Get him out of here now!" a distant voice shouted, interrupting Kara's thought.

"No! I'm the king of this land. I will stay with my wife," Derrick yelled, his authoritative voice loud enough to be heard throughout the infirmary despite being laced with sheer panic.

"I knew something was wrong!" Kara exclaimed as she quickly rounded the corner following his voice.

Her loyal and protective comrades all yelled for her to come back, but she ignored them and quickly found Derrick being pushed out of room 104.

"We are doing everything we can to help your wife your majesty. I can assure you that she and the babies will have a much better chance if you just let us work," Suzie said hastily, closing the door of the infirmary room in the king's face before he could protest again.

"Dad, what's going on? Are Misty and the babies okay?" Kara spoke meekly and fearfully, rolling up behind him.

Jumping at the sound of her voice, Derrick turned around, his eyes wide and full of a mixture of sadness and worry. "Kara, sweetheart, what are you doing here? I told you to stay with–"

Trembling, the little girl's fear and nausea simultaneously quadrupled as she looked to her adoptive father. *You can do this*, she assured herself after taking a few deep breaths. *Just be brave.*

"No!" the curly-haired ballerina shouted, pushing through her fear to cut him off. "Something is wrong. I heard you yelling at the nurses and I can see it in your eyes. I am tired of being in the dark. Tell me what's going on," she demanded.

Pinching the bridge of his nose, Derrick shut his eyes.

Unable to stand his silence, Kara persisted. "Please talk to me, Dad."

After a moment the king's eyes fluttered open and he wordlessly lifted her from the Dance Dazzler.

The pint-sized royal opened her mouth to protest but stopped short, surprised to realize she felt safer in his embrace than she had in weeks. *So much for demanding answers*, the princess mused as she rested her head on his shoulder.

Kara was once again surprised as Derrick carried her out to the waiting room, whispered something to Stella and accepted a quick half-hug from the eccentric woman, before she and everyone else in the waiting room cleared out, leaving the terrified royals alone.

Uh oh, if Derrick sent everyone away just to talk to me, things must be really bad. The princess took another breath, struggling to stay calm as the king, who she quickly noticed was also shaking, sat her down in a waiting room chair, and then sat down next to her.

After a long moment, he turned to face her and spoke, his voice hesitant and quiet. "Women having more than one baby sometimes struggle through their pregnancies, sweetheart. Unfortunately, Misty has had a few complications throughout her pregnancy," he explained.

"Misty and the babies are going to be okay though, right?" the princess interjected innocently.

"Well, uh," breaking eye contact with Kara, the loving husband and father looked at his hands.

Uh oh, Derrick wasn't even this nervous the night that his and Misty's parents reunited, Kara realized as she was hit by yet another wave of nausea.

"You okay, sweetheart?" Derrick asked, his eyebrows wrinkled with worry.

Taking another deep breath, Kara shook her head vigorously. "Please don't change the subject," she begged. "Just tell me what's going on."

After another long moment of silence, Derrick spoke, his voice quiet and strangely timid. "Every bone in my body is telling me that

Misty and the babies are going to be okay, but Tabitha and the doctors here aren't so sure. Misty and I didn't want to worry you, but, the truth is, her blood pressure has been high throughout the whole pregnancy." Derrick's usually confident, steady voice trembled and shook the princess to her very core.

This can't be happening. This is a nightmare. I'm going to wake up tomorrow at home in the castle and everything will be fine. This is just a horrible nightmare, the little girl told herself as she struggled to keep listening to Derrick.

"Sweetheart, the truth is, right now Misty's blood pressure is so high that it is putting her and the babies in danger," Derrick explained as moisture built up in his eyes.

"What do you mean her blood pressure is putting them in danger? The doctors and nurses can help, can't they?" Kara's voice was fretful and full of urgency.

Reaching for Kara's hand, Derrick squeezed it gently. "The only way for the doctors to make sure Misty and the babies are okay is for them to deliver the babies as soon as possible. The nurses are preparing Misty now," he enlightened her, his voice still trembling.

"No, they can't!" Kara cried. "It's too early. It's not safe!"

"Shh," Derrick cautioned. "We need to keep this quiet. We don't want to worry anyone."

"How can you be worried about anyone other than Misty right now?" the princess almost scolded, her voice shaking even more than that of her adoptive father by then. "How can you let this happen? You're king for cryin' out loud. Can't you make Tabitha and the doctors help Misty without delivering the babies?"

"I wish I could," Derrick murmured. "Being king gives me a great deal of power, but it doesn't allow me to play God."

Sighing, Kara protested, "I know but–" she began.

"Sweetie, I know this is scary but it's not in our hands. All we can do is hope that everyone will be all right," Derrick encouraged, squeezing her hand again. "Can you do that for me? Can you be hopeful?" he pleaded.

Looking into Derrick's eyes, Kara saw nothing but fear and utter sadness. *I wished that Misty wasn't pregnant anymore, all of this is my fault*, the little girl realized as she burst into tears.

"It's okay, sweetie. It's going to be okay," he soothed while pulling her into a hug.

Breaking away from Derrick, Kara shook her head. "No, no it's not and it's all my fault," she sniffled as tears continued to stream down her face.

"What are you talking about, sweetheart?" the loving father asked, his voice laced with confusion in addition to sadness. "None of this is your fault."

Kara opened her mouth to explain herself, but instead became nauseous yet again. *Now is not the time to be sick,* she groaned inwardly.

"Sweetheart, you're as white as a ghost, are you sure you're okay?"

Taking another deep breath, Kara grabbed her stomach. "My tummy hurts a little," she admitted sheepishly.

"Aww, sweetie. I'm sorry. I could tell something wasn't right. What do you need?" Derrick questioned, his voice full of the concern that only a loving parent can have. "I may not be able to help Misty right now, but I can certainly help you."

"I'm okay. I just need to..." Kara's voice trailed off as she began to feel dizzy in addition to nauseous.

"Do you want some water?" Derrick's forehead wrinkled with worry as he eyed her. "I'm going to go get you some water," he said before running off. "Sweetie, have you been taking your stomach medicine?" Derrick asked as he walked back to her with a cup of water.

Kara opened her mouth to answer but stopped short as dizziness overtook her; the next minute everything went black.

Chapter 18

"Wahh, wahh, wahh…" Startled awake, Kara scanned her surroundings and realized she was no longer in the waiting room of the infirmary but was, instead, in a patient room.

"Shh shh… quiet loves," Misty whispered sweetly as Derrick wheeled her into the room. "Your big sister is resting."

At the sound of Misty's gentle, melodic voice, Kara sat up in bed. "Oh my gosh! Misty, it's so good to see you. Are you okay? Are you holding who I think you're holding?" she blurted out the questions in seconds, her voice full of excitement and anticipation.

Misty chuckled, her eyes full of love. "I'm fine, sweetie. More importantly, I'm glad to see that you're okay. I have two people here who were so ready to meet you they decided to wake you up."

Even though Kara had been dreading the arrival of the twins for weeks, in that moment, as she saw the joy on Misty's face, she wanted nothing more than to hold the babies herself.

"Let me hold them. Let me hold them, please, please, please. Let me hold them," she exclaimed, flashing a cute smile.

"Okay, we'll do one at a time," Derrick said before gently lifting a baby from Misty's arm. He smiled down at the baby for a long moment before turning his attention to Kara. "Sweetie, I'd like you to meet your brother, Luke Michael Denison. Be sure to support his head as you hold him," the proud father advised, gently placing Luke in the crook of her arm.

The joy and excitement Kara felt as she anticipated holding the twins disappeared after she looked down at Luke and saw Derrick's soulful blue eyes as well as Misty's radiant smile and instantly began to sob.

"Aww, sweetheart, what's wrong? Why are you crying?" Misty asked worriedly.

Derrick frowned. "Is it your head, sweetheart? The doctors said you may wake up with quite the headache."

Forehead creased in confusion, Kara looked to Derrick. "I'm not crying because of a silly headache… even though I do have a big one," she sniffled. "I'm crying 'cause the babies look just like you and Misty," she admitted quietly.

"Sweetie, I know it's a bit unfortunate that the little ones take after me in the looks department, but it's nothing to cry over," he joked.

The pint-sized majestic shook her head, still crying. "This isn't funny, I–"

"How are my favorite royals doing?" Suzie asked as she walked into the room, interrupting the princess.

Turning his attention to the red -haired nurse, Derrick smiled. "Well, if it isn't the best nurse in the kingdom."

Nodding, Suzie returned his smile. "I'm happy to see all of you together and doin' well."

Kara's eyebrows furrowed in confusion. "Wait. What are you talking about?" she queried, wiping tears from her eyes. "How did you guys meet?"

Turning his attention back to Kara, Derrick answered. "Suzie did an amazing job helping both you and Misty last night. Honestly, she helped save both of you and, for that, I'll be forever grateful," Derrick explained, his voice full of the gratitude he felt toward the nurse.

Waving a dismissive hand, the healthcare professional dismissed the idea. "Super Dad here is just being modest. If it weren't for him giving us the space to help Misty and then bringing you to us after realizing your shunt malfunctioned, we'd be having a very different conversation right now."

Kara's mouth dropped slightly. "Wow," she exclaimed. "Derrick, I didn't know you knew anything about shunt malfunctions."

Derrick looked at her, wide-eyed and slightly bewildered. "Sweetie, you're my little girl. The very moment you came into my life, I tried to learn all I could to care for you properly," he explained as though it were the most obvious thing in the world.

Wow, I never realized how much Derrick cared about me from the very beginning, Kara thought, as moisture filled her eyes once again.

Quickly picking up on the little girl's renewed sadness, Derrick shifted his weight from one side to the other and looked to Suzie. "I know you need to take some blood samples from the twins. Would you mind taking them to the nursery afterward so we can have a few minutes with Kara, please?" he queried kindly.

"Sure thing, Super Dad. I'll just scoop up the babies now and give y'all some privacy," Suzie said before doing just that.

Silence settled between the three of them for a long moment until Derrick finally spoke. "Sweetie, it's time we all had a talk," he suggested.

"It sure is," Misty agreed. "We want to know what's going on in that pretty little head of yours. Why are you so sad?"

In that moment, as Misty and Derrick looked at her, their eyes expectant and full of a mixture of love and concern, Kara couldn't help but answer them honestly.

"Now that you guys have two cute little babies that look just like you, you're going to forget all about me. I won't get to be your daughter or a princess anymore, you are going to love them more than me and send me away," she explained as tears streamed down her cheeks.

Shaking her head vehemently, Misty disagreed. "Aww, sweetheart, that will never happen. Why would you think that?" she tried to give her assurance.

"I know other kids who have been adopted but had to come back to the group home after babies were brought into families. It happens," she sniffled.

"Well, it's not going to happen to you. You are a Denison. We love you. We could never forget about you," Derrick declared.

"Really?" the little girl asked pointedly. "Misty forgot about our girl time twice, and you gave up dance class," she explained before wiping at her tears again.

Misty sighed. "Sweetie, I'm so sorry. I'll admit that my pregnancy and its complications have had me very distracted, but I never meant to make you feel like I forgot about you or that you didn't matter. You are one of the most important people in my life. I could have a thousand babies and that wouldn't change. I chose to be your mother because I've always felt that we have a deep connection and I love you very much," the loving mother and queen explained before she, too, started to cry.

"We both love you and we both chose you," Derrick reassured her. "Sweetheart, you are a Denison whether you like it or not. I thought you were able to activate our family's enchantment last night because you finally understood what it means to love the way you dance. That's a motto we Denison's live by, sweetie. Sure, I helped a little by playing the Fairy Lullaby on Misty's music box, but the rest was all you. Truth be told, I can't even take credit for having the music box. I only had it on me because Misty insisted that its music might be the encouragement you needed to make it through last night's ordeal."

Nodding in agreement, Misty's sniffled. "Mother's intuition, I suppose."

After giving Misty's shoulder a reassuring squeeze, Derrick turned his attention back to the little girl, his gaze thoughtful. "Sweetie, the point is even with your mom's intuition and a little help from me, you never would have been able to call on the magic of the Denison ancestors if you were not one of us."

"I never would've had to call upon the Denison ancestors if I hadn't done what I did," the little girl admitted shamefacedly, as fresh tears fell down her right cheek.

"What do you mean, sweetie?" Derrick inquired, his eyebrows furrowed in confusion.

No reason to stop being honest now, Kara decided. Sighing, she looked from Derrick to Misty and back before explaining to them that she had gone to Victrollia because she'd been mad. She then told them about how she didn't word her wish properly and had unknowingly put Misty and the twins in danger.

Eyes wide and full of disbelief, Misty looked to her loving husband. "We have really made a mess of things, haven't we my love?" Her voice was solemn and quiet.

"What are you talking about?" Kara asked. "This is all my fault. My wish put the whole kingdom in danger."

"Yes, it did sweetheart," Misty agreed. "But it is certainly not all your fault. Derrick and I have kept a lot from you over the last several months because we didn't want to scare you, but I now understand that we should have communicated with you more, trusted you more, and tried harder to make you a priority. I'm so sorry we didn't. I hope that you can forgive us and understand that we will be family forevermore," She explained, her voice sweet and full of love for the little girl.

Nodding, Derrick smiled. "Same goes for me. I love you just as much as I love Luke and Liliana and I am going to try my hardest to prove that to you. I'll start by talking to you about why you want Starrycrest to establish a kiddo keeper program so badly."

Kara's eyes lit up with excitement. "I have something important to show you, but can I meet my new brother and sister properly first?"

With that, Derrick retrieved both babies from the nursery and brought them back to Kara's room where the royal family spent the afternoon becoming reacquainted while feeding, rocking, and otherwise doting upon their newest additions.

***

Oh my gosh, the whole kingdom is here. What was I thinking? Kara wondered as she waited backstage in Starrycrest theater.

"Hey sweetie, how are you? You look so pretty," Misty gushed, her voice a whisper as she and Derrick approached.

"What are you guys doing here?" Kara whispered worriedly. "You shouldn't be back here. I'm going to be on in just a few minutes. Where are the babies? Is everything okay?"

Grinning, Derrick gently grasped her shoulders, "Sweetheart, everything is fine. Take a deep, cleansing breath," he encouraged, demonstrating how to do so.

Chuckling, Misty agreed, "Everything is fine. Don't worry about the twins. Edna and Fred are keeping an eye on them. I wanted to sneak back here so I could get closer look at this contraption that your dad told me about. It's so tall and you don't even look like you're sitting in anything. I've never seen anything like it," she whispered excitedly, examining the unique wheelchair, wide-eyed.

Kara giggled, exposing her beloved dimples. "I'm not supposed to look like I'm sitting in anything, Mom. The whole point of the using Dance Dazzler is to have people focus on me and not my disability. Stella says that someone who dances as beautifully as I do deserves to be an audiences' only focus."

Nodding, the beautiful majestic smiled. "You'd think, as a queen who loves to dance, I'd get to try the Dance Dazzler first. Maybe I should have a little chat with Stella," Misty teased.

"Oh. Well, I'm sure after tonight—" Kara began.

"Sweetheart, I was only joking. Stella picked the best dancer in the kingdom to try the Dance Dazzler first and I couldn't be happier. The real reason your Dad and I snuck back here because we have something for you," Misty explained, holding out a wrapped present toward the little girl.

No time like the present to accept a present, Kara mused as she accepted the gift and enthusiastically ripped it open.

"Oh my gosh, are these what I think they are?" the little girl gushed, her voice a mixture of excitement and disbelief as she eyed the gift.

Derrick chuckled, his eyes sparkled with love for the little girl. "If you're thinking it's your own pair of custom pointe shoes then you'd be right."

"They are so pretty. I love the color!" Kara said in excitement as she admired the lavender, crystal adorned pointe shoes.

"I'm so glad you like them. Here, let me help you put them on." Derrick suggested, reaching for the box on her lap.

Gripping the box so that he couldn't take it, Kara shook her head. "That's okay, Dad. I've got it."

"Are you sure, sweetheart?" he queried sweetly. "I don't mind helping."

"It's okay," she assured him, easily slipping the shoes onto her feet. "Being away made me really grateful for you, Mom, and the castle staff and showed me that I should only ask for help when I really need it."

.Kara glanced down at her feet as Derrick and Misty looked at her, their expressions full of love and pride.

These are the coolest, prettiest pointe shoes I've ever seen, the tiny dancer mused. "The left shoe fits my clubfoot perfectly," she exclaimed excitedly. *I can't believe it. I'm finally going to look like a real dancer.*

Smiling, Misty nodded, moisture building up behind her eyes. "Sweetheart, you are a wonderful dancer. The best, in my opinion, and you deserve to look and feel as beautiful as you truly are when you dance. We really hope these pointe shoes will help you with that." Pausing, she sniffled, then added, "But remember, pointe shoes don't make the dancer. Talent and dedication do, and you, Kara Denison, have that in spades."

The little girl nodded vehemently. "I'll remember. I promise," she assured, glancing down at her feet. "I just love my new pointe shoes," she said, continuing to admire them. "I've never seen anything like them. Where did you guys find them?"

"We went to a very kind and very old man named Nicholas Stevenson, the most recent in a long line of King Maxwell's apprentices. Turns out adaptive shoes were Maxwell's specialty. Nicholas used Maxwell's design and pattern, as well as a little help from Misty and I, to make them just for you," Derrick explained.

Kara's eyes widened. "That's so awesome!" she exclaimed. "I hope Maxwell would be proud that I'm wearing his shoe design."

"Of course, he would," Derrick agreed.

.Misty nodded. "Without a doubt. Now go and leave your heart out on the stage like the true dancer that you are, sweetheart," she encouraged.

Nodding, Kara took a deep breath and made her way onto the stage in the Dance Dazzler.

Nothing like a good shock to make The Nutcracker more exciting Kara mused as a collective gasp sounded from the audience.

The idea of all eyes in the kingdom being on her had Kara wondering a few moments earlier if she may throw up, but in that moment, with a new-found confidence from her new pointe shoes, she felt incredibly exhilarated.

Calm down. The Dance Dazzler takes fineness, the princess reminded herself. *Time to show the kingdom that you're the best Sugar Plum Fairy the Land of Sweets has ever seen.* Taking a deep breath, she studied the giant, glittery snowflakes, Christmas gifts, and candy cane props that served as her backdrop for a moment before slowly moving her body and gliding the Dance Dazzler through them in a precise and perfect figure eight motion.

Oh my gosh, that was my best figure eight yet, she realized as adrenaline began surging through her tiny body. *Misty's right. Nothing beats leaving your heart out on the stage,* the princess mused as the audience erupted in applause, which lasted until she danced off stage.

The adrenaline and excitement Kara felt after her solo was still present as she glided back onto the stage to dance with Tyler.

Uh oh, Tyler is really nervous, she realized as she spotted the fake smile plastered across his lips.

"We got this," she whispered, her voice low enough for only him to hear. "Let's just do what we do best. Let's just dance it out."

Being reminded of Stella's adviceseemed to calm Tyler. The fake smile across his lips was replaced in seconds with the quiet confidence that he only seemed to have when dancing.

The tiny royal struggled to maintain the same quiet composure, despite the adrenaline still surging through her.

Arms out in front of his chest and slightly rounded, Tyler positioned them into first while concurrently positioning his legs into fifth position. This position lasted only a moment, before he executed a beautiful battlement glisse with one leg while bending his other leg only slightly, presenting a textbook plié. Jumping into the air then, he brought his feet together in pointe and extended his arm out in front of him in a fluid stroke before landing with his feet in fifth position once again.

Yay, they're loving it, Kara realized, her body buzzing with anticipation for the upcoming lift as the audience applauded, following Tyler's beautiful assemblé. Moments later, he rose up onto his tiptoes and transitioned seamlessly into a gorgeous relevé before finally jumping into the princess's outstretched limbs. *Wow, either Tyler has suddenly become the lightest dancer in the kingdom or I have gotten really good at shoulder lifts,* Kara mused, lifting him high above her head and guiding him into a sitting position on her shoulder as though he were as light as a feather. *The only thing better than getting to dance and leave your heart out on a stage is getting to do it twice,* Kara decided as the audience once again erupted in applause.

***

What is Derrick up to? Kara wondered, her eyebrows furrowed in confusion, as he came up onto the stage of Starrycrest Theater after she, Tyler, the other starlets, and Stella had all taken a bow.

273

Aww, he's teary-eyed, the tiny dancer realized, as she watched him whisper something to Stella. *I hope it's only because my dancing brought him to happy tears,* she smiled as Derrick accepted a microphone from Stella and turned to address the kingdom.

"Good evening fellow citizens. Firstly, I wish to thank you all for coming out to celebrate the anniversary of our lovely kingdom and watching the Starrycrest Starlets' beautiful and imaginative performance of *The Nutcracker.* Secondly, I'd like to take advantage of the fact that we are all gathered to discuss some changes to our wonderful kingdom going forward," he explained, his voice full of the quiet authority he reserved for his constituents.

A few gasps and worried murmurs sounded from the crowd.

Shaking his head, Derrick gazed over the crowd, his eyes full of reassurance. "Please don't worry. Please trust in me as your king when I say these changes are going to make our kingdom an even better place than it already is."

Is he getting at what I think he's getting at? Kara wondered, her body once again buzzing with renewed excitement.

Pausing briefly, Derrick winked at Kara then turned back to the audience.

I wish I could read Derrick half as easily as he can read me, Kara groaned inwardly. *He winked at me so that means he has good news, right? He wouldn't drop a bomb on me in front of the entire kingdom, would he?* Taking a deep breath, the little girl steeled herself and focused on Derrick.

"As most of you know, my beautiful daughter, Kara, recently saved our kingdom from the wrath of Victrollia, Trovella's vengeful cousin, by calling upon our royal ancestors for help. What most of you don't know is that my daughter went to Victrollia and made a wish because she feared that my beautiful wife and myself would replace her with biological children. With all due respect to my sweet, little Sugar Plum Fairy, I thought the fear silly, and something built up in the mind of a child who loves us very much. However, my wife and I have both heard people whispering about the future of the monarchy since our beautiful twins were born and that has helped me to realize how my amazing daughter could have developed such a fear. So, while we are all gathered here, I intend to set the record straight."

What is he getting at? Kara groaned. *I wish he'd just spit it–*

Turning his attention back to the little girl, Derrick interrupted her thoughts, "Kara, come on up here, sweetheart."

Even though she had just been center stage dancing with Tyler, her heart pounded against her ribs as she approached Derrick. *This is ridiculous,* she realized. *I'm so nervous. Hopefully, he'll get to the point before I faint,* she mused.

Smiling at the princess, the loving father addressed her directly. "Kara, sweetheart, I love you. You did not come to Misty and I in the same way that Liliana and Luke did, but we love you just as much as we love them."

"That's right," Misty, who was sitting in the front row, holding one of the twins in each arm, agreed. "Sweetie, you may not have been born from my womb, but I promise you that you most certainly were born in our hearts," she explained as moisture welled up in her eyes.

Kara opened her mouth to respond to Misty but stopped short as Derrick continued, "Misty and I know, without a doubt, that you,

Kara Marie Denison, were not only meant to be our daughter and a sister to Luke and Liliana, but also to change this kingdom for the better so, without further ado…Edward, if you please."

Edward only comes out of retirement for the most significant royal decrees. What could be so important? Kara wondered as an elderly gentleman with short, white hair and kind, green eyes who'd worked as the kingdom crier, announcing decrees for Starrycrest and the surrounding kingdoms for three times as long as she'd been alive, stood up and cleared his throat.

"Hear ye, hear ye: On this day, the 16th of December in the year 764 of King Derrick and Queen Misty's reign, Derrick Michael Denison, in his official capacity as King of Starrycrest, decrees that his eldest daughter, Kara Marie Denison, will henceforth be acknowledged as the future queen of Starrycrest and his rightful heir."

Did he just say 'future queen'? Kara wondered as her eyes widened in disbelief. Excited all over again, the little girl's heart thumped against her ribs. *I can't believe it. I'm still a princess and even going to be queen someday. But the best part is Derrick and Misty really love me. We really are a family. Me, Derrick, Misty, and the babies.* The moment Kara thought about her new sister and brother her excitement faded into sadness. *What about Luke and Liliana?* she frowned. *They're as much as part of the family as I am. I'm excited to be queen one day, but I don't want either one of them to—*

The feel of a hand on her shoulder distracted the little girl from her thoughts. "Sweetheart, take a deep breath and just listen," Derrick urged as though he knew exactly what was running through her mind. Listening to his suggestion, Kara tried to calm herself and focus on Edward.

"Additionally, the king's youngest daughter, Liliana Marie Denison, and his son, Luke Michael Denison, will be known as the Duke and Duchess of Starrycrest respectively," the kingdom crier declared, his voice brimming with sincerity.

Tears formed in Kara's eyes as the reality of Derrick's latest royal decree began to sink in. Blinking, she looked to Derrick. "You really do love me just as much as the twins. We really are a family!" she exclaimed, happiness exuding from her voice.

As the crowd began to cheer, Derrick discreetly led the princess backstage.

"I brought you back here so we can talk privately about something very important," the proud father explained. After scanning the small prop and costume-filled space to ensure that he and the princess were alone, Derrick knelt to her level and said, "First things first. Of course, we're a family, sweetheart, that's what Misty and I have been trying to get you to understand. We will reiterate it as many times as it takes for you to know it in your heart, sweetie," he reassured, pulling her into a tight embrace.

"I think I'm starting to get it. I just can't believe you actually believe in me enough to name me the future queen," she gushed backing ever so slightly away from his hold. "Do you really think I can make the kingdom a better place?" she asked, looking up at him, her eyes full of love and hope.

Nodding vehemently, Derrick continued to reassure her. "Sweetheart, I have no doubt that you will improve this kingdom by leaps and bounds. In fact, I believe in you so much that I'm going to let you use your authority as princess and the future queen to make this decree official," he explained, pulling a piece of folded parchment from his chest pocket he handing it to her.

Unfolding the piece of paper, Kara skimmed it carefully. "Oh my gosh! Is this what I think it is?" Her eyes widened in disbelief for the second time in minutes.

Derrick chuckled, his eyes sparkling with love for his daughter. "If you think it's a royal decree establishing a kiddo keeper program here in Starrycrest then you're right," he whispered sweetly.

"Seriously?" Kara exclaimed, her voice brimming with a mixture of skepticism and excitement.

"Yes, sweetie, after reading Maxwell's journal and speaking with you again, the family and I are all on board."

"Oh my gosh!" the princess yelled with delight. "Thank you, thank you, thank you. This is going to be great for so many boys and girls in the kingdom. You won't regret it. I promise." The princess fidgeted in the Dance Dazzler, struggling to contain her happiness.

Chuckling, Derrick placed a hand on her shoulder. "Take a breath sweetie. Starrycrest doesn't need its future queen jumping out of her fancy Dance Dazzler. I'm excited and I'm sure the kingdom will be too," he assured her.

"I sure hope so. How exactly do I make it official?" she asked excitedly.

"You have to give it your seal of approval and then tell the fine people of Starrycrest," Derrick explained, his voice brimming with pride.

Nodding vehemently, Kara flashed an excited smile. "Do you have a quill? Where do I sign?"

Chuckling, Derrick shook his head. "Sweetheart, you don't seal it using a quill, you use your ring," he explained.

"My ring… what do you mean?" her eyebrows furrowed in confusion.

Gently taking Kara's hand, Derrick admired her ring for a moment and then looked into her eyes. "Sweetie, your ring, the ring that Misty and I gave you is much more than a ring."

"Yeah, I figured that. History shows that trolls don't go for costume jewelry," the tiny royal joked.

Throwing his head back, Derrick laughed. "Very true, sweetheart, but not where I was going. Your ring is special because from this day forward it will not only be a ring, but also the seal you use to make all your royal decrees official," he explained.

"What do you mean?" Kara queried, her eyesbrow furrowed once again. "Ink can't be good for the crown jewels, can it?"

Pulling something out of his other coat pocket, Derrick flashed her a proud smile. "I love that you're thinking about protecting the crown jewels. It shows that you truly learned something from the whole ordeal with Victrollia."

Shaking her head, Kara reassured him. "I sure did. I'm never going to let another creature or person mess with our family ever again. That's a promise."

"I trust you, sweetie. You don't need to worry about that and you don't need to worry about the royal jewels either because when sealing a royal decree we use this magic ink that only reacts to parchment and won't harm them in any way," Derrick explained, showing her the small vial he'd retrieved from his coat.

Smiling from ear to ear, Derrick wordlessly, carefully opened the vial, dipped his finger into the ink, took it out and showed the princess it was indeed stain free. Chuckling at a wide-eyed Kara, he took another small piece of parchment from his coat pocket.

"What else are you hiding in your pockets?" Kara queried, her voice full of amusement.

"Watch," the king urged before stamping his own ring into the piece of paper, leaving behind a distinct print.

"Oh my gosh, that's awesome," Kara exclaimed.

"You're awesome and you're going to do an amazing job making this decree official." With that, the royals returned to the stage where Derrick found Edward and explained what was about to happen while Kara prepared to address the kingdom.

Chapter 19

*T**his can't be real. Just a few weeks ago I thought everything was falling apart and, now, here I am in front of the entire kingdom with a real power to make a difference,* Kara realized as tears welled up in her eyes.

Taking a deep breath, she wiped them away and addressed the audience. "I feel like the luckiest little girl in Starrycrest," she declared.

Murmurs of agreement sounded from the crowd before she added, "But not for the reason you think."

Uh oh, I've barely opened my mouth and I'm already doing this wrong, Kara thought as many members of the crowd responded with looks of confusion and wonder.

"Wah," a small cry from Liliana stole the princess's attention. As Misty put the baby over her, shoulder preparing to burp her, she flashed the little girl a smile.

"You got this, sweetheart," she mouthed.

Comforted by Misty's silent vote of confidence, Kara took another deep breath and addressed her fellow citizens again. "Don't get me wrong, I'm honored to be your princess and future queen, but the real reason that I am the luckiest girl in Starrycrest is because I have a mom and dad who chose me and they love me more than anything in the world."

Whoa, it feels good to call Misty and Derrick Mom and Dad. The princess was surprised that the terms of endearment had rolled off her tongue before she realized, but she was even more shocked by how natural and right it felt to do so. As she looked out into the audience and saw that both Misty and Derrick were smiling from ear to ear with tears rolling down their cheeks, she had to bite her lip to keep from bursting into happy tears herself.

"Every boy and girl in this kingdom deserves the love of a mom and dad, but many orphans in this kingdom have never gotten the chance to experience that love. The fact the orphans of this kingdom have a home at all is because my great, great grandfather, Maxwell Denison, a cobbler-turned-king who was orphaned himself opened a home to ensure that children without families would always have somewhere to go."

"Thank goodness for that," Stella yelled from the crowd.

Nodding, Kara giggled. "I couldn't have said it better myself. I will always be grateful to King Maxwell for giving the orphans of our kingdom a home. I wasn't lucky enough to get to know the king while he was alive, but I have been lucky enough to get to know him through his journal. His journal explains how, in his heart, he hoped that someday all orphans would have the chance to leave the group home and gain the love that a family provides. With that said: Edward, if you please."

Smiling, she held her breath, as the kingdom crier opened the scroll she'd signed and cleared his throat.

"Hear ye, hear ye: On this day, the 16th of December in the year 764 of King Derrick's and Queen Misty's reign, Kara Marie Denison in her official capacity as the future Queen of Starrycrest, decrees the creation of Starrycrest Kiddo Keepers. From this day forth, the aforementioned program will allow families and children in need to get to know one another on a trial basis in the hopes that children in need of finding their forever families do so and that families in the kingdom reach new levels of happiness and completion."

Kara let out a breath that she hadn't realized she'd been holding as the crowd cheered following her decree. The princess's lips broke into a smile as the crowd showered her with praise saying things like, "Way to go Princess!" and "That's a wonderful idea."

This is working out better than I ever could have imagined, Kara realized. *I'm so glad that other orphans in Starrycrest are going to get a chance to find their forever families and I can't wait to help them but, for tonight, I am going to spend time with my family*, she decided before making her way off the stage and joining the crowd to do just that.

***

"Betsy may seem a little cold at first, but she'll warm up to you in no time," Kara assured the twins as the Denison family walked into Starrycrest Group Home a few weeks later.

"Well, if it isn't my favorite royals," Betsy said by way of greeting. "What brings you here?"

"There are some people I want you to meet," Kara explained, her eyes sparkling with love and excitement as she looked from Betsy to her siblings and back.

"Oh, my heavens! It's about time you brought those babies to meet me!" Betsy let out.

Kara giggled as the elderly woman leaned forward to get a closer look at each of the babies who were in bassinets on each side of a double stroller.

"Awww… how cute are you?" she queried sweetly, flashing an ear-to-ear smile at Liliana. "Just as beautiful as your sister and mama."

"I appreciate that," Misty said. "But I personally think that both of my adorable girls have me beat in the looks department."

Looking at Luke, Betsy broke into another smile. "Well, with all due respect to Your Majesties, I must say, that little guy has out done his daddy in terms of looks. I could just eat those dimpled cheeks right up," she gushed, reaching out to pinch the baby's right cheek.

Kara rolled her eyes. *Poor Lukie*, she thought. *I hate it when people pinch my dimples*. "Betsy, I know you probably needed a baby fix but, c'mon, give the little guy a break."

Betsy nodded, chuckling. "You're right, little one. I needed something to make me smile. If your kiddo keeper program continues to go as well as it's been goin', I'll be out of a job soon. Five kiddos have found their forever families in the last month alone. I only wish I could figure out a way to make Ralph and Shirley understand that they cannot take in every child in the kingdom."

Derrick shook his head. "Don't talk like that, Betsy, there will always be a place for you here in Starrycrest," he assured her.

"Of course," Kara agreed. "I'm glad the program is working out so well. I'll have a talk with Shirley and Ral—"

"Waaahh, waahhh, waahhh," the soft yet persistent cries of the duchess quickly filled the space between Betsy and the royals, interrupting the princess.

"Aww, Lilly, what's wrong love?" Derrick questioned sweetly as he lifted the crying baby out of her bassinet.

"Phew, I think I smell the culprit," Misty said after a moment, her nose scrunched in distaste.

Uh oh, dirty diaper alert, Kara mused. "On that note, I'm goin' to go talk to the other kids." Slowly backing away from the group, she looked to the still crying baby. "Don't worry, little sister, Dad's got you."

Winking, Derrick flashed her a smile then turned his attention back to the baby.

Just as Kara was heading to the room that Tiphany and some of the other orphaned girls shared a loud thud made her jump. *What the heck is going on?* she wondered as Tyler practically burst into the group home, slamming the door behind him.

Eyebrows wrinkled with worry, the tiny royal looked to her dance partner. "Ty, what's wrong? What're you doing here?"

"Kara, you have to help me. You can't let this happen. You just can't."

Uh oh, something is really wrong, Kara realized as she noticed the boy was trembling. *Tyler never sounds this serious and his eyes look all red and puffy like he's been crying.*

"Whatever is going on, it's going to be okay," she assured him. "Just take a deep breath and tell me what's wrong."

"I can't tell you here," he whispered after a long moment. "I don't want Betsy thinking it's good news."

What could Tyler possibly be so upset about that Betsy would think was a good thing? Kara wondered as she followed him outside.

The spiky, red-haired boy stayed quiet as the two settled into an old wooden playhouse that had been in the yard of the group home for as long as the little girl could remember. *I'm used to having fun in here, but something tells me this conversation isn't going to be fun at all.* Kara's cheeks grew hot as silence settled between her and her dance partner.

"C'mon, Ty, you're scaring me," she complained after a long moment. "I can't help you unless I know what's going on."

After another long moment of silence, Tyler looked to the tiny royal and said, "Zoe has become a kiddo keeper," he shuddered as the words fell from his mouth, pain practically radiating through his eyes.

Eyebrows furrowed in confusion, Kara shot Tyler a questioning look. "Zoe who?" A moment later, Kara remembered the last time she'd seen so much pain in her friend's eyes. "Wait a minute, Zoe as in…" Kara paused, hesitant to finish the sentence.

"My bio mom," the boy finished, his voice forlorn and quiet.

Kara's eyes widened in disbelief. "You've got to be kidding!" she exclaimed. "Zoe gave you up. I understand that she was young then, but she rejected you a second time not too long ago because she was too busy being famous, and now, all of the sudden, she is ready to take in other kids? I don't think so."

"No, no, you don't understand," Tyler insisted. "Zoe says she became a kiddo keeper because she wants a third chance. Long story short, I told her I didn't want to give her a third chance, but she insisted so we went to court." Pausing, he let out a defeated sigh. 'I am being removed from Stella's care and into Zoe's tonight," he explained, a single tear rolling down his right cheek. "I have to go tell Betsy right now."

In that moment, as Kara saw the sadness and despair in her friend's eyes, the apprehension she'd been feeling was replaced by anger. "I don't understand," she shouted. "Zoe gave you up. She told you she didn't want you back a few years ago and now, all of the sudden, she gets to change her mind. What is Judge Clairmont thinking?"

A sad chuckle escaped from Tyler's lips as he quickly wiped the tear from his cheek. "I dunno. I told him my history and about how I've been doin' pretty darn good at Stella's for a little while now. He said he's glad Stella and I have been doing so well, but the court must give Zoe priority as my biological mother."

Rolling her eyes, Kara let out a huff. "Why do people think biology is so important?" she questioned rhetorically.

"Ya got me," Tyler shrugged. "The worst part about this is I was dumb enough to think that Stella was really happy with me, but even she thinks I should give Zoe a third chance," he admitted his voice meek and quiet.

Kara shook her head. "Ty, you're not wrong. You make Stella happy. You, she, and Tony have something special. I've seen it with my own eyes."

"Obviously, what we had doesn't matter," he retorted his voice coated in a mixture of anger and sadness. "Zoe shed a few fake tears in court and, just like that, the last few weeks didn't matter anymore."

Fake… that's it. This is all fake. It's all an act. It has to be. That's the only explanation, Kara grasped. As that realization sank in for the princess, she became even more determined to help her friend.

Eyeing her warily, Tyler sighed. "You're cookin' up another plan, aren't you? I can see it in your eyes. Please don't do anything too crazy. I can't afford to rock the boat and end up back here at the group home," he cautioned, frowning.

Kara waved a dismissive hand. "Don't worry. I got this. Just hang in there and you'll be back where you belong in no time," she assured him. "Now, go talk to Betsy while I head to the castle and figure out how we can get you home once and for all."

My plan to start Kiddo Keepers here in Starrycrest worked out. My plan to help Tyler is going to work out too, she decided as she headed to the castle, more determined to dance out her problems and help Tyler than ever before.

***

"How are the cutest babies in the kingdom?" Kara pronounced by way of greeting as she walked into the twins' nursery the next morning.

A putrid smell hit her nostrils a moment later, instantly making her eyes water. *Uh oh, Lilly's got that look in her eyes,* Kara mused as she scanned the room for the source of the smell. *Aww, Dad's got bags under his eyes. He must've had a rough night,* she realized.

"You look exhausted this morning, Dad. Everything okay?" she asked.

"Good morning, sweetie. Lukie and Lilly are bright-eyed and bushy-tailed this morning. Mom and I not so much. The babies were quite the tag team last night and still haven't let up."

Kara chuckled and looked into the beautiful blue eyes of her baby brother. *Lukie might not be who the smell is coming from, but he sure looks like he's had his fill of milk,* she realized as she looked at the baby, who despite being half asleep looked like he was about to burst into tears. "Did you and sissy keep Mommy and Daddy up last night?" she asked, her voice sweet and quiet as she carefully lifted the baby from his bassinet.

"Sweetheart, I fed Lukie and now he's ready to be burped, but the duchess needs a change and your mom is off in search of very, very strong coffee. Mind lending a hand?"

Kara giggled. "I'm way ahead of you," she explained, gently patting the baby on his back. "I got this. As soon as I saw the little guy this morning, I knew he needed his big sister's touch. Isn't that right, Lukie?"

A smile stretched across the princess's face as her baby brother snuggled into her, resting his head on her shoulder. "But first, Lukie and I are going to my room where no air freshener is required."

Throwing his head back, Derrick laughed. "I see how it is," he joked before turning his attention to Lilly.

***

Lukie looks so peaceful. If only I could sleep that contently, Kara thought as her baby brother slept in her arms.

289

The mere thought of sleep made her yawn, but before she could join her brother in slumber, a quiet knock on her door made her jump slightly.

"Sorry, sweetie," Derrick whispered. "I didn't mean to startle you. I just wanted to check on you two. How are you doing?"

"I'm a little tired," she admitted. "But I'm definitely enjoying all the baby snuggles I'm getting today."

Derrick flashed a smile then turned serious as he studied her for a moment. "You do look a bit sleepy," he agreed. "Did you not sleep well last night?"

Shaking her head, Kara sighed. "No, I didn't. But it wasn't because of the babies. It was because I'm worried about Tyler."

Derrick nodded. "I'm not surprised. Mom and I have been worried too. Stella told me about how Zoe popped up out of nowhere and uprooted Tyler. Honestly, the whole thing seems fishy to me. Why does a young ballerina at the top of her game want to be the mother of a ten-year-old boy?"

The princess nodded, eagerly agreeing, "That's exactly what I've been wondering. It just doesn't make sense."

I know. It's a shame we can't just have the royal guard follow her around and investigate a bit," the king said lightheartedly.

Kara's eyes lit up with excitement. "That's a great idea," she agreed, her voice quiet but full of anticipation. "Wait… why can't we do that?"

Derrick chuckled. "Sweetie, I was joking. As royals, we are sworn to protect our fellow citizens of Starrycrest not stalk them."

"Yeah. I guess you're right," Kara sighed. "I just wish that there was something I could do."

Reaching for her hand, Derrick gave it a gentle squeeze. "I know. I'll tell you what, I can promise you this. Whatever happens to Tyler, your mom and I will always watch out for him and make sure he's okay."

I know Derrick is trying to comfort me, but I can't help but think that Tyler deserves his own family to stick up for him. "Will you take Lukie?" she asked after a moment. "I'm going to head to the studio and dance my frustrations out a little."

"Sure, sweetie, but don't take too long. Jason and Jayla are coming this afternoon to have lunch and meet the babies."

Kara groaned, "Why do we pretend to like them?" she whined. "They're so annoying."

The loving father chuckled, his eyes sparkling with amusement. "Jason and Jayla are a bit eccentric, but I like them just fine. They're our friends."

The princess stared at him, wide-eyed. "Our friends? How can you consider them to be our friends? They lied to us and tried to take Mom away."

Nodding, Derrick agreed. "Yes, sweetie, they lied. But they had a reason for doing so. They were under royal orders. By no means does that justify them lying, but it does explain it. You and I both know how scary Reginald can be sometimes." Pausing, Derrick chuckled. "Put yourself in Jason and Jayla's shoes," he urged.

In that moment, Kara felt as though a fifty-pound weight had been lifted from her chest as a solution came to her. *Derrick and*

Misty would never approve, but desperate times call for desperate measures, she decided. "You're right, Dad," she relented after a moment. "The important thing is that, in the end, Jayla and Jason came clean and let us stay together. I promise I will be nice to them."

"That's my girl," Derrick praised. "Now go dance your heart out."

With that, the princess kissed Derrick on the cheek and went to the dance studio hoping to calm the nervous excitement she felt before, hopefully, recruiting two partners in crime.

Chapter 20

*W*hoa, I must've missed a memo on the dress code for this get together or something, Kara mused when Jason and Jayla showed up to the castle in a purple, sequin-covered, floor-length dress, and a white dress shirt and black slacks respectively.

A quick glance at her wide-eyed parents, confirmed that they, too, felt underdressed. *This should be an interesting afternoon,* she realized as Derrick led their excited guests into the informal dining room of the castle.

"You two look snazzy," Derrick complemented as they all sat down to lunch. "Is the university hosting a dance tonight or something?"

Laughing nervously, Jayla shook her head. "It's not every day we get invited to the castle. We weren't sure what to wear," she admitted.

Misty smiled. "Oh, I see. Well, Derrick is right. You both look very nice, but please know you don't need to dress so formally just to visit. We're all friends here."

"That's right," Derrick agreed. "These days I only give the castle chef time off to cook for our friends. I hope you like baked ziti."

"Awesome!" Jason exclaimed. "I'm starving and I love pasta. Did you make garlic bread too?"

These two make quite the pair, the princess mused, biting down on her bottom lip to stifle a laugh as Jayla elbowed her boyfriend's side. "Ow," he exclaimed. "What was that for?"

Kara focused on the plate of cheese covered pasta in front of her to keep from bursting into laughter as an angry look from Jayla made Jason practically jump out of his chair. "I-I, I mean, we- we're here to meet the twins," he stammered.

Shaking her head, Jayla let out an angry huff. "What Jason means to say is: it's great to see all of you. We appreciate this wonderful lunch and would love to meet the newest members of the royal family while we're here if that's okay."

After finishing a bit of ziti, Misty nodded. "Of course, you can meet the twins. They should be up from their afternoon nap in just a few minutes."

"Great!" Jayla exclaimed. "Tell us, what's it like having two new babies in the castle?" the young woman queried, her voice laced with excitement.

"Caring for the babies is a lot of hard work, but we love them and wouldn't have it any other way," the queen explained, her voice full of love and pride.

Derrick flashed a smile. "That's for sure," he agreed before biting into a piece of bread.

After finishing a bite of pasta, the princess shook her head vehemently. "A lot of work is an understatement. I love the twins, but I don't want a baby for a long time."

Chuckling good-naturedly, Misty looked at the little girl. "I'm glad to hear that sweetie. You have a whole life to live before you should even start thinking about babies."

"That's exactly right," Jayla agreed. "Jason and I are going to wait until after university, aren't we, hun?"

"Yeah. Whatever you say," the pimple-faced 20-something confirmed before shoveling a fork full of ziti into his mouth.

"Smart man," Derrick joked, eyeing the boy. "Seriously though, you two are young and have your whole lives ahead of you," he advised after a moment.

"Yep. And if you need a baby fix in the meantime, you're always welcome to help with Luke and–"

"Waahh, waaahhh, waahhh," the shrill, persistent cries of a baby in need sounded at that moment, interrupting the majestic.

Moments later, Marie rushed into the dining room, holding baby Lilly. "My apologies for the interruption of Your Majesties. I cannot get Miss Lilly to stop crying. I've fed her, changed her, and rocked her. I even sang a lullaby and she won't stop." Letting out a heavy sigh, the personal care assistant looked to Kara. "I think she needs her big sister's special touch."

Smiling, the princess backed away from the table and held her arms toward the crying baby. "Come here, baby sis," she coaxed. "We'll snuggle and make things better."

"Wow, you really do have a special touch," Jason complemented after the baby fell asleep on Kara's lap in a matter of minutes.

The little girl flashed a smile, exposing her beloved dimples. "Thank you. Mom and Dad say I'm a natural."

"Waahh," a distant cry once again stole the attention of the royal family and their guests.

"Master Luke awaits," Marie declared, standing up from the table. "Thank you so much for your help with the duchess, princess. I should be going now."

Shaking his head, Derrick disagreed. "Nonsense. We're almost finished with lunch. Let us tend to Lukie while you take a break."

Yawning, Marie nodded. "I could use a nap. Master Luke has already had his midafternoon feeding, so he probably just needs a good burping."

"Sure thing. Super Dad to the rescue," Derrick joked before taking Lilly from Kara and leading the family and their guests to the baby nursery.

Uh oh, looks like Lukie is still having a bad day, Kara realized as she and the others walked into the babies' room only to find the Duke of Starrycrest wailing in his crib.

"Aww, what's wrong little dude?" Jason asked, warily eyeing the sobbing baby.

"His tummy is probably upset. Marie said he needs to burp," the princess reminded them.

"Don't worry, Lukie. Daddy's here," Derrick soothed, lifting the baby out of his crib.

"Waaahhh, waahhh, waahhh," Lukie's crying intensified as the loving father gently patted his back. "Maybe Dad doesn't have this," he admitted after a couple of minutes. "Anyone else want to try and help my little man here?"

"I'll give it a whirl," Jayla offered, reaching her hands toward the baby.

The hazel-eyed, bubbly young woman smiled from ear to ear as Luke rested his head on her shoulder. Her smile fell into a frown moments later as he spit up, instantly sending milk down her sparkly dress.

Misty's cheeks instantly turned crimson. "Oh no!" she exclaimed. "Jayla, I'm so sorry. We should've thought to cover your dress. Marie is pretty good at getting stains out. I'll go–"

This is my chance to finally pull Jason and Jayla aside, Kara realized. "It's okay, Mom," she assured, quickly interrupting Misty. "Don't disturb Marie's nap. I got this. Jason, Jayla, come with me to the kitchen."

"Why do I gotta come?" Jason asked, his forehead wrinkled in confusion.

The princess let out a nervous laugh. "Well, I guess you don't have to come, but if ya do I'll show you guys where the good desserts are."

"Dessert? You don't have to ask me twice."

I hope I don't have to ask him what I'm about to ask him twice either, Kara mused as she led the young people to the castle kitchen.

"So, where did you get this dress anyway?" the princess dabbed at the spit stain with a washcloth.

"I actually made it myself," Jayla admitted, her voice meek and quiet.

"Wow, you made this gown yourself? It's gorgeous! You're really talented," Kara complimented as she dabbed at the stain a second time after adding baking soda to the washcloth.

"See? I'm not the only person who thinks you're talented," Jason said excitedly. "Tell her princess. Tell Jayla she should choose fashion design as her major," he urged.

Smiling, Kara nodded vehemently. "He's right. You could definitely be a designer. I can tell just based on this beautiful gown that you're really something."

Grinning, Jayla blushed. "Thanks, so are you. I can't believe you got the stain out that quickly," she looked at her wet yet otherwise blemish free dress, wide-eyed.

The princess shrugged. "It's nothing. I saw Betsy do it all the time at the group home."

"I bet things have really changed at the group home since you introduced the new kiddo keeper program. That was a really awesome idea by the way," Jason praised.

It's now or never, the tiny royal told herself as she worked up the nerves to tell them about her idea. Taking a breath, she looked from Jason to Jayla and back. "It's funny that you brought up Kiddo Keepers," she began.

"What do you mean?" Jayla questioned, her voice full of curiosity.

Over the next few minutes, Kara told them about Tyler and how his biological mother, the famous Zoe Hempster, suddenly popped back into his life with what she feared were not honest intentions.

Hanging his head, Jason sighed. "I'm sorry to hear that princess. Sounds like your little buddy Tyler has had it rough."

Shaking her head, Jayla frowned. "Yeah and I agree Zoe popping up out of nowhere after so many years seems fishy but I'm not sure what anyone can do about it. Zoe is his mother after all."

Fidgeting in her chair, the princess looked down at her feet. "Funny you should say that," she admitted. "I was hoping you guys could look into Zoe for me."

Eyebrows furrowed, Jason eyed the little girl warily. "Look into her how?" he asked.

Taking a deep breath, the princess divulged her idea to have the two of them go undercover and befriend Zoe to find out her true motivation for becoming a kiddo keeper.

Frowning, Jason bent down to Kara's level. "I know you want to help your friend, little one, but I'm not sure my girl and I goin' undercover again is a good idea. If queen Misty hadn't talked her father into havin' mercy on us, we would've been the youngest prisoners in Starryton history."

The princess opened her mouth to object, but closed it when Jayla spoke first, eyeing Jason, annoyed.

"Oh c'mon, babe, where is your sense of adventure? You know I've always wanted to meet *the* Zoe Hempster. This is the perfect way to not only meet her but get to know her and help the princess at the same time. Please say we can do it," she urged excitedly.

Groaning, Jason hung his head. "Our adventures are always getting us into trouble. Can't you go on this one without me?"

Pouting, Jayla reached for Jason's hand and squeezed it. "You and I both know going on an adventure solo is no fun. Help me and I'll do your algebra homework for a month."

Flashing a mischievous grin, Jason relented. "Make it two months and ya got yourself a deal."

I can't believe I actually talked them into helping me, Kara mused as she grabbed one of Tony's peanut butter pies from the fridge. *Now I just have to hope we can all help Tyler,* she realized as they headed back to the informal dining room to enjoy the pie.

***

"Oh my gosh, Ty, are you okay?" Kara asked by way of greeting as her dance partner walked into the schoolhouse with dark circles under his eyes. "You look like you haven't slept." Pausing, the princess lowered her voice. "And I think your shirt is on inside out," she pointed out, eyeing him warily.

Yawning, Tyler shrugged. "I'm lucky I've even got a shirt on. I'm so tired. Stella may act like a drill sergeant sometimes, but she ain't got nothin' on Zoe."

The princess scrunched her eyebrows in confusion. "Huh?"

The spiky-haired boy yawned again, wiping sand from his eyes. "All Zoe ever wants to do is dance," he divulged. "And she is constantly yacking about how I need to become just as good, if not a better dancer than she is. I look forward to school these days just for the break," he admitted.

Kara's mouth dropped open in disbelief. "Whoa, if you're actually looking forward to school things must—"

"Good morning boys and girls," Ms. Ryder declared, cutting off the chatter of Kara and Tyler as well as many of their classmates as she entered the schoolhouse.

How am I supposed to concentrate on anyone's history presentation when I know that Zoe is about three seconds away from turning Tyler into a dancing zombie? Kara mused as she struggled to concentrate on Tiphany's presentation about Edwin Peterson, who founded the kingdom's library. *I knew that Zoe becoming a kiddo keeper was fishy. If the way she's treating Tyler doesn't prove it then I don't know what will.*

Sighing, she shook her head. *Who am I kidding? Mom and Dad will need more proof than that before doing anything to make things right. I hope Jayla and Jason get the dirt soon. They may be the only hope Tyler has at being happy again.*

A moment later, the young couple appeared at the door of the schoolhouse as though they had heard the princess's thoughts.

Miss Ryder let out a huff as Jason tapped lightly on the door. "Miss Brewer, Mr. Anders, didn't you graduate a couple of years ago? Why are you interrupting my students' history lesson?" the teacher demanded, eyeing them suspiciously as she approached.

Taking a step back, Jason put space between himself and the frustrated educator.

"We did graduate, Miss. Ryder," Jayla insisted, her voice coated in anxiety as she spoke up. "We're here to discuss some urgent business with the future queen. It should only be a couple of minutes and we even have a note from his majesty," she explained, shifting her weight from one side to the other while handing Miss Ryder a piece of parchment.

Accepting the note, the teacher glanced at it briefly and sighed, relenting. "Okay, go on ahead, but make it quick," she urged. "The princess has a class to get back to and an education to continue."

Having heard what the anxious young couple said, Kara joined the conversation. "Thank you, Ms. Ryder, Jason and Jayla are my friends. If they have an urgent message, then I should hear it. I promise we'll be quick," she said before joining the twenty somethings outside.

"What's up, guys? Did you find out why Zoe became a kiddo keeper?" the princess pried once they were out of earshot of anyone in the classroom.

Grinning from ear to ear, Jason nodded. "We sure did and let me tell you you're never gonna believe the reason behind it. I mean I hardly believe it and she told me herself."

"For once this goofball is right. The reason is unbelievable," Jayla agreed.

The princess sighed, rolling her eyes. "Guys, please just spit it out already. Ms. Ryder said we gotta be quick."

"The producers of Dare to Dance told Zoe that they will replace her if the show's ratings don't go up in the next couple of weeks," Jayla blurted out.

The princess's eyebrows wrinkled in confusion. "What do the Dare to Dance ratings have to do with becoming a kiddo keeper and getting Tyler back?" she asked.

"Zoe's tryin' to make your little buddy as good a dancer as she is, so he can become her partner on the show and save it," Jason explained.

The princess stared at her older friends in disbelief, her eyebrows still wrinkled in confusion.

"I used to admire Zoe, but the more we got to know her the more I realized she's just plain selfish," Jayla admitted. "She pretty much told me that she doesn't have a maternal bone in her body. She's just trying to take advantage of Tyler's 15 minutes of fame and exploit the mother-son angle."

How can anyone be that cold? Kara wondered as silence settled between the three of them.

"I'm sorry we don't have better news, little one," Jason offered a moment later, his voice solemn and quiet.

"Me too," Jayla agreed. If there's anything else we can do to help you or Tyler let us know."

Tears filled Kara's eyes as she returned to the classroom. *How do I tell Tyler that Zoe only wants him in her life because she's using him? Knowing your parents didn't want you is one thing but knowing that they are using you is another thing entirely. I can't even imagine how sad and angry he's going to be.*

As the princess pulled up to her desk next to him, Tyler leaned over and whispered, "You okay there, partner? What did Tweedledee and Tweedledum say? Ya look like they told ya romantic comedies were outlawed or something."

Fidgeting in her wheelchair, Kara looked down at her feet as she contemplated her response.

She opened her mouth to answer, but instead let out a sigh of relief when Ms. Ryder spoke first, "Mr. Hempster show your classmates respect and cease talking during presentations please."

A spelling test, a discussion about photosynthesis, and an introduction to pottery made it easy for Kara to avoid her dance partner for the remainder of the afternoon, but the moment the bell rang, signaling the end of the school day, Tyler looked to her expectantly . "Okay, spill. You've avoided me all day. Tell me what's going on," he insisted.

I guess I should rip off the band-aid so to speak, the princess decided. Taking a deep breath, she told her dance partner about how she'd gotten Jayla and Jason to investigate Zoe and what they had subsequently found out.

"I knew it," Tyler muttered before practically storming out of the schoolhouse.

"Ty, where are you going?" Kara called as she raced after him.

"I'm going to take care of this issue with Zoe," Tyler spoke as though his explanation was painfully obvious as he continued walking. "You can come with me or go home to the castle. It's up to you, but if you're gonna come along try and keep up," he urged.

"Ty, I'm not going to let you go off by yourself when you're all angry and upset like this. I don't think this is a good idea. You should take some time to calm down and think about what you want to say before confronting Zoe," she suggested.

"Did you take any time to calm down before you went to see Victrollia?" the spiky-haired boy asked through gritted teeth.

The princess sighed. "Oh, all right, I'll come with you, but, if we get grounded for this, you have to tell my parents that leaving school was your idea and I shouldn't lose my dance studio privileges."

Tyler groaned. "If ya would shut up for a second, you'd recognize this neighborhood and know I'm not confronting Zoe," he yelled.

Stopping cold, Kara glanced around, taking in her surroundings. *Tyler wants to confide in Stella,* she realized, instantly recognizing the sky-blue shutters on the front of the dance instructor's house. *I hope Stella knows what to say to make Tyler feel better,* the little girl thought as he knocked on the front door.

The pink-haired woman's eyes went wide as she opened the door. "What are ya kiddos doin' here?" she asked, her voice full of alarm. "Is everything okay?"

"It's good to see you too, Stella," Tyler said. "I need to talk to ya. Can we come in?"

Stepping aside, Stella gave the children room to enter, "You guys are always welcome here. Come on in and tell us what's on your mind."

"Us?" the children questioned simultaneously.

"Hon, who's at the door? Your tomato soup is gonna get cold," a familiar voice called out.

"Tony, my man, what ya doin' here?" Tyler questioned as they walked into the kitchen.

"Hey, bud, I could be askin' you the same thing. We haven't seen you for a bit. How're ya doin'?"

"I'm good. I just came to talk to Stella. Did I hear somethin' about tomato soup?"

"Sure did. Made grilled cheese too. Grilled cheese and tomato soup go together like peanut butter and jelly. There's plenty to go around. Come have a seat." Smiling at the princess he added, "You too, little lady. Come tell us what life is like as a big sister."

"Being a big sister is great," Kara said as she pulled up to the table, "but we're actually here to talk about something more serious."

"Okay, kiddos. We're ready. Spill your guts," the larger-than-life chef urged, after serving the others and joining them at the table.

"In short, we're here because Zoe is a lyin', connivin' snake and I don't wanna live with her anymore. I'd really rather be with you, Stella, so I was wonderin' if ya would go with me to talk to Judge Clairmont about it. What do you say?" the young boy rushed his words, enthusiastically chomping into his grilled cheese sandwich.

Wow, apparently Tyler's not going to sugarcoat this. Oh, who am I kidding? Kara mused. *Tyler never sugarcoats anything. This should be interesting.*

Eyes widened, Stella deliberately put down her spoon and looked at Tyler. "I'm gonna need a little more information here, kiddo."

Tony, who had also stopped eating, scoffed. "Hold the 'little'. You owe a lot of explainin'."

"What's there to explain?" Tyler questioned. "When this whole mess with Zoe screwed up the good thing that we had goin' you said I could come to ya if I ever needed anything. Well, I need somethin'. I need to live somewhere where I won't go insane or risk my toes fallin' off." Tyler spoke as though the solution to his predicament were the easiest thing in the world to understand, but the bewildered looks on Tony and Stella faces told Kara that they thought it was anything but easy to understand.

Her suspicion was confirmed when Stella eyed him once again, her eyebrows wrinkled in confusion. "Huh?"

I better help Tyler before they get any more confused, the young royal decided as she continued to eat her soup.

After a moment, she put down her spoon, smiled and offered, "Allow me to shed some light on the situation."

Over the next few minutes, Kara brought Tony and Stella up to speed, telling them what had been discovered about Zoe's motives for becoming a kiddo keeper.

When the tiny royal had finished her explanation, Tony shook his head in disgust. "What kind of person takes advantage of a child?"

"Like I said, the woman is an absolute snake. So, what do you say, Stella? Are ya willing to put up with me again?" Tyler asked eagerly. "Can I move back in with ya?"

Fidgeting with her chest, Stella focused on her grilled cheese sandwich, avoiding eye contact with the young boy.

Uh oh, why does Stella seem so uncomfortable all the sudden? Kara wondered as she watched the dance instructor's cheeks turn from pink to red.

Reaching for Stella's hand, Tony grasped it as though he too sensed her uneasiness. "Who lives here isn't just up to me anymore, Ty," she said after a long moment.

"What do ya mean?" Tyler asked after finishing the last of his grilled cheese. "This is your house."

Shaking his head, Tony grinned. "Correction. Stella and I share this house now. I moved in last week."

Tyler's eyes brightened with excitement. "Awesome. I'm totally down to live with both of you guys."

Oh my gosh! Kara mused. *It's about to happen. I just know it. Tyler's going to be with his for–*

"Not so fast, bud," Stella cautioned, interrupting the little girl's thought. "Do ya have any proof of Zoe's motives?"

Tyler shrugged. "What proof do ya need? Isn't my word and the word of the future queen enough?" he asked pointedly.

Uh oh, this isn't going to end well. The tiny royal cringed as she struggled to think of a way to diffuse the tension.

Nodding, Stella agreed. "I know you're a young man of your word, Ty, but Judge Clairmont may need a little more convincin'. You made it clear last time we saw him that you would rather live with me than Zoe and he said that would only happen if he was given substantial evidence that she's an unfit mother. Do you really think that havin' a couple young people confirm your belief that she only took interest in you because you can dance is enough?" Stella chuckled as she posed the question as though the very idea of such evidence holding up in court was absurd.

Shaking his head, Tyler scoffed, "I don't know, Stella. From where I'm sitting, it sounds like you need a little more convincing of my character too. Well, ya know what? I don't have to convince you or the judge that I'm being honest. I am gonna get that proof," the young boy declared, his voice edged with anger.

Whoa… this is totally not where I saw this conversation going. Tyler is really angry. I better do something to ease the tension fast, Kara decided as she continued to ponder how to do so. *Oh, I know. I'll tell them about how Lilly giggled for the first time the other day. No one can be angry after hearing a story about a cute little baby.*

Flashing a nervous smile, the princess opened her mouth to tell the story, but stayed silent when Tyler spoke first, his voice laced with a mixture of anger and disappointment.

"And after I have proof, I am gonna find people even better than you and Tony who are happy to have me as part of their family."

Tony shook his head. "C'mon, bud, don't say that. Ya know Stella and I care for you very much."

Nodding vehemently, the hazel-eyed woman agreed, "That's right, we care about ya. Tyler, please understand. I didn't mean to make it sound like—"

"Save it," Tyler yelled, cutting her off. "I know when I'm not wanted," he insisted.

Standing up from the table, the young boy looked to his dance partner. "Thanks for tryin' to help, Kara. See ya at school tomorrow," he murmured before turning to leave.

"Tyler, wait!" Stella pleaded, tears forming in her eyes her eyes.

"Please just give us a minute to explain, little man," Tony added urgently.

Ignoring the adults' pleas, Tyler wordlessly walked out the door without looking back.

*****

So much for diffusing the situation, the princess sighed as she backed away from the table and turned to leave.

"Kara… wait!" Stella called out, her voice breaking slightly as tears streamed down her face. "Please try and make Tyler understand. He changed everything. I just don't think I could bear to lose him a second time," she sniffled, continuing to cry.

"What are you talking about?" Kara asked, rolling back to her spot at the table.

After giving Stella's hand a supportive squeeze, Tony spoke for her. "After losing Madam Sterling, Stella promised herself that she would never become a kiddo keeper because she couldn't bear the possibility of losing a family again, but you and your scheme changed that." Pausing, he flashed a sad smile then continued. "Tyler went and wormed his way into her heart." Shaking his head, Tony let out a sad chuckle. "Heck, the little man captured both of our hearts if I'm bein' honest."

Nodding, a still crying Stella agreed. "Exactly," she sniffled. "That's why I asked him to stay even after you went home to your family. The three of us were just beginning to feel like a family of our own when we lost him to Zoe. I can't go through that again. I just can't!" Overcome with sadness, Stella collapsed into Tony's shoulder and broke into heaving sobs.

I knew I wasn't off-base. I really need to learn to trust my instincts. Despite the melancholy moment, the idea that things might still work out after all filled the little girl's heart. *It's clear that*

Stella, Tony, and Tyler care for each other and want to be a family. I just need to help them see it. In that moment, a piece of advice that both Derrick and Stella had given the little girl popped into her head. Flashing a sad smile, she addressed her friend and dance instructor. "Stella, I know it doesn't seem like it now, but it's going to be okay. I really should catch up with Tyler, but I'll leave you with this piece of advice. Learn to love the way you dance. It makes life much more fun."

"Ty, wait," Kara shouted as she raced out of the house to catch up with him.

Shaking his head, Tyler refused. "No, I can't slow down. I have to get to Zoe's and figure out how I'm gonna prove that she's a lyin', dancin' dictator."

"About that… I was remembering what Jason and Jayla told me about Dare to Dance and if you'll go along with just one more of my crazy plans, I have an idea that would allow you to show the entire kingdom what Zoe Hempster is really like."

Oh, thank goodness! I can finally catch up. Kara let out a sigh of relief as her dance partner slowed to a stop, contemplating his response. "Oh, what the heck?" he murmured after a moment. "It's not like I have any other ideas."

With that, Kara divulged her plan in hopes it would be as successful as her plan to establish a kiddo keeper program in the kingdom and Tyler could be happy again.

Chapter 21

"You ready for this, Ty?" Kara whispered, sneaking up behind him as he waited backstage in Starrycrest Theater.

"Oh, jeez," Tyler exclaimed, jumping at the sound of her voice.

"Sorry. Didn't mean to startle you. I just wanted to come check on ya and make sure you're still up for this," Kara explained, her voice still stiff and quiet.

"It's too late to back out now," Tyler scoffed.

"Don't worry. Everything will be fine," Kara assured him. "You're just helping people to see the truth. Things will change for you once everyone catches a glimpse of the real Zoe Hempster."

Tyler's eyes widened as he heard Andre Anderson, the host of Dare to Dance, say, "The next person competing to be the lovely Zoe's partner is her long-lost son, Tyler. Zoe, my darling, do you think Starrycrest's most popular young male dancer has what it takes to be your partner?"

"I hope you're right. Here goes nothing," Tyler whispered as he waited for his cue to go on stage.

Kara joined Misty and Derrick in the audience just in time to see Zoe grab the microphone from Andre and declare, "Oh, I don't think it. I know it. Tyler takes after me. I can confidently say he's the hardest working young dancer in the kingdom."

Chuckling, Andre nodded and took back the microphone. "Obviously, Zoe is not what one would call impartial, so we brought in three dance experts to help judge her partner hopefuls," he explained. "Each of the amazing Zoe Hempster's potential partners has been asked to prepare an original dance piece. The judges will score each dancer and their performance on creativity, form, and execution, but before we get to all that fun, let's meet our esteemed judges, shall we?"

The princess tried to concentrate as Andre began introducing the judges, but her mind had other ideas. *I hope this works out like I think it will. If it doesn't and Tyler looks dumb in front of the entire kingdom, he'll never forgive me,* she fretted internally.

"Sweetheart, Tyler's up next," Misty whispered from her seat next to the little girl. "Cross your fingers."

Oh, my gosh! What are Misty and Derrick going to think when they see this? Should I have let them in on the plan? she wondered. Shaking her head, the tiny royal quickly dismissed the thought. *Nah, if I had, they would've never agreed to push for Dare to Dance to be recorded live here in Starrycrest. Now all I can do is hope for the best,* she decided, sucking in a breath as Tyler raced onto the stage, causing his pointe shoes to come off in the process.

After racing through the process of lacing his shoes back on, Tyler laid down and rolled from one side of the stage to the other. Despite the nerves she'd been feeling, Kara burst into laughter as her friend topped off his performance by getting on all fours and crawling off stage. *For such a talented dancer, Tyler really does know how to throw a performance,* she mused. *That wasn't even dancing. That was... I'm not sure what it was.* Glancing at the confused expressions of the judges told the princess that they, too, were puzzled by Tyler's performance. *That's my cue,* Kara realized as a thin-lipped, wide-eyed, Zoe headed backstage after Tyler.

As Kara went to set the next part of the plan into motion, Misty put a gentle hand on the princess's shoulder and whispered, "Where are you headed?"

"After a performance like that, I really need to see what's up with Ty."

"That's so sweet of you! Your dad and I will see you in a bit." The doting mother whispered.

Smiling from ear to ear, the princess made her way over to the television crew. "Excuse me, sir," she said sweetly as she approached a man with a long beard and ice blue eyes holding a camera. "I think there's something goin' on backstage you need to see."

Resting the camera on his shoulder, the man held his hand out to the little girl. "The name's Roger."

Accepting his hand, the princess shook it. "Nice to meet you, Roger. I'm–"

"I know who you are, princess. What do you think I need to see?"

"Follow me and bring your camera," the tiny royal urged, leading him backstage. *Whoa, I knew Zoe would be mad that Tyler threw his performance piece, but I didn't know she'd go nuclear. Poor Tyler,* Kara's eyes widened when she and Roger snuck backstage just in time to see the famous ballerina back her dance partner into a corner.

"How dare you embarrass me in front of the entire kingdom after all I've done for you. You made me look like an idiot. You better hope my agent can think of a way to spin this and save my career."

Chuckling angrily, Tyler shook his head. "You haven't done anything for me!" he shouted. "Everything we've done since you blew up my life by comin' back into it has been to try to save your stupid career and make you look good."

Uh oh, now things are gonna get really interesting, Kara realized, her eyes grew even wider as her parents, Stella, and Tony headed backstage just in time to hear Tyler say, "Well, I'm done. I threw the performance because I don't wanna be your partner. I don't want anything to do with you anymore."

"Kara, sweetheart, what's going on here?" Derrick whispered urgently.

"Just hold on. You'll see," she assured. Biting her lower lip, the princess fidgeted nervously in her chair as Zoe lowered herself to Tyler's level, so they were nose to nose.

"I am a famous ballerina and you're nothing more than an ungrateful little brat. You don't get to leave me. I'm leaving you. I don't want you. I never wanted you," the irate ballerina said curtly. "And I'll tell you one more thing," she added, practically spitting the words at him. "After seeing that pathetic performance, no one else in the kingdom will ever want you either."

"Mom, Dad, let Tyler say what he needs to say then you can step in, okay?" Kara pleaded, grasping Derrick's hand as he stepped forward to intervene at Misty's whispered urging.

Scoffing, Tyler shook his head at Zoe. "I wouldn't be so sure about that. People may change their opinion of me when they find out why I threw my performance."

Throwing her head back, the ballerina let out a sarcastic laugh. "No one is going to find out. Even if you try to convince this kingdom's pathetic little princess, no one will believe either of you because, like I said before, I'm a respected ballerina and you're a nobody."

Glancing at Roger, who was still recording, Tyler smirked. "You're the one who is going to be a nobody once the kingdom sees who you really are. Isn't that right, Roger?"

Nodding slightly, the camera man agreed and continued to record. "Smile for the camera, Ms. Hempster."

Following the cameraman's voice, Zoe's eyes widened in horror as she realized they had an audience and were being taped. "Oh my God! You set me up!" she screamed.

"I just helped people see who you really are," Tyler said smugly, flashing a smile at the camera.

"That's it!" Zoe declared, her face turning a deep shade of crimson. "I don't care who sees, or what happens to me, I'm going to wipe that stupid grin right off your face," she shouted, raising her hand to him.

Whoa, I've never seen Tony move so fast, Kara mused as the larger-than-life chef charged forward and grasped Zoe's hand while it was still in midair. "Touch one hair on that little dude's head and I swear on my Grandma Anita's chicken parm recipe, I'll twist ya into a pretzel and you'll never, ever dance again," Tony grumbled angrily, tightening his hold on her hand.

"That will not be necessary, Tony," Misty assured, using the authoritative tone she typically reserved for personal audiences. "Zoe is no longer welcome in Starrycrest. These fine gentlemen are going to personally make sure she gets settled far away… perhaps in Embersville," she explained, before two 300-pound gentleman came and escorted a still red-faced, screaming Zoe out of the back door of the theater.

"That was epic!" Tyler let out as the door closed behind Zoe and her escorts. "Kara, I can't believe your crazy plan actually worked."

Rolling her eyes, the princess shook her head. "Whatever. My plans always work."

"Mind letting us in on what you kiddos are talking about?" Derrick inquired, looking from Kara to Tyler and back.

"Well, in short, I told Stella and Tony, that Zoe only became a kiddo keeper because she wanted to take advantage of my dancing ability and Stella said she needed proof before she'd do anything about it. So, Kara and I came up with a way to show her and the rest of the kingdom the real Zoe Hempster," Tyler explained, smirking proudly.

Derrick nodded as the boy's explanation sank in.

"Kara, did you talk Mom and I into letting Dare to Dance film here in Starrycrest just to help Tyler?"

"A future queen's gotta do what a future queen's gotta do," the princess chuckled. "Besides, if you can't count on your dance partner, who can you count on?"

The loving father flashed a proud smile. "You, my sweet girl, are really something."

"Ya can say that again," Stella agreed. "You kiddos both keep us on our toes." Looking at Tyler, the pink-haired dancer sighed. "I'm so sorry you had to go through all this to prove your point, bud. I should've listened to you," she said solemnly.

"We should have listened to you," Tony corrected, grasping her hand as he approached.

"Whatever, man, thanks for saving me from a handprint to the face. Throwing a performance is actually pretty exhaustin', so I'm gonna find Betsy and see if I can go back to the group home and call it a night," he responded, walking toward the door to the theater auditorium.

"Ty, wait, stop, I was hopin' we could talk," Stella called out.

The boy shook his head, continuing to walk away. "What's there to talk about? You made it clear you don't want me."

"No, you don't understand!" the dance instructor exclaimed, her tone desperate. "That's not it at all. I love you as if you were my own."

Stopping in his tracks, Tyler turned to face her, eyebrows furrowed questioningly. "You do?"

Nodding, Stella pulled him into a hug. "Yes, bud, I do," she assured, giving him a tight squeeze.

Tyler gave Stella a quick squeeze back then pulled away, looking even more puzzled. "Then why did you say the things you said when Kara and I came for to see you?" he asked.

"I was scared, Ty," Stella admitted, her pink cheeks turning a deep red.

"But you never seem scared of anything," Tyler argued.

"Well, 1 feared losing you again. I just didn't think I could survive it a second time."

"What are you sayin'?" Tyler questioned, his eyebrows furrowed even more than moments before.

Why can't these two just stop being so stubborn and listen to each other? Kara sighed as she hid in the corner quietly, listening to the exchange between her friends despite Misty advising her to give them privacy.

"Hon, why don't you tell him what you told the princess the other day," Tony suggested.

Taking a deep breath, Stella looked Tyler straight in the eye and said, "Kiddo, as much as I fancy myself an independent woman who needs no one, I've always wanted a family. Madam Sterling was the closest I came. It was so painful when I lost her that I promised myself I'd never open up again." Pausing, the ballet enthusiast flashed a smile. "Well, all of that changed when I met you. You opened me up. What I'm sayin' is I'm open to the two of us being a family if you'll have me."

The princess smiled as Tyler responded by pulling Stella in for another hug and saying, "'course I will."

"Uh, well, I'm sure you two are going to make the best family around, but I'd like to suggest somethin'," Tony said after a long moment. "This isn't exactly the way I planned it and it probably would be cooler if I wasn't pullin' a page from his majesty's book, but what the heck, there's no time like the present, right?"

The tiny royal, who was still watching couldn't help but giggle quietly as Tyler and Stella both eyed him, confused. *How are those two so oblivious?* she wondered. *Tony couldn't be any more obvious if he tried.*

The princess smiled as the beloved chef dropped to his knee and pulled something from his pocket, confirming her suspicion.

"Can I join your family as a husband and father?" he proposed, his usually confident voice quiet and slightly shaky.

Yay! I called it! I knew they'd make a perfect family for each other! Kara smiled as Stella threw her arms around Tony and answered, "Oh, my goodness! Yes, of course, that'd be wonderful!"

Smiling from ear to ear, Tony slid a ring onto her finger.

Stella gasped as she looked at her ring finger and saw that she wore a delicate rose gold band featuring a shiny, cushion cut opal. "Oh, my gosh! Is this what I think it is?" she gushed.

Tony smiled, his eyes sparkling with love and amusement. "If you're thinking it is Madam Sterling's, then you're absolutely correct, sweetheart."

"Unbelievable," she gasped. "I admired this ring whenever I noticed it in her old photos. The rose gold has always reminded me of pointe shoes. Before she passed, I got up the nerve to ask her for it and was disappointed when she told me she'd given it to a boy who stayed with her briefly and became like a son. I can't believe that was you and that now ya have given it to me."

Tony nodded, still smiling. "Believe it, darling. When Madam Sterling gave it to me, she told me to make sure I gave it to the perfect woman for me, and well, I can't think of anyone that fits that bill more than you, my lady," he explained, kissing her lips softly.

"Eww, must you guys do that in front of me?" Tyler joked, shielding his eyes as the newly engaged couple continued to kiss.

Pulling away from Tony, Stella laughed, her hazel eyes alight with love. "Sorry, bud. I got carried away. I should've talked to you before sayin' yes. After all, you and I are a package deal now."

Flashing, a hesitant smile, Tyler eyed them. "So, you two are gonna be my mom and dad now… like forever?"

"Yes, bud, you're stuck with me," Stella confirmed.

"Me too," Tony agreed. "At least that's the plan if ya are on board."

"Totally!" the young boy almost screamed his response.

After the three shared a group hug, Tony smiled at Tyler. "I'm glad to hear you're on board with us becoming a family, Ty. I have somethin' for you to help commemorate this occasion as well."

Kara couldn't help but giggle again as her dance partner eyed Tony and said, "Hey man, I'm cool with you bein' my dad and all, but I'm not the ring wearin' type. Ya know that don'cha?"

Throwing his head back, Tony laughed and retrieved something else from his pocket. "Don't worry, little dude. I don't have a ring for ya. Instead, I have this," he exclaimed, holding the gift out to the boy.

Tyler's mouth dropped open as he accepted the gift from Tony. "Is this real gold?"

"It sure is. This was my grandfather's pocket watch. He always wanted me to pass it on to my son someday, and now, I am," he explained, his voice thoughtful and quiet.

"Are you sure ya want me to have it?" Tyler questioned, skeptically eyeing the family heirloom.

How is Tyler still questioning him after everything that just happened? Sighing, the princess came out of hiding.

"Ty, for cryin' out loud, just thank him for the watch and accept that this is happening. I was right. You've found a family. Now, all you have to do is love them the way you dance."

"Says the girl who took over two years to refer to her parents as Mom and Dad," Tyler quipped.

"Exactly! I don't want you to make the same mistake I did," Kara urged. "If our time with Stella taught me anything it's that, to be part of a family, you have to embrace them and allow them to embrace you. You don't let worries and self-doubt get in the way when you dance. Well, you can't let those things get in the way of your life either. You have to live and love the way you dance," she insisted.

"Kara's right," Stella urged. "I wouldn't have the courage to be part of a family with you and Tony had she not reminded me of that."

"Okay, I get it," Tyler nodded. "Obviously, I'm new at this family thing but I will do the best I can," he smiled, carefully placing the heirloom watch in his pocket.

"Great!" the princess exclaimed. "I guess this means that another one of my crazy plans worked. I knew as soon as I saw the three of you together that you were meant to be a family."

This is so great! If Tyler and I both found our forever families, then there's no reason every orphan can't find theirs as well, Kara realized, feeling more confident in Starrycrest's Kiddo Keepers than ever, as she and her parents took their friends to the castle for a night of celebration.

Epilogue

Three months later

"I can't believe I let Derrick talk me into this," Kara whispered as she entered a packed Starrycrest Square with her family as well as Tyler's family to be in tow.

Throwing his head back, Tyler chuckled. "Says the girl who sweet talked me into taking over Dare to Dance."

The smells of chocolate and fried dough wafting through the air, coupled with upbeat melodies, a giant glittering Ferris Wheel, an enthusiastic face painter, an eager magician, and the overall sense of happiness that filled the atmosphere should have brought her joy, but the overall magnitude of what was about to happen left her stomach in knots.

"I can dance in front of all these people any day, but this is different. This is so important. It's a start to a whole new life for many people here."

Tyler nodded. "You're right. Today is the start of a new life for many of us, includin' me, who wouldn't have a new life if it weren't for you. Bein' a princess may not have been your birthright, but you were born to do it. Today wouldn't be possible at all without ya."

"I couldn't have said that better myself," Derrick agreed, kneeling to Kara's level. Taking her hand, he squeezed it gently and attempted to reassure her. "Ty is right. You were born to do this. Days like today are part of your destiny. I know you can do this and that you will continue to do great things for Starrycrest. That's why I named you future queen."

Nodding, Misty flashed a smile. "I agree. This, sweetheart, is only the beginning of the great things you'll do for this kingdom. Now get on up there," the loving mother coaxed. "Judge Clairmont is starting."

"I need to see my favorite twins first for good luck," she insisted. After placing a gentle kiss on each baby's head, Kara focused on the judge as he approached the podium that had been constructed and placed in the center of Starrycrest Square just for the occasion.

"Good afternoon everyone. Thank you for being here to mark this momentous occasion," the elderly man began. "I have to admit that I never thought a day like this would come. As an old man, I've lived long enough to understand that family bonds are about more than biology or DNA. Time and wisdom have shown me that true familial bonds require nothing more than unconditional love and acceptance. I've been trying for years to help my fellow citizens understand that, and well—" Pausing for a moment, he smiled from ear to ear, considering what to say next. After a long moment, he chuckled and said, "Despite my best efforts, I was outsmarted by a little girl. She was not just any little girl, but a little girl who this kingdom has come to know, love, and respect due, at least in part, to the miracle of adoption, our beloved princess and future queen, Kara Marie Denison."

Aww, why did he have to go and start crying? Kara sighed as she spotted moisture behind the elderly man's eyes. *Now I'm gonna go tearing up before I even get up there. Oh, what am I thinking?* the princess mused. *I'm going to cry a ton of tears today anyway. At least the tears are tears of happiness,* the little girl thought as she smiled and tried to focus on what the elderly judge was saying.

"I had the esteemed honor of signing the princess's adoption into effect a couple of years ago. While I like to think I've done a lot of good for this kingdom, I know I will never do anything better for us than when I signed that piece of paper. When I signed it, I legally made that little girl a member of the royal family and gave her the power to make a difference. Adoptions were once a rare occurrence here in Starrycrest, but thanks to the princess's introduction of a kiddo keeper program here in our kingdom, we are here today to make multiple adoptions official. This momentous day would not have been possible without the princess and her unwavering persistence; so, it seems only appropriate for me to pass the torch, so to speak, and allow her to mark this extraordinary occasion. So, without further ado, princess, will you come up here please?" Judge Clairmont addressed, his voice sweet and full of excitement.

Smiling from ear to ear, Kara wheeled her way up to the podium and addressed the crowd. "Hello everyone and welcome to Starrycrest's first annual Forever Family Festival. Today, I am beyond excited to have the honor of making seven forever families official. That's more adoptions than have ever been signed in one day in Starrycrest. I am ecstatic to be saying that and I want to congratulate each of the families here for having the courage to open your hearts to one another. I know from firsthand experience how difficult that can be, but I also understand just how beneficial it can be to your life. It all clicked after my friends and family told me to love the way I dance."

"You're so pretty when you dance," a toddler with beautiful amber eyes and long chestnut brown hair standing at the front of the crowd complimented sweetly.

Kara smiled at the tiny girl, her eyes bright with happiness. "Thank you, sweet pea. You are very pretty too." Still smiling, the princess turned her attention back to the entire crowd. "I am often given compliments like the one that beautiful little girl just gave me because when I dance I lead with my heart. I've learned that, when it comes to being part of a family, you must also lead with your heart. As your families become official today, remember that it isn't a piece of paper that makes a family a family, but rather the love you feel for one another, and when it comes to love you must lead with your heart. Now, let's get some adoption papers signed so we can enjoy the Ferris Wheel, shall we?"

"I can't believe you're makin' us go last on a day like this," Tyler said, as he, Tony, and Stella approached the podium after six other families. "What kind of friend and dance partner are you?" he joked.

Smiling, the tiny royal waved a dismissive hand. "Oh c'mon, Ty, you gotta know I saved the best for last."

"You got that right," Stella agreed, grinning from ear to ear, her eyes sparkling with love and happiness. "Now let's do this so that we can get on with celebratin' and stuffin' our faces with funnel cakes."

"Sweetheart, I can make ya funnel cakes at home anytime ya want. Ya don't need a festival as an excuse," Tony assured her.

The pink-haired woman's eyes widened as she looked to her significant other. "I knew there was a reason I married you," she gushed, kissing him softly on the lips.

"Gross," Tyler exclaimed, scrunching his nose in disgust. "Can we please do this before they get any more lovey dovey?"

Looking from Tyler to a still kissing Stella and Tony, and back, the future queen of Starrycrest laughed. "Okay, okay, I'll sign it, but you have to promise me something first."

Rolling his eyes, Tyler grinned. "From now on, I promise to love Stella and Tony the way I dance. Now, will you sign the stupid paper?" he insisted.

"Remember what she said, kiddo," Stella urged, placing a hand on his shoulder. "We're a family because we love each other. Not because of some piece of paper."

"Your beautiful mama is right," Tony confirmed. Looking at Kara he smiled and added, "Little lady, I guarantee that the Mrs. and I will lead with our hearts when it comes to lovin' this knucklehead."

With that, Kara dipped her ring into ink, proudly sealed the order making her dance partner's adoption official, and spent the rest of the day with her family enjoying every attraction and treat the festival had to offer. From that day forward, the Denisons, the Cacciatores, and every other forever family in Starrycrest lived happily ever after.

ABOUT THE AUTHOR

Allison M. Boot, otherwise known as the Wheelin' Wordsmith, wrote this story to spread a message of self-acceptance to young adults and children traveling paths similar to hers. She earned a Master of Arts in Mass Communication from the University of Dayton and currently resides in Urbana, Illinois with her husband, Dylan. In addition to writing books, she also advocates for the rights of those with disabilities as a contributing writer for Yahoo Lifestyle and The Mighty. She is also the owner of an extensive troll doll collection, started at the tender age of three, after being told that they bring good luck. To this day, her large collection continues to grow and do just that.

WANT TO CONNECT WITH THE WHEELIN' WORDSMITH ?

Join her mailing list by visiting www.allisonmbootauthor.com, where you can learn more about her and her books today! Also, don't forget to "like" her on Facebook and Pinterest as well as follow her on Twitter at @WheelNWordsmith and Instagram at @Wheelin_Wordsmith